# THE DEVILS OF
# BAKERSFIELD

# THE DEVILS OF
# BAKERSFIELD

A Jack Liffey Mystery

JOHN SHANNON

PEGASUS BOOKS
NEW YORK

THE DEVILS OF BAKERSFIELD

Pegasus Books LLC
45 Wall Street, Suite 1021
New York, NY 10005

First Pegasus Books edition 2008

Interior design by Maria Fernandez

Library of Congress Cataloging-in-Publication Data is available.

ISBN: 978-1-933648-29-3

10 9 8 7 6 5 4 3 2 1

Printed in the United States of America
Distributed by W. W. Norton & Company

*For my editor Michele Slung*
*who has contributed so much and so selflessly*
*to Jack Liffey's world.*

I want to thank all those whose help in researching this book was essential, but especially Randy Beeman, social historian par excellence, Ken Meier, friend and mentor, Mike Russo's bookstore and his staff, Marci Lingo and the librarians at Bakersfield College, the librarians at the Beale Memorial Library, Rowell Greene, Bakersfield native, and Jim and Nan Heitzeberg, artists and friends. All the mistakes in the book are my own.

JOHN SHANNON

You don't know me but you don't like me
You say you care less how I feel
How many of you that sit and judge me
Ever walked the streets of Bakersfield?
—Buck Owens and Dwight Yoakam,
*Streets of Bakersfield*

I'm rollin' out of Bakersfield
My own private hell on wheels
But this time I'm gone for good
And I've never gone this far before
Beyond the slammin' of the back screen door
—Martina MacBride,
*Cry on the Shoulder of the Road*

I was driving home early Sunday morning through
  Bakersfield
Listening to gospel music on the colored radio station
And the preacher said, You know you always have the
  Lord by your side
And I was so pleased to be informed of this that I ran
Twenty red lights in his honor
Thank you Jesus, thank you Lord.
—Mick Jagger,
*Far Away Eyes*

Well since I left California, baby, things have gotten worse
Seems the land of opportunity for me it's just a curse
Tell that judge in Bakersfield my trial'll have to wait
Down here they're looking for a Cadillac with Tennessee
  plates.

—John Hiatt,
*Tennessee Plates*


I'll never swim Kern River again,
It was there that I first met her, it was there that I lost my
  best friend.
And now I live in the mountains, I drifted up here with
  the wind,
And I may drown in still water, but I'll never swim Kern
  River again.
I grew up in an oil town but my gusher never came in.

—Merle Haggard,
*Kern River*

# THE DEVILS OF
# BAKERSFIELD

Chapter One

# DECENT FOLK

S pin around, he thought, then open your eyes. Maybe the actors have changed, the flats depict a different scene, the props are newer, older, more colorful. Context is everything. You learned your lines but you may now be Hamlet declaiming to Willy Loman in his back yard. Mother Courage staring at a strange glass menagerie.

Jack Liffey smiled at himself. It was just a moment of fanciful alienation, really. He had them, even when he was with his daughter who tended to keep him grounded. Maybe it was the spectacle in front of them.

Powerful underwater lamps lit the steep-tumbling whitewater

of the Kaweah River right below the restaurant, and he could tell that in a half hour or so, when the last sun was gone, the inner-lit rapids would be a magnificent if weirdly artificial display. Now in the dusk you could still see northward along the broken terrain of the Sierra foothills. The western slope was a gradual meandering rise to the really high peaks that were well out of sight, a lot less impressive here than the abrupt wall of the eastern Sierras that he loved.

"Those hills out there," Maeve started, nursing her Shirley Temple or whatever they called it these days. Jack Liffey himself just asked for a ginger ale. "They look like white elephants."

Uh-oh, he thought. The famously oblique Hemingway story in which the dread word *abortion* is never uttered. Maeve was back on task.

"I get it. But I'm not pushing you, hon," he said.

"I know," she said glumly. "You've never even stated a preference, though I know what it is."

Right then they should have been settled into a campground amid the giant sequoias, having this nice father-daughter chat around a soothing campfire. That had been the plan, except some fatuous guru, unknown to either of them, had declared this very weekend and Sequoia National Park the date and site of an Indigo Child Harmonic Convergence, whatever the hell that was, and every aging wing nut on the loose had descended on all the camping spots and begun to chant and dance and practice some fairly unmentionable behaviors out in the trees. Jack Liffey and his daughter had retreated to the town of Three Rivers at the park entrance only to find that booked up, too. The pixie dust had spread that far.

"'Have some Anis del Toro,'" Jack Liffey said. "'It tastes like licorice. Everything tastes like licorice.'" That, too, was from the story and ought to shock her. At one point in his life he had nearly worshipped Hemingway, but like most men he'd eventually backed away from all that male sentimentality, that steeping bath of laconic intensity, Gary Cooper on steroids.

"No fair," she said. "I didn't really want to talk about Hemingway."

"Okay. We can talk about the baby now if you want, hon."

"Baby? I'm only six weeks gone."

"Fetus then. It sounds so clinical. I just—"

The waiter came up to interrupt as waiters always did, this one slim and handsome and about eighteen, and Jack Liffey could see that his daughter was truly in a distracted state because she didn't even notice him. She'd really been in love with Beto, a feckless gangbanger who'd got her pregnant, and Jack Liffey kept reminding himself that a teenager's first loves and losses were every bit as dire and consequential as his own fiftieth attempts, maybe more so. And the first pregnancy dumped it all into a bath of hormones and mommy-passion.

"How do you make these horrible decisions?" she asked. "I know I should go ahead and have . . . the operation, but it's going to wipe me out emotionally. I know it will. And I'm always going to wonder what the kid would have been like. Or *be* like. I sound like I've decided but I haven't. Not really."

A hundred platitudes crowded his brain and he managed not to let any of them escape. "Have you talked to your mom about it?"

She gave him a dismissive look, her face bunched up like a prune. "She wants to kill Beto. With a thumbtack so it would take a really long time. You know exactly what she'd say."

3

"Did she tell you about hers?"

Maeve looked thunderstruck. He wasn't sure he'd ever seen her jaw drop quite like that.

"Oops," he said.

"Are you serious, Dad?"

That was a cat that Kathy should have let out of her own bag, but it was too late now. Another lapse his ex would hold against him. He was astonished she'd never told Maeve. "It was before we were married and I was in graduate school. She learned she was pregnant and made her decision without telling me a thing. It was a different time, you know. She thought she was being brave, and I think it was considered mildly gallant of me to pay for the abortion after the fact. But to be honest, I wouldn't have tried to talk her out of it. We weren't ready to be parents."

"Was it my ex–older brother or ex–older sister?"

"Hon, that's like asking the shape of the asteroid that didn't hit the earth. The fetus probably still had a tail and gills when she ended the pregnancy."

"Interesting euphemism." Neither of them could stay away from words—the intent of words, the sound of words.

"When she bumped it off. I'm not afraid of words. Or acts. I stood by her and would have if she'd made a different decision. But I probably would have come to resent it a bit. Back then it seemed so important to get my master's. As it turned out, with a master's in English lit, as they say, and three dollars, you can get a Starbucks." In fact, after a long career as a technical writer and after the final layoffs during the collapse of the aerospace industry in L.A., he'd never reached his peak salary level again. But had he tried? What he'd been doing was making himself about half a living as a finder of missing children, while his IRAs and savings dwindled away.

A couple dressed like refugees from Woodstock were arguing at the door with the headwaiter, who was obviously insisting that the restaurant was booked up even though a couple of tables were visibly unoccupied.

"How did Mom take it? I mean after."

"I won't lie to you. It surprised her how much it walloped her. She thought she was a toughie. But she got over it."

"Meaning, I will, too."

"Sure, you're a toughie. But if you tell me you've got to go through with it, I'll stand by you all the way to hell and back. I mean it, hon. I'll go to Lamaze with you and hold your hand while you're learning to pant."

She touched his hand. "Thanks, Dad. I appreciate the thought, but I'm not sure I wouldn't prefer a big nudge in the other direction."

He smiled. "That's honest. Responsibility's a sonofabitch, isn't it?"

A Mexican server showed up with his fish and her vegetarian delight and set the platter on a folding trestle that he snapped open with a flourish. This one she looked at, possibly out of loyalty to the father.

"Where are we going to sleep tonight?" Maeve asked.

"There's no real problem. Bakersfield is only an hour and a half down the road and it's a pretty big town. There'll be motels galore. We'll be there in time to watch Leno if you want."

"Is he the one with the chin?"

——

## Artifact: 1877

If it please the court, and the gentlemen of the jury, of all the low, miserable, depraved scoundrels that I have ever come in contact with, these defendants, without any grounds for defense, are the most ornery rascals that I have ever met, and I think the best thing we could do is take them out and hang them as soon as possible.

—The *defense* counsel, Bakersfield trial of alleged horse thieves. They were hanged only minutes later. [1]

——

Maeve was dozing as Highway 99 led him toward the surprising sprawl of Bakersfield, a glow ahead. Just outside town was a billboard all in black letters on white, overrun with underlinings and exclamation marks like a teen's love letter: JESUS SAYS *IMPEACH!* ALL THOSE WHO SUPPORT *SATAN'S* ONE WORLD GOVERMENT!!!

He liked the fact that the "n" in government was missing. Someone had actually taken credit for the sign, but he was past before he could read the smaller print.

He split off on business 99 and picked out a likely neon sign, neither a big overpriced chain of "suites" nor one of those gone-to-seed Kozy Kabins, just something called Rancho Bakersfield that seemed middling and hopefully free of roaches. The desk clerk who answered the bell seemed to be Vietnamese. It was the first time he'd seen that. Usually it was East Indians.

Maeve was wide awake now and clutched his arm ostentatiously. "Oh, Humbert, can we have a really big soft bed?" she announced mischievously.

He glared at her for a moment but the clerk didn't seem to have a clue.

"A daughter who's almost eighteen deserves the privacy of her own room," he said, enunciating "daughter" and "own room." "Two rooms, please. Single beds will be fine."

"Please, Humbert, at least have them close together." She leaned into him and gave a stage whisper: "I'll sneak over later."

"Could you put one of us here and the other in Fresno?" Jack Liffey said. It only confused the clerk and he waved his remark away. "Anything. This is embarrass-dad night."

Maeve calmed down and found a rack of tourist brochures to study as he finished up with the clerk.

"What was all that?" They'd gone back outside to retrieve their camping bags from the pickup.

She held his arm again fiercely. "Humbert, don't you know all daughters are in love with their dads?"

"Okay," he said. "You can't really get any more pregnant so we may as well make love, just so Freud is happy."

He could feel her stiffen and let go. "*Dad!*"

"You started it. Don't you know the gods have burdened fathers with a kind of automatic self-loathing about incest? I can't even think it. I'd be struck by lightning and turned into a cinder where I stand."

"You know that's not true of all dads," she said.

"Yeah, I do." In fact, he'd run across the dispiriting aftermath of incest often enough in his child-finding career. "Anyway, I'm very happy, thank you, with Gloria, as you know."

Sgt. Gloria Ramirez was the LAPD officer he lived with in East L.A., though, for unstated reasons of her own, she would not marry him. He was crazy about her strength of character and her sense of independence. He wasn't quite as crazy about the confused sense of self she'd been saddled with by Latino foster parents who'd brought her up to despise the fact that she was a near full-blood Paiute Indian.

"Can we do something tomorrow to make up for this fiasco?" Maeve said.

"We could visit where César Chávez used to live, or we could go to the remains of a black farming village called Allensworth that was founded by Civil War veterans . . ."

"That doesn't quite cut it."

"We could even go back and chant to the big trees with all those purple converging harmonicas."

"We got one walk through the sequoias," she said. "That was enough to recharge my nature batteries for a while. They really are amazing trees."

"Yeah. It's good to be overwhelmed once in a while by Mother Nature. Here's your key for 108."

The door key was actually a plastic card with a mag stripe. Most motels used them these days. He was in 114, three doors down. He resisted the urge to go into her room first and look under the bed, and into the bathroom and closet to make sure she was safe from whatever.

"How 'bout I call your room about eight tomorrow morning?"

"I'll try to have my face on by then."

"I'm really sorry the camping didn't work out, hon. Maybe we'll find something better to do."

"Serendipity." She grinned, then pulled a face.

"Sure. Or rationalization. They're about the same."

Jack Liffey's motel room hadn't gone ratty yet but it was just waiting for someone to look away for a few minutes. There were ruffled flounces on the beds that were a different shade of bilious green from the spread itself, and a framed print of a shaggy Highland cow sat over the dresser, the like of which he hadn't seen in years. He had just sunk wearily into an easy chair with knotty pine wings when a man's voice boomed at him, startling him upright.

"God holds them over the pit of hell, just as we would hold a spider or a loathsome snake, and He truly abhors them. He is dreadfully provoked . . ."

Slowly an image gathered out of the void on the old TV and Jack Liffey realized he must have sat down on the remote. A handsome man with severely raked-back silver hair was pacing in front of a giant wood cross wearing a navy blue robe that swirled at each turn of his legs like a great flightless bird.

"His wrath will burn them like fire; they are worthy of nothing but to be cast into the fiery abyss. He cannot bear to have them in his sight, they are so vile, they are ten thousand times more abominable in His eyes than—"

Finally he found the device under him, and the first button he hit in a panicky stab was the mute. He watched the minister pace back the way he'd come, his mouth now chewing away angrily in silence. He wondered if the tirade were live somewhere in the Pacific Time Zone, a midnight service for those needing a little hellfire pick-me-up. More likely it was taped. He popped the mute on-off on-off.

"—*venomous* serpent—"

"—God has held you up—"

"—*Nev*-er would you dare—

He tired of the game and shut the set off. The picture irised down slowly to a spot and then expired. Such ideas of hell annoyed him immeasurably. For some reason he thought of Loco, his slightly naughty half-coyote of a dog that Maeve's love was beginning to tame into domesticity. If Loco doesn't get to go to heaven, he thought, I want to go where he goes.

— —

He must have been buried under several slabs of sleep exhaustion, because when an unfamiliar ring burred somewhere in space-time, his eyes came open like a speared cat's. He had no idea where he was. His hand found the phone before he was quite ready for it.

"Wha—?"

"Is that you, Jack? You sound funny."

"Funny." His mouth tried the word a few ways, as if chewing it over. "I don't really think so. I'm not laughing. Is this Gloria?"

His eyes danced over the murky room and a sense of orientation assembled itself. Not his home bed. Motel. Bakersfield. Trip with Maeve.

"Slap yourself a couple of times," she said.

"I don't think so. I'm almost touching down. There it is. Three-point landing. Taxiing now. I'll be at the gate soon." He picked up his wristwatch and squinted to make out that it was just before 4:00. "Are you okay, Glor?"

"I might ask the same. Bakersfield P.D. woke me a few minutes ago to ask me about one Maeve Margaret Liffey—as they said— and then they handed her the phone. Only time I've heard the middle name is when she's getting chewed out."

"It's the way cops deal with driver's licenses, as you well know. She's with me, three doors down in this motel fast asleep."

He was going to add something snide about presidential assassins always having three names on the news, but it began to penetrate his haze that he might be wrong about his daughter's whereabouts. "What the hell did she say?"

"She's not in your motel, Jack. That's what I'm trying to tell you. They've arrested her for prostitution."

"*Prostitution?*"

"You heard me. They've got her at the main sheriff's station, which is in some place called Oildale, but they're going to be taking her to the Central Receiving Facility in downtown Bakersfield for booking."

"*Booking!*"

"Jack, please stop shouting random words that I say. I know you're upset, but listen. This was her rights call and she phoned me because she didn't know how to get the motel and she was afraid they'd cut her off if she used her one call on Information. She remembered the name of the place, though, and I got the number from the operator. Do you want me to come up there?"

He rested his forehead on his palm. "This is crazy. Some crazy mistake. I'll let you know if I need you. Did she say anything else?"

"She sounded a bit cocky and not very worried."

"Oh, great. You cops love kids with attitude. Thanks a lot, Glor. I'll put some clothes on and take care of this."

"Nice picture to leave me with."

"I miss you, too."

— —

He woke up the young night clerk, who was no longer Vietnamese and had a plastic nameplate on his shirt that said SLICK, and was grizzled and skinny. He was young but looked a lot like someone who'd be found holding up a WILL WORK FOR FOOD sign at a freeway off-ramp. It took some convincing to get him to run off a new card key for Maeve's room.

Her bag was zipped open on the made bed but he didn't see anything obvious gone. He felt slightly guilty poking around in it, but not guilty enough to stop. At least there were none of the hooker-look clothes from only a few weeks back when she'd been running with the bangers. Gloria had shown him the red bra and shorty spaghetti-strap top and what even Gloria called fuck-me pumps with four-inch heels. He sighed.

Leaving her room, he walked out past the Rancho Bakersfield sign that creaked a little in the wind high above Union Avenue, and just on general principles he headed in the direction that looked like it led toward town. A little fog hung on the air and the pools of deep shadow among the run-down motels were not very inviting. One shadow seemed to stir and flex with the retreat of a human shape.

He assumed Maeve had gone out for a walk. You could never teach her prudence.

Before long a tall young woman with hair blasted white by chemicals came out of a bus shelter wearing a short skirt and a tube top. She looked up the road as if for a bus. "Want a date?" she asked languidly in a gravelly voice.

"I think the prom is over," Jack Liffey said.

"Are you lost?" There was an almost genuine concern in her voice.

"How about I give you some money and you answer a few questions."

"Depends. You want some nice French?"

"*Mais, non.* My daughter is missing. I wonder what the cops are like around here. I wonder what 'around here' is like around here. Would the cops tend to arrest a girl just for being out at night here?"

"You mentioned money, amigo."

He took out a twenty, which didn't seem princely, but he wasn't exactly flush after blowing a lot of his cash on the lit-rapids-enhanced dinner, and he handed it to her. She took it the way she might a used-up bus pass.

"This is the row," she said. "Actually you're in the hot spot for boys. Rough trade and all that." She grabbed at her crotch like Michael Jackson, and there seemed to be something there so he guessed all at once that he was probably talking to a pre-op trans-sexual. They were getting a lot better at faking it.

"The local cops hot to trot?" Jack Liffey said.

"Don't you know."

"Know what?"

She whistled once on a descending note. "Twenty bucks don't buy much, amigo. But I were you, I'd get my daughter and just book out. I can tell you're probably L.A."

"Are you saying the cops are dirty here?"

She laughed, with genuine humor. "Even God is dirty in this town, pard." Then she turned her back and hurried away from the road along a path worn through the weeds that took her into the shadowland between motels.

"Thanks!" he called. "I think you like your job too much."

She paused in her stride just for an instant. "Life is all the same shitbag when you ain't got a choice, L.A."

—-—

The central jail was a low structure wearing big horizontal louvers, hunkered down behind the tall glass Bakersfield courthouse like a baby seal protected by its vigilant mother. The fog had thickened a little, and he remembered warnings about the valley's tule fogs that could go quickly to whiteout in the late fall, causing fifty- and hundred-car pileups on Highway 99. The fog now was mostly ribbons and wisps from the cloudbank overhead, carved free by street poles and the light breeze. There was a false sense of impending dawn, probably just city lights making the cloud incandesce. A handful of beat-up cars disturbed the eerie silence as they carried early risers to whatever crummy jobs required them this early.

He parked in a huge lot behind the jail. Inside, nobody had ever heard of a Maeve Liffey.

"Could it be because she's still being booked?"

The officer on duty cocked her thumb over an ample shoulder to a glass door that offered a clear view of a big empty room with a counter and several unoccupied desks.

"That's Booking. You see anybody in there?"

"I got a call relayed from the sheriff's office in Oildale."

She pursed her lips as if deciding whether he was worth taking the trouble. He waited. She went back to the one-piece computer that had notes stuck all around its edges, and she typed for a few moments and peered at the screen.

"Okay, there was a girl out there—was she wearing a long-sleeved blue workshirt?"

"Yes."

"She's not there no more."

"Could they be on their way here?"

She shook her head. "That was hours ago."

"Can I have the arresting deputy's name?"

"You got to go to Oildale for that."

"Look, pretend it's your daughter and you're on vacation in a

very pleasant faraway town, full of nice people, and she's suddenly gone missing and you get a call that she's been arrested but
she's not at the jail when you try to find her. What would you do?"

"I'd probably scream bloody murder until I had her back
again, but I don't recommend that."

"What do you recommend?" He did his best to hold back a
gathering temper.

"She's okay, I'm sure. Don't you worry. This is a very law-and-
order-times-ten kind of town. They don't let nobody get out of
line here, not even the neeg-rahs and the Mexicans. Why don't
you go home and wait for a call."

"I had my call," Jack Liffey said. His patience was astounding
even to him. "Could you tell me how to get to Oildale."

"It's up Chester just across the river."

She gave him directions and it was an easy trip, three miles
through a bit of town that got pretty rough-looking, just across
the mudflats and a stream that passed for a river. The Kern
County sheriff's headquarters was a flat campus of buildings
under cottonwoods at the edge of a shuttered airport. But Maeve
wasn't there either, and he started to get frantic in front of
another puzzled officer who'd just come on duty.

— —

Just the usual screw-up, he thought when the sun was finally
coming up on the solution to the mystery. They'd already let her
have her call at the sheriff's station when they'd discovered she
was under eighteen, and they'd driven her to Juvenile Hall out in
East Bakersfield instead of the jail.

He caught the night social worker or whatever they called her coming off shift in the parking lot. She must have weighed 300 pounds and gave him the fish-eye from within a hooded sweat-shirt thrown over commodious green scrubs.

"Give me a break here," he said. "I'm a father and we just dropped off the highway to grab a motel to sleep."

"Well, she'll be asleep now. Why'ncha let her snooze it off?"

"Can you just clue me in to what went down?"

"They caught her cruising the row on foot. It's not a good place. The deputies might have let her off on the 647b—that's prostitution—but they found three quarter-bags of crystal meth in her shirt. We're not a town that winks at that, I'm afraid."

"My daughter did not have meth on her. Believe it."

The big woman looked him over. "I wouldn't take that attitude if I was you. Maybe it's somebody else's shirt. That might work. Maybe it's *your* shirt."

"I don't even drink, but if I were going to ingest something it wouldn't be a trailer park drug." He regretted it as soon as he said it. In his defense, he thought, he was very very tired.

"I'm from proud Okie stock, mister. They's a lot us here and we come up in the world a lot."

"Bless you, ma'am. Forgive me if I insulted anyone at all, truly. But my little girl is a paragon of virtue. There must be a mistake."

She unlocked the door of an old Ford Escort that was too small for her and then painstakingly wedged herself behind the wheel. "I don't care what sort of polygon she is. You both better straighten up and fly right. People that buck the morals of decent folk go down hard here, and that sure goes for smart-ass hippies."

Chapter Two

# LOCKDOWN

After a years-long history of dealing with the police in a number of very unproductive ways, Jack Liffey had finally come to the conclusion that step one was always to get a lawyer. He remembered that Goldie Jewison, one of the early ex-wives of his old friend Mike Lewis, taught California history at the local state college, and to get a lead on a likely defense attorney he went to a phone book. He found Goldie's number and dialed it.

"Four-nine-eighty-six," came a woman's quick voice.

"Is this Goldie Jewison?" he asked.

"Generally," a voice replied.

"Not specifically?"

"Let's see what it is you want."

He let it lie. He liked something about the alert tone of her voice. "I'm a friend of Mike Lewis's and I'm only passing through town and I need some advice."

"*Oooh*-kay."

"My name is Jack Liffey. My daughter and I checked into a couple of motel rooms on Union Street last night, and I guess she went out for a walk in the dark, and somehow the cops busted her in the wee hours. For some pretty absurd charges. I think I'm going to need an attorney who knows the ropes, if you can recommend someone."

"Oh, I've heard of you, Jack. I'm surprised we never met." All of a sudden she was friendly. "Mike always liked you. What are these absurd charges?"

"I'm told prostitution and possession, meth. It's all crap. She's a good kid. Not even some crazy runaway rolls into town and starts hooking the first ten minutes. She's at the juvie now, but I think I'd better get help."

There was a long pause. A shadow flashed across his face and he glanced west at a buzzard circling in the pale morning sky, as if the bird knew something.

"Listen, Jack, you have a right to know what you walked into. We tend to have some serious police oppression in this town. These days the great enemy is . . . wait for it . . . godless hippies. Nobody expects the Spanish Inquisition."

Only an ex of Mike's would have quoted Monty Python. She actually struck him as a bit overwrought. "Maybe you'd better let me and the lawyer worry about Savonarola. Can you recommend someone?"

"The very best. Jenny Ezkiaga." She spelled it out and gave him a phone number.

"Seriously, don't—I mean, *don't*—underestimate the trouble you can get into here. It's a town with rules of its own."

"I can't think about that right now. The noise from 99 kept me awake most of what I had for a night. And now this."

"Never disparage that highway, Jack. It's the fastest way out of here."

—–

They picked their way down the switchback path toward the Kern River flats. Delia Di Giorgio and Rob Hise were wearing the flesh-covering clothing that their youth counselor required, long-sleeved shirts buttoned to the neck and for Delia, a long skirt that swished along the path—yet despite the decorum of their dress, they held hands fervidly, occasionally bumping hips, almost as if by accident. Fifteen-year-olds. Even this morning hike together was very much frowned upon by the Olive Grove Evangelical Church.

The sparkle of water out beyond the reeds, the croak of a frog, the mists burning off—it was one of those early winter mornings in Bakersfield that promised a near perfect day ahead. Besides, they were very much in love.

As usual they did their best coming down the path to ignore the industrial muddle beyond the river, the horizon-to-horizon Tinkertoy hodgepodge of oil pipes, tank farms and nodding pump jacks of the Kern River Field No. 1, once the richest oilfield on earth. They no longer even noticed the faint smell of tar on the air.

Outsiders always found the view from the mansions along Panorama Road atop the cliff a bit ridiculous, but the blighted landscape didn't matter in the least to the young couple. They were conscious of very little beyond the sensation of holding hands, a mild but still frowned-upon sin.

Later they would wonder if that was what had invited Satan into their lives. Pastor Kohlmeyer had preached on Teen-and-Tween night that the Fall was always summoned with seeming innocence, touching bodies at a school dance, watching a fleeting kiss in a movie, reading a romance novel. Holding hands. Such transgressions gave the Devil his invitation to slip through a cranny into your life.

"Rob!"

Delia saw it first, just beside some brush on the mudflat, and she pulled away from his hand to cover her mouth reflexively with both of hers.

"Get thee behind me!" Rob blurted. Thinking only of Delia, he turned her shoulders away so she wouldn't see, then squatted for a closer look himself. He touched the infant's neck the way he guessed an ambulance driver would, but the skin was so cold that the state of the baby was obvious. Pinned to the diaper was a typed note with an upside-down cross drawn crudely above the text.

> Amen. Ever and ever for the glory and the power. The kingdom is Thine for evil from us. Deliver not but temptation unto us. Lead us against those who forgive trespasses. Forgive bread daily, our day, give us this heaven as earth. Done be thy will, come thy name, Kingdom. They be hallowed in heaven who Father Art Not.

It took him several moments of utter mental whirling before the profane words came close to making sense. The delay was in part because the note was based on some other version, and their church used only the King James, the language that God himself spoke and inspired others to write.

Had the word 'trespasses' been 'debts,' he would have known at once that the note was a nearly backwards rendering of the Lord's Prayer. With a few alterations to make it even more blasphemous.

Before taking out his cell phone, Rob Hise blessed the dead infant as best he knew how, hoping to undo whatever damage had been done to its newborn soul by obvious Satanists.

— —

Pastor Kohlmeyer read the appalling note at his desk three times with a ratcheting-up sensation of apprehension. He had done his best to make himself ready, but how did you ever know for sure you were prepared for the great challenge? The police had Xeroxed the note and let the boy give him a copy, and the pastor had a call in now to Channing Pelt, Olive Grove's youth leader, his trusted adviser.

He had seen at once that the message was some perverse travesty of the Lord's Prayer, and it struck him that this was just the way the devil would make the first public announcement of his arrival, thumbing his nose at the Lord. He wanted to hear Pelt's impressions, because Bakersfield's largest and most prominent evangelical church had sent the youth leader earlier that year to a week-long seminar in Laredo, Texas, to learn about the plague of devil-worship that was now sweeping border areas of the country. Pelt had brought back an entire suitcase of publications, brochures, and action kits.

They had already followed the directions in one of the kits for setting up an early warning system to spot Satanic activity in its earliest stages in Kern County. Twice a week the pastor's secretary called around to all the local dairies, checking for any unusual incidence of spoiled milk. Members of the Youth League who worked at libraries and bookstores watched for a sudden interest in material on the occult or a spike in checkouts of Harry Potter or Michael Moore. Other members of the Sword of God took regular drives around town to look for new graffiti, particularly inverted crosses, pentagrams, and drawings of men with goats' heads. A woman who worked at the Cooktown shop at the mall was alerted to watch for teenagers buying butcher knives or large stew pots. Down at the animal pound, a young man watched for mutilations. And a devout computer student had set up what he called the anti-Satan algorithm. Every Sunday at Olive Grove and a few other churches people tossed old cash register receipts into a cardboard cylinder at the door, and they were collected so the boy could scan them all into his computer program that looked for unusual occurrences of the number 666 or other Satanic nonprime numbers. Every Saturday without fail Channing Pelt convened the Anti-Cult Committee to examine all the data that had been collected and prepare an omnibus report.

Dennis Kohlmeyer sat back slowly and looked at the large painting of Jesus healing the sick on the wall of his office. For once it gave him no comfort. The weight of things was coming down on him. Father, if thou be willing, he thought, remove this cup from me: nevertheless, not my will, but thine, be done. He hoped he was up to the challenge, if this event indeed marked the arrival of the devil in their town, bringing infamies in his wake.

The one trial that had been sent to him as a youngster had just about crushed the faith out of him, and his father, who had founded Olive Grove and built it from a pulpit on the back of a truck in a farm field to about half what it was today, had scoffed at him.

We all live in the ruins of our childhoods, he thought, in an uncharacteristically sour moment of reflection.

He wondered suddenly if not the dead infant, but *this* was the way the Devil arrived. If it began with an inkling of your own weakness, knowledge already present to him and working to dishearten him. He knelt to pray.

--

"The name is Basque," she said. "I don't actually speak much of the infernal language and I'm not absolutely certain anyone else on earth does either. My granddads were brought here as shepherds and sent off into the hills one by one with flocks of sheep. Now we're honored pioneers. Some of my uncles even own things like markets and gas stations."

She was a chunky woman with short jet-black hair. She wore a navy blue business suit, and her fierce manner was thrown a little off kilter by the fact that one eye was greenish blue and the other brown.

"*Jenny no es un nombre vasco,*" he said, showing off, though he wasn't sure he was getting it right.

"Yeah, I can manage Spanish. If you insist, I was christened Gotzone. It means Angel in Basque, which is utterly unlike every other European language. It's said we came down from the hilltops to trade with the Romans after we'd hidden in the Pyrenees since the Stone Age. I personally think we twirled down on a flying saucer."

"That's fine. I've run into a lot of the unusual in my job." He'd already told her that he made much of his living finding missing children. And now, for the moment at least, Maeve was more or less missing. "A certain percentage of the people I've met passionately believe something just about as preposterous as saucers from space. I find it's best to treat it as part of life's occasional inclination to be entertaining." He was so tired he didn't know quite what he was saying, and he decided he'd better put a lid on it or soon he'd be telling lesbian jokes, and a sensitive antenna told him that would not be a very good idea, not even warm-hearted, tolerant, and agreeable ones.

She smiled. "The varieties of human experience. If you'd rolled into town two decades ago it might not have been so funny to you, unless you enjoy the idea of massive rings of child molesters, hanging their children nude from hooks in motels, and selling them to strangers for unspeakable sex acts. Of course *none* of it ever happened. The sheriff and the D.A. simply went out of their skulls, led by some pretty weird recovered-memory characters."

He said nothing, and she gave a little dismissive shake of her head. "A bad time, all are agreed. Though it was worse for the hundred or so ordinary moms and dads who went to prison, but the convictions have all been overturned." She looked at him. "Unless they decide to waive your daughter's juvenile status, it may not be a question of charges, as such. They'll probably just turn her over to you. At very worst—which won't happen, believe me—they could try to declare her a status offender. Which in other towns just means a kid who skips school every day and the parents find uncontrollable, but, for the moment, around here it seems to apply to certain kids that the local watchdogs are calling hippies."

"Does anybody still use that word?" He remembered the social worker he'd met in the parking lot talking about smart-ass hippies, but he hadn't taken her seriously.

Her desk was old and oak and much-dented as if it had served a rural post office for generations. There were a couple of certificates on the wall between the prints of inoffensive landscapes, and he wanted to get a good look at them to see where she'd studied.

"We're a bit behind the times. You'd probably call them Goths or freaks. They're just disturbed kids trying to seem interesting to each other, really, but it riles our hardshell Christians no end. And it worries all the more secular locals whose main ambition is to live out their lives in a Norman Rockwell painting."

She snorted. "Some of these kids today *are* pretty extreme, I have to admit. All the piercings and in-your-face tattoos. I defended one street kid down from Fresno who actually had plastic horns surgically implanted in his forehead, I swear to God, and another one who had a tattoo on his neck that said Atheists for Jesus."

"Strangely enough there isn't as much extreme stuff in L.A. as you'd think," he said. "But my daughter is pretty ordinary looking. I'm not sure why they busted her—though she does have a mouth."

"Meaning?"

"She doesn't mind telling you about her rights."

"Ah, the authorities always love that."

"I know. She gets it from me, I'm afraid, but I'm bigger than she is. She's been through a lot, but she's not half as tough as she thinks."

A short man with red hair and freckles poked his head in without knocking. "Oh, sorry. Jenny, have you got the papers on the Tennyson appeal?"

"Come in, Sonny, I want you to meet a client—Jack Liffey. Sonny Theroux. Sonny is the investigator I use. Long ago and far away he was a cop, and he was a real hero here toward the end of our Salem-type insanity. He came up with the tapes of the sessions where they'd questioned the kids, browbeaten them, really. For months all officialdom had denied the existence of any tapes of the interviews. When Sonny dug them up, they showed pretty clearly that everything was coerced."

Sonny stepped in and shrugged, all five-two of him, and Jack Liffey stood to shake his hand. His hair was the red of a Scots warrior and the freckles suggested it was all real. "There's a few mean souls still in the D.A.'s office," Sonny Theroux said, with hints of the south in his voice.

"How'd you get the tapes?" Jack Liffey said.

"Sources. It's a long story." The man had obviously had some subliminal signal from the woman to move along. He hoisted a cardboard carton from the sideboard. "Nice to've met you, Mr. Liffey."

But Jack Liffey wasn't quite ready to relinquish him. Whenever he had to root around, he liked to collect the wounded, and this man seemed a prime candidate. "You're not from around here, are you?"

Sonny chuckled. "I was born in bayou country near New Orleans, but my parents moved along a lot. South Carolina, Georgia, Kentucky, East Texas. Pops always had a dream a minute and a ticket to the next train. His head was full up with stump water that didn't nobody want to drink. But I've been here in Kern a long time now and it's my home. I got to see a man about a squid."

"Squid?"

"It's a joke of hers. Bye, Jen." He closed the door behind him.

"Sonny is a first-rate investigator," she said. "I just can't believe how he gets along in this town. He tells everybody the unvarnished truth, insults them to their face, all in that cornpone idiom—and they worship him for it. I try to emulate him and they just get annoyed. Where's the justice?"

"Ms. Ezkiaga, can we talk about my daughter?"

"Oooh. *Ms.* I'd better give you a few Miss Manners tips. That's a devil-word in this town, Mr. Liffey. It announces to all and sundry that you're probably an agnostic. Secular humanist. Maybe even a novel reader."

"I've been known to read a novel."

"Don't let it slip out."

"Aren't you afraid of some sort of backlash against you?" Jack Liffey asked, taking a risk.

"My family is old Bakersfield. It's kept me safe so far. Basques and Okies. We can get away with a lot these days. But you, you should consider this area the Deep South—and then maybe figure you look a little dusky, if you get my meaning. Sorry for all the melodrama, but I'm guessing you'll thank me some time soon." She levered herself upright. "Let's see right now if we can get in to see your daughter."

— —

Before they could leave the old frame office building that had once been a Victorian house, Sonny Theroux stopped him in the hall.

"Mr. Liffey, mind if I ask your profession?"

"I hunt for missing children. Sometimes I even find them."

"A brother at arms. That's how I'd call it. If you're ever in need of some professional courtesy in town, please." He tucked a business card into Jack Liffey's jacket.

"I always thought professional courtesy was a school of sharks deciding not to eat a lawyer."

The investigator chuckled. "Present company excepted, of course. Being landlocked, we stock our jokes differently here. Ours tend to rely on carrion, roadkill, dead snakes."

"Come, Mr. Liffey," Jenny said. "Let's get your girl out of the system as quick as we can."

—-

## Artifact: 1910s

Allensworth, California

The small town of Allensworth was founded in 1908 by Col. Allen Allensworth, a former slave who had fought in the Civil War. As elected leader of a group of former slaves from the Los Angeles area he purchased 800 acres, thirty miles north of Bakersfield, in a promising area of abundant wells, artesian springs, and a small river called Deer Creek. The colonel led the pioneers to the area, and the town they founded became the only all–African American farming community in California.

At its peak the town held 300 families, and contained a hotel, school, library, post office, bakery, machine shop, and many other businesses serving the surrounding farms that raised alfalfa, sugar beets, and livestock.

The town became a transfer point for the Santa Fe Railroad, and a bustling African-American center grew up, offering concerts, plays, and club meetings. A small black college on the order of Tuskegee Institute was planned. Unfortunately the town was surrounded by powerful corporate farms that used upstream diversion and massive groundwater pumping to meet their own water needs. Deer Creek was mysteriously diverted. The Pacific Farming Company, which had sold Col. Allensworth the land, did not deliver on its promise to continue providing water.

As agribusiness all around Allensworth prospered, the black town and black farms were starved of water. Col. Allensworth died in a traffic accident, then the railroad was diverted, businesses folded, and the town gradually died.

—Tourist brochure distributed at the Allensworth site.[2]

— —

"So go on, what *is* your favorite way to get back at a guy who's hassled you?" Maeve Liffey played along.

Her new friend smiled. "Just promise him something really special in the way of sex and then show out a tube of K-Y, but lube up his weenie with Mentholatum."

They grinned at one another, then dissolved into giggles.

"This is even better," Toxie said, and she patted her chest, hunting for something. "I forgot. They took it away last night. I got a necklace with the tip of a guy's dick who tried to force me to suck him off."

"Really!"

"I bit it off. It's been shriveling up for a year, but he's sure not around any more to bug me."

"Jeez, I'll bet."

"I just got to dangle it at a guy to get some respect."

It was late morning, but they hadn't slept much the night before in the itchy county-issued gray sweats, and, like teen campers the first night, they sat cross-legged and woozy on their hard cots. Their slap-happy lovefest had started when they found that—back in the day—they both had had a passion for *Jane Eyre*. Not just that, but Nick Cave, Zen Killer, Unfit to Plead, Portishead, Vomit Scream, and the transgressive feminist art collective called Hair Pie.

Maeve was astonished to find a kindred spirit up here in Bakersfield, even one who had been so obviously forced to the extremities of acting out. "Toxie Shock," who refused to answer to any other name, had the sides of her head shaved bare and the top formed into rigid spikes of fluorescent blue. She had too many tattoos and piercings to count, and the only way Maeve kept up at all was by showing Toxie the genuine gang tattoo from East L.A. on her left breast, which up until that moment she'd tried fervently to wish away. Even her dad didn't know about the tattoo, as stubborn a reminder of her month-long passion overload as the pregnancy itself, but since it was a true mark of ownership from the Greenwod *klika*, the baddest gang in Boyle Heights, it pretty much equaled the whole of Toxie's gallery.

"What are they going to do to us?" Maeve asked.

"This is your first time. They'll probably just let you go if your dad bothers to show up."

"Of course he'll show up." That spoke volumes about Toxie's parents, she thought. To Maeve, showing up was what parents did. "What about you?"

The girl rubbed her eyes a little and sighed. "I've already done their Pathways thing. That's where they put you in the be-a-zombie program. Luckily you're not allowed to do Pathways twice, as if it's some fucking great privilege. Next is Teen Court and I've done that, too. Ah, I can't bear it."

She groaned theatrically. "There's, like, a jury of teener Jesus freaks deciding what to do with you. Oh, fuck, man. The last time, the cops even dragged my mom out of some gutter to come watch it all. There she was with her crazied-up eyes as the Jesus Jumpers sentenced me to three months of cleaning toilets at some big Church of the Perpetual Shit-Eating Grin out in the burbs. Why can't they just leave me alone?"

"What did they bust you for this time?"

"Just hanging out at Joseph's Pizza after midnight. Curfew, you know. It's federal here to want to be different. Don't go thinking I'm being super paranoid. They got the power and they use it."

"I believe you."

"I got kicked out of high school for ratfucking my social studies teacher." She smiled. "But I deserved that. What a prune. She was a slave to all her apeshit habits. Every day, she stepped into the classroom at the exact second the bell rang and then sat on the edge of the desk and glared at us forever until we got quiet. So Mike Toobin and I oiled up the front of her desk with superglue with ten seconds to spare and she went and plopped down right on it. She glared forever and then nearly tore her butt off trying to stand up." Toxie giggled so hard she coughed several times. "It was worth every damn thing that happened to me."

Toxie chuckled some more. "Keep it real, girl," she said. "There's some bad shit here. And I hear a real jack-up is gonna come down."

--

A pleasant looking middle-aged woman met them in the weirdly homey lobby, carrying a manila folder. She wore a crisp khaki shirt that suggested some kind of uniform and baggy green scrub trousers.

Jenny Ezkiaga had decided it would be best to negotiate this herself.

"Please sit down," the supervisor said, indicating the knotty pine furniture next to them.

That wasn't a good omen, Jack Liffey thought, and a complicated series of frowns suggested that the lawyer agreed with him. Neither of them moved.

"What's the problem?" Jenny Ezkiaga demanded.

"No problem, really." The woman consulted her folder. "The arresting officer came in at the crack of dawn and retracted his report. He said he'd made a mistake."

"You mean he found out the girl had connections and decided he'd better not have planted dope on her."

Jack Liffey was really beginning to like his new lawyer.

"I wouldn't put it that way," the woman demurred.

"Of course you wouldn't. Why don't you just bring us Maeve Liffey, and we'll forget all about the inconveniences she's suffered."

"We'll be letting her go as soon as we can. Unfortunately, we're in total lockdown right now."

The lawyer rolled her eyes. "What have you got, a bunch of kids pulling their hair? I hope she isn't hurt."

"It's not internal, I promise. Every facility in the county is in lockdown, jails and all. I can't tell you any more right now."

The lawyer tried hard to pry out more information. But they learned nothing more, and all they were told in the end was to phone back in the afternoon. Outside, they squinted in the sudden brightness.

"Have you ever seen something like this?" Jack Liffey asked.

"Yeah, maybe," she said thoughtfully. "Back in the bad old days, whenever somebody brought in a few new kids to work on, they'd put the freeze on for a while. So nobody who was already in the can could talk to their relatives and compare stories. It's worrying."

"You think the hysteria is back?"

"No. Whatever it is now, it'll be different, I'm sure. Got any idea why that cop ate his report about the dope?"

A fat black bumblebee the size of a thumb streaked suddenly toward him and he flinched. It was gone in a flash, as if erased from the brilliant morning. It reminded him of the way fate could arrive and vanish without warning.

"I can guess," Jack Liffey said. "I've got a woman friend who's an L.A. cop. She or one of her colleagues called up here."

She nodded. "That would do it. What an embarrassment that would be, planting evidence on another cop's kid."

Jack Liffey smelled peppertree on the air as they crossed the small parking lot, and he experienced a floating, locationless feeling, a kind of unfocused nostalgia with a touch of dread. Where he'd grown up in San Pedro it had smelled just like that. He wondered if his stateless feeling had anything to do with being without Maeve. His anxiety level on her behalf was whipping up fast.

Chapter Three

# CLARITY IS THE OPPOSITE OF TRUTH

J enny Ezkiaga drove him a few blocks to the offices of the *Bakersfield Bee*, and her chutzpah walked them right past a lobby receptionist who barely demurred and into an old Otis elevator heavy with darkening brass. "Someone on the city desk will be on this lockdown like white on rice. They've become a pretty good paper the last few years. Acting like a pit bull when it comes to minor and obvious scandals—which is about the best you can expect of a newspaper."

The elevator joggled upward, emitted a brief metal-on-metal shriek between floors that Jack Liffey could taste behind his eyes, and stopped abruptly about four inches below the third floor.

Someone had duct-taped the safety latch, and she flung the accordion grate open. They stepped up into a big room, crossing to a T-shaped array of desks where a balding man was bent over a stack of paper.

"John Jones," she said peremptorily. It seemed a pretty unlikely name, but his rumpled white shirt was monogrammed JJ. "How does a newsman say, Fuck you?" she challenged.

Without looking up, the man smiled and his pen dipped to strike out a word. "Trust me," he answered. It seemed to be an old joke between them. "Hello, Jen. So what does a Polish lesbian do at a party?"

Her eyes narrowed. "Picks up a man, of course. Do you know why all the Kern jails are in lockdown? That's not a joke."

Finally his head came up, but he merely glanced at her and then studied Jack Liffey with watery blue eyes, as if he might be the particular answer to some problem he was contemplating. She made no move to introduce them. "Dead infant," he said. "Riverwalk. Satanic note pinned to its diaper. Give you a bad feeling, Jenny?"

"Who've you got on it?"

"Karl and Melissa. Malcolm and F.A."

"Well, then you've got a bad feeling about it."

"Why are you interested?"

"Lawyers always are. Ambulances speeding away, etc."

"You might want to duck this one," he said simply. "A dead baby and Satanism." He shook his head. "The fundies will be in full roar. I don't want to get behind the curve on this one."

"The *Bee* wasn't even near the curve last time. You weren't in town then, but this paper repeated everything the D.A. and sheriff said, like an echo chamber. The good ol' boys might as well have been writing the paper themselves."

35

"Things change," he said. "You wouldn't take my advice even if it came with a gold seal, would you?"

"Everybody lives in some relation to danger," she said. "It's when you try too hard to protect yourself that you get sucked into it."

She cocked her head at Jack Liffey and then nodded to the exit, and he followed her back out. He was liking her more and more. The elevator grate clanged shut, and he braced for a bad descent.

"You picked yourself an evil time to drive through here, Jack Liffey. Let's get your daughter out of the *pinta* the minute we can and send you on your way."

"And you who must go on living here?"

"Maybe nothing. Maybe I get burned at the stake."

— —

Maeve waited alone in what they'd called a dorm room, having given up reading the tiny print on translucent paper of the King James Bible that was the only book in the room. Undertakers' time, Toxie had called it. Dead-on-arrival time, unmeasurable and unusable. There were no clocks in the room.

The room had been decorated as if it weren't a cell at all, with cheery blue-and-yellow plaid curtains over the wired glass window and two small knotty pine desks. But the locked metal door had a thick glass peephole in it, and behind a modesty partition in the corner there was an ugly stainless steel toilet and washbasin in a single unit, just in case you had any doubts about where you were.

A fluorescent fixture was recessed behind filthy glass in the ceiling and there did not seem to be a switch to turn it off. The effect was of not quite enough light, and it was making her eyes smart a little. Over each cot there were shelves where you could store clothes if you were going to be here for a while, but the ones she'd come in wearing were not there. Nor were Toxie's, unless she'd come in wearing another pair of gray sweats, which seemed pretty unlikely. There was a sweetish chemical smell, too, probably disinfectant, the kind that clung to your nostrils.

Toxie had to have been gone more than an hour. She'd been taken out without explanation. The woman who had come for her had spoken to Maeve briefly in a voice devoid of humanity. Soulless and menacing at the same time.

"You are not to speak."

"Do you know how long?" Maeve had asked, foolishly.

It had seemed to please the woman not to acknowledge the question. Then she had done something with Toxie's hand to make the skinny girl gasp and go compliant as they left.

Maeve lay back and finally managed to nap through some of the frozen time. It might have been a few minutes or an hour when the door coming open jolted her awake.

Toxie took one look at Maeve as the door closed behind her, then threw herself down on her cot with her back turned. The change in her mood was alarming.

"Toxie!"

Her companion just shook her head, so Maeve came over her and hugged her.

"It's going to be okay."

Cockiness had been so much a part of her persona that with it gone Toxie seemed about half her original size.

"Did they hurt you?"

She shook her head, but still Maeve could not put scenes from women-in-cages movies out of her mind. She'd never actually seen one, but they were a standing joke among the guys at school. And she'd seen the covers of those creepy magazines in liquor stores, with the snarling men in Nazi caps gloating over helpless women in torn slips.

"Come on, tell me what happened."

Toxie remained silent. She chewed her lip and started to stay something.

"I mean, come on, you're scaring me."

"You gotta get yourself out of here," she brought out finally. "They're way sicko."

"So what did they do?" Maeve was patient.

Relentless, boring, insane questioning was what Toxie at last described, by a tag-team of four of them. They'd asked about her friends and their activities, promising tougher sessions to come.

"They had some hair up their butt about the Devil. Assholes. They thought I sneaked off with my buds and worshiped Satan, and they kept asking me where our black mass was held. What a bunch of dorks!

"I told 'em if I didn't buy into their Sunday fairy-story God, what made 'em think I'd believe in the flip side? But they just kept insisting that they *knew*. They had evidence connecting *me* to this Devil shit. One of 'em had this way of describing completely crazy scenes—sex rituals and tortures, and insisting I'd been there and that other people said so. I'd been *named*. I was the high priestess, for Chrissakes.

"It was all whack. Maeve! Crap about stabbing babies on altars and total sicko shit. You just know it came out of their own

CLARITY IS THE OPPOSITE OF TRUTH

evil minds. They kept on and on at me. You start to feel crazy just hearing it."

"Does anybody you know ever *play* at Satanism?" Maeve asked.

Toxie shrugged. "Maybe some kid doodled SATAN RULES! on a binder cover, but that's just giving your old minister the finger as you walk away." She seemed to remember something and her tentatively returning bravado evaporated. "They took pictures of my tats. This ugly bitch photographed every one close up."

"So?" Maeve had seen a lot of the tattoos and they were pretty—butterflies and animals and flowers.

"I mean, there's some you haven't seen. They made me undress."

"Gross," Maeve said.

"It's just a joke, you know."

"Can I see?" Maeve asked.

Toxie looked a little sheepish. Then she got up, tugged down her sweatpants and pulled at the elastic of her black panties to reveal a cherubic girl devil in diapers. She was holding a stretched-out slingshot ready to let fly. Looking at it, Maeve couldn't help giggling.

Toxie sighed heavily. "So, there it is, the case against me. At least three of my friends have the same one. We did it together. It's the Little Debbie Devil."

"Cool," Maeve said admiringly.

"Not here," Toxie said. "These people are crazy. Scary crazy." She lay down and just before pulling a pillow over her head, she said, "Sorry, I need to get away from linear time for a while."

—-—

## Artifact: 1921

14 February, 1921
Rosedale Colony,
Near Baker's Field.
U.S. of A.

. . . I must tell you that recently one has experienced here new and particularly vexing troubles. Several unpleasant fellows who come from the nearest town have shown the effrontery to demand from me a vote that would assure their continued domination over the Kern County Agricultural Alliance. Making themselves ridiculous, they ride around at night draped in bed linen, carrying torches and threatening their enemies. It would be laughable if they were not so stupid as to fail to understand where such theatrics and the volatile emotions stirred up by them might lead. As Englishmen, we who have settled here at Rosedale, and hope only to succeed with our ranching scheme, additionally find ourselves subject to mockery regarding our "outlandish" ways whenever we must venture into town.

Through it all, I must say that Creighton Whitehead has remained a staunch friend and splendidly dependable ally. It gives me pain, however, to report that he has been singled out for the swinish attentions of those ill-wishers I have mentioned and once actually was recklessly struck by a piece of rock, hurled by persons unknown, as he was walking into the feed-store where we procure the main part of our supplies. . . .

Such worries as any of this account may arouse in you I ask you to keep from Father, and only make sure to say to him that his last cheque to me was over a month delayed. I remain as always deeply grateful, you may tell him, for his continued indulgence.

Your affectionate, if too far distant, brother,

Geoffrey

—Excerpt from letter written by Geoffrey Carmingler
to his brother William in East Sussex[3]

——

"You'd best stay with me for now," Jenny Ezkiaga said as she blew through the red light and swung her Passat recklessly onto a busy roadway that he guessed was headed west from downtown. She was a terrible driver, as if she'd learned late and carelessly, but the car had airbags and you had to either go with it or get out, Jack Liffey thought. "I'll get about six calls the instant they lift the lockdown," she said.

She grimaced and came to a very late stop about six feet into a big intersection. She made no attempt to back up to her proper place and ignored the drivers in the cross-traffic who glared as they had to crowd the center lane to get past her.

"In the meantime, I need to find out how this is going down. How do you feel about evangelicals?"

"They have the same right to their beliefs as Rastafarians and Scientologists and cargo cults, as long as they don't think any of their rules apply to me," Jack Liffey said. "The same goes for Presbyterians, Hassidim, and Shiites."

"And when you're not being tolerant?"

"I try not to go to the other place." The light changed and she jackrabbited away, then ground the shift into second.

"If they ever get total power, you and I'll have a big problem," she offered.

"I don't worry about it much," he said.

"Why's that?"

"The only way fundamentalists could have that kind of power would be at some local level, and it would be miles from where I live."

"Where will you be?" she asked.

"Somewhere else. Preferably where a lot of competing ideas are still buzzing around. Even lame ones."

"One can never tell where one'll end up."

"Oh, yeah. One can tell about *that*."

She waggled a finger pointing straight ahead like a guide pointing out a new ecosystem. "This here's the southwest part of town. Look familiar?"

Past a big strip mall, the housing tract he saw reminded him of Orange County, in fact. Two-story earth-toned houses with fanlights and too many gables. They were set shoulder to shoulder behind a continuous concrete block wall that shut out the highway. It was the white-flight middle-class suburb of any American city, he thought, and it looked like there was an awful lot of it. "Whitebread Meadows," he said.

She nodded. "Good people, of course. Work hard, go to the PTA, backyard barbecues—but there's also some germ of fear at work out here. I don't really understand it. Law and order is the password in this town. It's as if they carry some tragic burden from the past that might catch up at any minute, like Faulkner's Mississippi.

"I've been in a lot of places and this one's different," she went on. "I've never seen so many folks worried about the Other sneaking up on them when they're not looking. Not just blacks and Mexicans. They're worried sick their own kids will turn teenage and sass them. It's like the whole place is so brittle that the smallest lapse'll shatter it."

"I'm only one guy," Jack Liffey said, "and I don't have enough duct tape to hold a whole suburb together." He wasn't sure what she was after.

"You told Sonny you corral missing kids. That's a fine calling. You work for one of those big fancy agencies?"

"Not big, not fancy. Just me."

"Really? Does it pay?"

He made a face. "A couple times it paid okay but not often enough. Mostly I get to be the Eagle Scout who leads the survivors down off the mountain."

He glanced at the big ugly houses, walled and wired against intruders, and considered what she'd said. These people were right about it being a tough world, he thought, but not for the reasons they always thought.

Her cell phone rang. He looked away and braced himself a little. Her driving was bad enough when she was undistracted.

"Ezkiaga. Oh, hi, hon. No, I can't make it home for lunch, sorry." She braked hard and then changed lanes and sped up again. His peripheral vision returned inexorably to the controls as if he might have to grab for them. She shifted with the phone in her right hand and had to yell down at it for a moment. "Something's up in town. I'll tell you about it tonight. Sure, anything but pasta. Um-hmm. Me, too." She rang off without ramming the car into anything solid.

"My partner," she explained. He wanted to say something that indicated that her gender preference was perfectly cool with him, but didn't quite know what it should be.

"Here we are," she said, saving him from fretting out a response.

The building looked like a gigantic flying saucer that had touched down on an equally large ring of stained glass windows. The lake-sized parking lot was nearly empty, and a low sign at the entrance said it was the Olive Grove Evangelical Church. A bright electronic section of the sign flashed a crawl at the world: YES, GOD PUNISHES SIN. YES, YOU CAN BE SAVED.

They parked near a handful of cars, and nearby a man was talking to a couple of painters who were raising the mercury level of a giant thermometer signboard. ADVENTURE IN GIVING, it said, and it shocked Jack Liffey a little to see the temperature reading calibrated in tens of millions of dollars.

Jenny told him that he was looking at the pastor here; amazingly, he was the very man-of-God he'd seen briefly on TV in the motel. In person his face looked younger than it should, Jack Liffey noted, wondering if he might have had a peel. His hair was a wavy steel gray and swept straight back from a high forehead, though less rigidly than it had been on camera. Don't prejudge, Jack Liffey told himself. He is what he is, and it may be just fine.

The pastor had a nice line in friendly smiles, bestowing one on the lawyer and then another on Jack Liffey for good measure. It really did seem sincere.

"Blessings, Miss Ezkiaga. It's always a pleasure to run into you."

"You, too, Denny. To me you're always the guy who puts the fun in fundamentalism."

He laughed, and she introduced Jack Liffey with a passing reference to being stuck in town for a day or two because his daughter had had an accident. Relatively true. The handshake was firm and not excessively hearty.

"Just a moment, please," the pastor said. He went back to talking to the sign painters. Jack Liffey could hear him quizzing the men about some banner he'd ordered for a harvest festival. "I don't want any gourds or turnips, anything that might be a pumpkin. You know how we feel about Halloween."

"Yes, sir, Pastor K. Are corncobs kosher?"

Jack Liffey smiled a little to himself. Were corncobs *kosher*? he thought.

In an inner courtyard a group of teens appeared to be rehearsing a pageant. They looked very clean-cut.

"What brings you out our way?" Pastor Kohlmeyer asked as he led them toward a low structure that jutted off the side of the huge nave.

"I'd like to know if you've heard about the dead infant down by the river . . . and the circumstances."

His face lengthened and he nodded gravely.

"You mean the emergence of the Satanic underground. We've warned of precisely this for years, Miss Ezkiaga. Milk production declined last month all over the county with no known cause."

Jenny halted for just an instant but then walked on as if changing her mind about something.

The pastor proceeded as if she hadn't just seen her shadow. "We're assuming the infant was unbaptized since no one is claiming her. In the *Malleus* handbook they say Satanists need the blood of an unbaptized child. The enemies of the Lord have been waiting out there, lurking for years—for what purpose we don't know. But we *will* fight back. It is necessary and has been foretold. As you are aware."

"I'm aware of no such thing, Denny. Jack, would you wait here?"

"Sure," he said. He'd heard too much, and he wanted only to get Maeve out of this town fast.

The two went into the office through a glass door. Jack Liffey took a deep breath and slowly made his way back to the passage that led to the inner courtyard. The teens were waving their arms hammily. Watching them, he tried to still his uneasy mind. An irrational fear had taken him over concerning Maeve, as if she were being stalked by some malevolent force here, a demon-faced killer in this town searching her out.

"Why has my wheat turned sour on the stalk and why have the leaves all shriveled?"

It was a young male voice that fluted a little at the end. The boys all wore long-sleeved silver T-shirts with an emblem on the back.

"Because you have done the unspeakable!"

"Because when the evil spirit sprang upon you, you *did not* resist!"

Jack Liffey moved a few steps closer and noticed that the design on the T-shirt was a hand holding a sword that had a wide handguard. The sword, cleverly, threw the perfect shadow of a cross. SWORD OF GOD, it said.

A girl in a white robe stepped forward. "The demons them-selves believe everything that you believe! Your belief is no better than theirs unless the true terror of hell rules your life!"

As the boy prostrated himself abruptly before the girl, Jack Liffey found himself backing hurriedly out of the passage. Thank-fully, after only a few paces into the open air, ambient acoustics swallowed the fanatical and maladroit dialogue of their play. He felt he'd been dropped for a moment into a faraway country whose gestures and warnings he could not quite construe.

Before long the office door opened and Jenny Ezkiaga strode out first, looking exasperated, followed by Kohlmeyer. "Where are you going with this, Miss Ezkiaga?" he asked. There was no answer.

She walked straight past Jack Liffey, but the pastor stopped facing him, only a few feet away. Aftershave perfumed the air. They watched each other for a lengthening moment.

"Mr. Liffey, have you accepted Jesus Christ as your personal savior?"

He didn't know what to say. There was no point in showing disrespect. Not to people here, not while his daughter was in town. Come on, he told himself, this isn't the Taliban, shooting people against walls. "No, sir, I'm afraid I haven't."

"You should tremble for your soul then, sir." He looked at Jack Liffey pityingly. "It will writhe and burn in conscious pain for all eternity."

He thought of walking away, but anger took hold of his better judgment. "Do you really believe in a God who's so sadistic?"

"It's your soul." Kohlmeyer's voice oozed concern, but his eyes were cold.

"Man, where does all that hate come from?" Jack Liffey said.

The minister smiled. It was frosty now, worse than his frown. "Look deep into yourself. I think the time is near. It's not me who hates, Mr. Liffey."

——

If anything, she was more reckless on the return journey, driving right up on other cars' tailpipes. Finally he had to say something.

"Slow down or I'm going to get out and walk."

"Sorry." She did slow down, though she wasn't much more attentive. "At least we know where Pastor K stands."

"He doesn't have much of a line in Christian love."

She looked over at him, then shook her head slowly. "This is just getting off the ground. I have to live here. Mark my words, Jack, it's not going to be pretty. Olive Grove has a congregation of over ten thousand people. It has congregants in social work, in the sheriff's office, and with the D.A."

She slowed the car a little more and was now going *too* slowly. But at least she was in the far right lane.

"Kids will be pointed out and taken into the star chamber and badgered until they admit they've seen the witches fly." She glanced at him again. "One or two may say they were molested by a middle-aged man from L.A."

"*Don't say that.* It creeps me."

"We had our fill of this poison in the eighties. You heard a little of it from Sonny, but don't sell it short. A hundred parents lost their kids and actually went to prison. All that rot about hanging their children up on hooks in motels and selling them for sex! Nobody ever found so much as a *screw-hole* in a ceiling. It's hard to believe, I know. People were so scared here that they were videotaping their own kids saying how happy and innocent they were and locking the tapes in safe-deposit boxes. The same mindless persecutors are still around, still sniffing into their neighbors' business."

"We had something like that in L.A."

"I know. McMartin Preschool. We were the proximate cause of that, Jack. Our interrogation teams sent people down to L.A. to show your prosecutors how you get kids to confess. How to insist and suggest and insinuate until you tease out those blanked-out memories. Even today, the accusers here and the D.A. think that they were right. It was just the evil liberal courts up in Sacramento that defeated them."

"Even now?"

She nodded.

He'd always wanted to believe that as time moved inexorably on, hurts healed and minds broadened, but maybe they didn't. He remembered a gruff neighbor from his youth, a seemingly ordinary engineer, who had disciplined his boys relentlessly with an old hacksaw blade. It was difficult as a child to judge an adult, but even then he thought he could see a man who was a little crazed, scared to death that someone would think him soft or weak or effeminate. He wondered what those boys were like now. He'd lost touch. Maybe generation after generation of violently disciplined children reproduced themselves, and rage accrued gradually within the human race like a toxin. Until brutality was everywhere and inescapable.

"They know absolutely that they're right, Jack. You can't shake them."

"You know what the physicist Niels Bohr said about that kind of certainty?" Jack Liffey said.

"No."

"He said clarity is the opposite of truth."

She smiled a little. "Yeah. I guess most people can't live with that."

"Let's not be elitists," Jack Liffey said. "If we can live with uncertainty, they can."

## Chapter Four

# AMERICAN BANALITY

T hey were told that it would probably be early evening by the time the lockdown was called off. So, around noon, Jenny Ezkiaga dropped him back at her office, and Sonny Theroux was kind enough to offer him a ride to the central library, where Jack Liffey felt he could burn off some down time.

"Where you and Jenny been at?" Sonny asked as they climbed into his van. Jack Liffey suspected the "at" was something of a cornpone affectation.

"We drove out to some church that looked like a mothership invading earth."

"Olive Grove. Where more than nine thousand enthusiastic souls are ministered to. Some kind of record. For a mid-size city west of the Pecos. Or something."

"Call me crazy, but I got a distinct whiff of fanaticism," Jack Liffey said. "Are you religious?"

"Not so you'd notice. And certainly not that strain. They ain't worth a bent nail, as we say down in swamp country."

Jack Liffey glanced skeptically at him.

Sonny grinned. "Okey-doke. If you prefer the words of the great James Joyce, I was a Catholic so I was raised in a logical religion. You can't expect me to go and join an illogical one."

Jack Liffey smiled. *"Portrait of the Artist*—strange book to come across in a swamp library."

A little runic smirk played on Sonny's lips. "I went and got me a degree or two from Duke, but don't spread it around. It was kinda accidental."

"Uh-huh."

"Mom did go and convert to the tongues when I was nine so I got my fill of Skeeter Bob's Jumpin' and Howlin' Church."

"I don't know which of your personas to focus on."

"It's possible to be many things in this world, Mr. Liffey. You know, in the South when we say I-think-I'm-losin'-my-religion all we really mean is I'm-about-to-start-swearin'. Eventually I argued that minister to death. That peckerhead was in a world of hurt trying to cope with my questions about some poor Burmese who never heard of Jesus. "

"I thought you were a cop," Jack Liffey said.

"Oh, yes, that, too. Ponder signs and wonders and then dismiss them."

Sonny dropped him at the main library, and Jack Liffey

cranked away at an old microfilm machine to read the *Bakersfield Bee*'s files on the last outbreak of local hysteria in the early 'eighties. It was a depressing read.

Toward dusk he wound the clattery machine to a small article that summarized the end of the trial for felony child abuse of a couple called, implausibly, the Smallbeers. The indictment had charged Randolph and Edna Smallbeer with hanging their nude seven-year-old daughter Tina Marie from the ceiling of their suburban ranch house and selling her for the pleasures of a number of strangers they had invited home from the Kern Rancho Motel. The name, reminiscent of his own motel, gave him a little chill.

It was reported that the D.A. insisted there was no significance whatever to the fact that the hookhole had been so expertly plastered over it could not be found, nor could any unaccounted-for strangers who'd ever stayed at the Rancho.

Jenny Ezkiaga's hand tapped his shoulder gently. "The lock-down's over, Jack."

He wasn't inclined to move right away. "Do you remember the Smallbeers?" he asked her.

"Um-hm. It wasn't my case but it was bad. I think the girl was their only child and she was taken away immediately and fostered. She was one of the last to recant all the nonsense the investigators planted in her head, and her parents' conviction wasn't overturned until they'd spent ten years in Susanville. I think they're living in Ohio now but the girl's right here in town. Six feet down in Union Cemetery. She couldn't face her folks getting out. Drugs and promiscuity got her first. Then self-hatred, I suppose. She seized it all like a whip and beat herself to death."

"Shit," he said.

"Let's get your daughter, Jack."

"Before she tells them I drink the blood of Christian babies."

"Don't even joke about it. Please."

— —

"Dad!" The door slammed behind her. Even at seventeen years and nine months, Maeve still managed to be all elbows and knees as she ran at him like a twelve-year-old. She flung herself around him in the lobby, and he was embarrassed a little by the fullness of her breasts against him. A dozen other adults waited nervously around the facility for their own children, watching him with envy and resentment. It was like a hospital lobby and his loved one had unaccountably beaten the cancer.

"Honey, it's wonderful to see you're okay."

"No thanks to this crummy place."

"Mr. Liffey, if you'll just sign here." He was handed a clipboard, a red X indicating where he was expected to play his part in this charade.

"Read it first," Maeve hissed. "You're probably giving up the right to sue."

"Those things are meaningless," he said softly, scribbling hastily on the paper. If anyone bothered to look closely, they'd see he'd scrawled JACK D. RIPPER.

"A friend of mine's still in there," Maeve insisted. She drew back a little as he tried to lead her away.

"Not right now, hon." He had visions of bone-chilling klaxons going off at the last instant and steel shutters coming down to seal them inside. "Let's get out of here first."

"Dad—"

"We'll talk about it, I promise."

He got her out the door as the sun was dropping into a glorious blaze of red cloudbank off to the southwest. "Have you had
anything decent to eat?"

"I'm not very hungry."

She settled into his pickup with a sigh, worried to death about
something—as usual—and he drove straight to the nearest coffee
shop, which was beside a rambling hotel. He hadn't eaten all day
and he was famished. Just to cap the day, there seemed to be a
convention of clowns at the hotel and every table was raucous
with false laughter emitted through greasepaint.

"There's this amazing girl in that place who's all alone now.
She didn't do anything but get a few tattoos."

He held up the flat of his hand. "First things first. Please. I'd
like to know how you got arrested."

"It's not my fault, dad."

"I didn't think it was."

The waitress came and Maeve found the vegetarian special
right off. In deference to her sensibilities he avoided red meat
and ordered the fried chicken.

She sipped at her water and swallowed carefully, as if testing.
"Okay, you know I dropped off to sleep in the car on the way
down from the mountains. I must have slept for an hour, and by
the time I got into the motel room, I found I was wide awake. So
I thought I'd go out for a little walk. The dark out there was scarier
than I thought, and when I saw a couple of women I went over to
talk to them. I guess they were hookers," she said sheepishly.

"But *I* hate clowns, too," a voice boomed, and several others
laughed.

"Miniskirts?" Jack Liffey said. "Deep voices? Lots of attitude?"

"Uh, I guess so."

"I think they were transvestites, hon. I made that round looking for you."

"Oh, wow." She thought about that for a moment. "If they're still sort of equipped like *guys*, what do they *do*? I mean—"

He smiled uncomfortably. "I think you can figure it out when you try. Is that when the cops showed up?"

"Yeah. They . . . the trannies, right? . . . they were just trying to shoo me back to the motel when the police car screeched up. They were really nasty to the—uh—women, and so I got angry and said they were just helping me and asked them to please be polite. They didn't like that and when I couldn't show them any ID—I'd left it back in my purse—one of them pretended to find some little Baggies in my shirt. I thought they only did that stuff in movies."

"They watch the same movies you do."

"They kept me at the station for a while, and when they figured out I was a minor, they got all freaked and took me to the juvenile hall. I'm sorry I had to call Gloria in the middle of the night. I don't know what she said to them, but they dropped the dope thing in the morning. Then there was the stupid blockdown . . ."

"Lockdown."

"Sure, but I'm glad there was. I got to make a really neat friend."

"Okay, now you can tell me about her."

She opened her mouth but stopped when the waitress brought their plates and fussed over them a little, as a table nearby erupted in laughter.

"I'm sorry about the other diners tonight," the waitress said, as if unable to use the word clowns. "They don't even tip good," she confided.

"We'll all survive," Jack Liffey said.

She left and Maeve dabbed at what looked like an eggplant and zucchini stew, poking and separating as if sure she'd find the hidden cutlet.

"Dad, so she's got a lot of tattoos and other stuff but I really liked her. She was really smart and her dad ran off long ago and her mom's a drunk."

"Define 'other stuff.'" He knew Maeve was forever picking up strays, and he wanted to be careful.

"Piercings and stuff. Honest, try to get over your prejudice. She's got a lot of earrings and one in her nostril and another one in her lip." She gave a mildly embarrassed smile. "And her hair's kind of extreme, too, I guess. But she's read *Jane Eyre*, dad. Toxie's got a really good mind and heart."

"Toxie?"

"It's just a nickname. She calls herself Toxic Shock."

He almost spit out a mouthful of the dreadful chicken. "Okay, I admit using a name like that takes guts. Almost as much as eating here."

Just then, a handful of teen performers ran in front of them juggling tableware from one to another, forks, peppermills, a Coke can, a jar of Tabasco. They wore silver sweatshirts that said JUGGLERS FOR JESUS.

The jugglers pirouetted together like a doo-wop group, and with a chill he saw the SWORD OF GOD on the backs of the shirts, then they swung back smiling, and on a whim he tossed an open salt shaker up into their mix. The shaker made it along the row twice before it began tilting and then spewed across the floor.

"Gosh darn!"

They bowed to the table and then trooped away, abandoning their little mess.

"Will you help me help Toxie?" Maeve insisted.

"I can't. But we'll talk to a lawyer I've met. She's got a good heart. But after that I'm getting you out of this place. I think it's a hard rain's a-gonna fall, hon."

— —

**Artifact: 1922a**

ERNEST WARNING
While the rabble with their thumb-worn creeds, their large professions and their little deeds, mingles with selfish strife—

FREEDOM WEEPS
Wrong rules the land and waiting, Justice sleeps.

To gamblers, gunmen, bootleggers, loafers, lawbreakers, nancys, guntzels, and perverts of every class and description, black, white or yellow—

BE WELL WARNED
If you are found in our town, we beg to advise you that however much you screech and wail, you will be dealt down without mercy."

Shafter Klan, No. 3, Ku Klux Klan, Kern Klavern, Realm of Kalifornia

—Notice distributed at night throughout the town of Taft, February 10, 1922.[4]

— —

As they came up the walk, a little girl with a head of golden ringlets burst out a screen door squealing and leapt off the porch. Jack Liffey wondered if he had the address of the tidy bungalow near downtown correct. But it was the right Passat in the two-track concrete driveway. He'd warned Maeve what to expect and she'd been mildly scornful that he thought he had to prepare her to meet lesbians.

"Olly-olly-oxen-free-free-free!"

A slender woman came running out behind. "That won't get you out of your bath, young lady."

"Oh," the woman noticed them waiting on the walk. "Are you for Jenny? Go on up."

"Thanks," Jack Liffey said, and then in a stage whisper he revealed, "She's hiding behind the car."

"No fair!" The blonde child rose up from where she'd been trying to shush them with elaborate gestures.

"Grown-ups stick together," he said darkly. "You may as well learn it now."

"Dad, you're mean," Maeve said.

"I'll do better later in life."

Jenny Ezkiaga was cross-legged on a hooked rug, gluing alternating orange and black construction paper strips into a long paper chain. Presumably for Halloween—the Devil's holiday, according to that pastor. He introduced her to Maeve.

"Please don't get up," Maeve said. She hurried over to shake the woman's proffered hand and then sat beside her and started sorting the strips to make the task easier.

"I'm glad to see you safe and sound," Jenny told her. She looked up at Jack Liffey. "I hope you're on your way to the highway. It's right on up 24th Street just six blocks west. Best on-ramp there is.

Don't even slow down until you're past the Grapevine and well on your way over the pass."

The Grapevine was a legendary stretch of road, once only a winding two-lane track but now a broad freeway, that was still the only real connection across sixty miles of mountains from the great central valley of California to Los Angeles.

"Maeve has something to tell you first."

But before Maeve could say anything, the woman they'd met outside came in carrying the child, who had obviously abandoned her escape plans and clung so hard to her neck he feared she would crush it. "Liffeys, this is Teelee Greene, and our rambunctious daughter, Catalin. Jack and Maeve."

The little girl was turned so she could greet them now, more formally. She seemed shy all at once.

"That's it for now," Teelee said. "Bath time!"

"G'night, Mommy J," Catalin said.

"I'll come tuck you."

When they had gone, Jack Liffey said, "She's lovely. Yours or hers?" He wasn't sure it was appropriate, but what the hell.

"Tee was the birth mother, and I managed to put the son-of-a-bitch who beat hell out of both of them away in Corcoran. The kid was Kathy until we all got together and then she wanted to take a Basque name for my sake."

"It's lovely," Maeve said. "My name is Celtic, too."

"Basque isn't really a Celtic language, dear. Then it would have been Caitlin or Caitriona. Basque is a pure mystery, with no known pedigree."

"And the name Teelee?" Jack Liffey inquired.

She shrugged. "A horse of another color." She didn't seem to want to go into it.

Maeve broke the uncomfortable pause by starting to explain about her new friend. When the outrageous name she'd given herself came up, Jenny Ezkiaga took it in stride.

"Can you help Toxie?" Maeve pleaded.

"I'll be honest with you. I don't know. My weather service says we've got a stage five fear-storm coming. What do they have on her?"

Maeve made a face and told her about the Little Debbie Devil tattoo. "It's a joke. I mean, it's got a *slingshot*. It looks more like Cupid than Damien in Omen 10."

The lawyer reached for the pack of construction paper and wrote Toxie's name on a sheet of thick orange paper. "Listen, around here, Cupid is considered a spawn of Satan, too. Do you know anything else about her?"

"She said the police picked her up at a pizza place."

She nodded. "That'd be Jerry's. The punks and the Goths hang out there."

"She's really smart and she's read a lot and I can't stand it that she doesn't have a chance. She says her mom is drunk most of the time and has a lot of men. And some of the men hit her or try to touch her up."

"A real name would help me a lot, Maeve."

"I'm sorry. I'm sure the other kids all know Toxie."

"I'll pay for your time," Jack Liffey offered.

Maeve looked over at him with such touching gratitude that he felt he had to add, "We'll take it out of your allowance for the next three hundred years."

"What allowance?"

— —

He had the good sense for once to follow the advice he'd been given and get right out of Dodge, up the inviting on-ramp to Highway 99 and south along the unending median of pink and white ten-foot-high oleander bushes. It was nearly pitch-dark but there was what looked like a bank of fog out to the west. L.A. was only two hours away, maybe a bit less. He wished that he'd kept on going two nights before.

"We never got much of a father-daughter chat," Jack Liffey said.

"Life always gets in the way when you make plans."

"Are you quoting somebody?"

"Me," she said. "Or maybe you."

"You're still off school for a few days. How about we go somewhere really peaceful tomorrow and talk."

"It's all good."

He assumed that meant yes. "Think about where and I will, too.

"Maybe we should go somewhere really weird," she said. "You know—like the stripper museum or the H of the Hollywood sign where that 1930s starlet jumped off to commit suicide." They had a standing game of finding L.A. oddities.

"Dammit, I deserve my share of American banality," Jack Liffey said. "This sort of father-daughter scene has to be performed in the style of an old MGM movie. Violins and a picturesque pond with bluebirds flying around."

"We're all from indie films these days, Dad," Maeve corrected. "You get smoldering trashcans in alleys."

——

It was about 11:00 when they got back home. Gloria greeted them from the porch barefoot with a beer in her hand. She'd been hitting that hard recently more and more, a professional hazard with cops, he knew. Their luggage was in the extended cab of the pickup behind the seats so he transferred it to the driveway and Maeve took her backpack inside. He rarely used the camper shell, didn't even lock it, because it had a bit of a mysterious leak when subjected to a long assault of rain. In fact, they'd passed through a squall coming over the Grapevine into L.A. but they'd been lucky and left it behind in a few minutes.

On a whim he tilted up the back hatch to see if any water had got in. It would be nice to be able to use the back once in a while. Glancing inside, he froze in his tracks. It took him almost a minute to decide to lean forward and look closer, but he wouldn't touch. Then he propped the tail-hatch up. Luckily Maeve had gone on into the house.

"Gloria, come here."

"No shoes, Jack."

"Fuck shoes. Look at this."

Not one to follow peremptory orders from a mere live-in lover, she backed into the house where she wriggled her feet into slip-ons by the door.

She came up beside him to see, and the only sign she gave was to inhale a little deeper.

"Is it real?" he said.

She reached down and lightly touched the severed infant's hand with the backs of two fingers. It lay in a pool of something dark that had congealed and then acquired a spattering of waterdrops.

"I'll call it in. Don't touch a thing."

"I'm on it."

"Do you ever have a little burst of *good* luck, Jack?"

"Last one was when I met you."

She shook her head, walking away. "I'm too tough to flatter, *querido*."

Chapter Five

# A MAN TO TIE UP NEAR IN A STORM

T hey got a special mass they say for cops killed down in
Lakeview," the big cop said. "They wave spears and
beat on jungle drums." His name was Tommy Etcheverry and reclining in his chair he was stocky enough to suggest a
barrel tipped against the wall. He had no discernible waist and
wore Sam Browne suspenders to hold up all the usual stuff hung
from his belt, the handcuffs and leather pouches with extra magazines for the Glock .40 that was not currently residing in his
shoulder holster. His jacket was off, his feet rested on an opened
drawer, and his fingers were laced behind his head.

"What do you say special about Loma when I'm not around?"

the other officer said, standing beside the desk. It was Lt. Efren Saldivar, if Jack Liffey remembered the name right, young and darkly handsome with a tidy mustache and an expensive suit. From his manner he seemed to outrank Etcheverry, though he'd never actually heard Etcheverry's rank.

"You know why they never run out of names for kids down in Loma?" Etcheverry counted off on his stubby fingers. "After Jose, they always got Hose-B, Hose-C, Hose-D . . . run out of letters, they got Hose-1, Hose-2—"

"I get it, you *vasco* sheepfucker."

Etcheverry laughed and Jack Liffey did his best to ignore the whole unpleasant scene from where he sat on a bench a few feet away, waiting for Scientific Investigation Division in L.A. to fax their report to the Bakersfield P.D. He'd driven back voluntarily so they could look over his pickup to doublecheck whatever L.A. told them, and maybe as a kind of moral hostage so they wouldn't bother Maeve again for any conceivable reason. The infant's hand itself was coming by medical messenger—one of those services the hospitals used to send around kidneys and livers.

Saldivar turned slowly to Jack Liffey. "I hope I don't have to tell you to keep this hand business mum. It's one of the details we aren't releasing to the press."

"*One* of them? Jesus Christ, was some other body part missing?"

"It could matter down the line."

Like cops everywhere, they never deigned to answer your questions. It made a certain sense, he knew, but he wondered what the human toll was. In his experience most people desperately wanted to share what they knew, and he wondered how long it took cops to train themselves so there would always be an insular *us* facing a probably culpable everybody else. It was part of his long-running problem with Gloria Ramirez, who barely opened up to him, even in bed, and he was never sure what she was holding back. In fact, she was masterly at leaving an edge on even the endearments she grudged him, probably just to arms-length him a bit.

But he was a big boy now, Jack Liffey told himself, and he could deal with a little chill at home. From the present company, as well.

"Your daughter was involved in this, too, wasn't she?" Saldivar said.

"No. Not at all. We were just passing through town and I got sleepy and I picked the wrong motel, the Rancho Bakersfield which I learned too late has a bad rep. That's my fault. She went out for a walk at night, the way wide-awake kids will, and you can guess who she ran into over there. If you want the truth, one of your black-and-whites rolled up on her for being where she was—that's understandable enough. But since he couldn't get anything else on her he palmed some Baggies out of her shirt pocket. Just so we all know that I know."

That got their attention. "He's since decided it was an accident."

They seemed to chew that over in a place that caused a bit of molar pain, but in the end let it pass. They discussed something amongst themselves for a while and looked over papers that Etcheverry held.

"How do you think that item ended up in the back of your truck?" Saldivar asked, looking up.

*That item.* Jesus. "I don't lock my camper shell because I never use it, and there's nothing back there but jumper cables and a work shirt. Nothing in there's worth the windows being broken for. The truck was parked at the motel for two days. Why me, why my truck?—I honestly don't know. I don't like coincidence any more than you guys do, but I can't figure why anyone in this town would want to set me up." He was talking too much and he knew it.

"And you were where at midnight?" Saldivar asked thoughtfully.

"In my room, asleep. Alone. I did talk to the night clerk about four, after I got a call about my daughter."

"Oh, detectives!" A beautiful blonde came in and waited on the other side of a low railing across the room. She was so stunning with pouty lips and a model's cheekbones that not one of them could take his eyes off her. "The L.A. fax you want is coming through. It's on the wrong machine up in the captain's office, that's why we couldn't find it. It's at fourteen of thirty-five pages so it'll be a while."

"Thanks, Susan," Saldivar called.

She had to step aside as a gaggle of black-clad youths with piercings, tattoos, and Day-Glo hair were herded in by two uniformed officers.

"Take your seats along the wall. Your number will be called when your prize is drawn."

One scrawny girl wearing shoveled-on mascara tugged at the cop's sleeve. "Ossifer, could you tell me who I have to suck off to get out of here?"

He yanked his arm away. "Hey! I'll have to have this shirt sterilized."

"Drake, what's *that* one's name?" Etcheverry called across the room. "The one who wants to suck somebody off?"

"Glow," the uniform called back. "But really, it's Cheryl Morgan."

"On what evidence?"

"Jeez, L.T., I don't know. I guess her mom told her."

"That's only hearsay," Etcheverry said. Saldivar sat forward and chuckled.

"She says she doesn't have a driver's license," the uniformed officer gave as an excuse.

"It was a joke," Etcheverry said, half under his breath. "Okay, Drake. Make sure *that* one goes into room three first. The minute Mrs. Orcutt gets here."

Saldivar glanced at Jack Liffey. "Your daughter look like them?"

Jack Liffey wanted desperately to dissociate Maeve from those lost and angry kids across the room, acting out who-knows-what parental abuse and neglect. But something told him it would sully Maeve, or himself, to read them out of the human race. He knew Maeve wouldn't have approved. For all he could tell, her pal Toxie might be one of those lost kids, though she was probably still locked up. There was a rule he'd followed, off and on, for many years, out of general cussedness—to insult only what could hurt him—and, though tempted now, he let that lie, too, out of a kind of weariness. I'm getting old, he thought.

"What kind of question is that?" Jack Liffey said. "My girl is a good kid."

"A question question. Maybe you should bring your girl up here for a chat. It looks like we're going to be talking to a lot of kids."

"Maybe you should—" Kiss my ass. But he stopped himself in time. "Have a look at my truck, so I can go home."

The lieutenant seemed surprised. "Your truck is impounded for the foreseeable future, Mr. Liffey. I thought you realized that. It was good of you to volunteer to bring it back, but we suspect a large number of serious crimes have been committed in this town, and your truck is the best physical evidence we have."

Jack Liffey noted the plural on "crimes." He wondered if there were more dead babies or if Jennie Ezkiaga's fears of a kind of hysteria had already begun to set in, linking untold incidents of spilled salt and missing pets and broken windows.

"May I leave?"

"You're not under arrest. But it would be good if you stayed in town for now."

"You can reach me through my lawyer, Ms. Ezkiaga."

"Not my idea of an attorney," Etcheverry said. "That rug eater."

"I like lesbians," Jack Liffey said. "They have a kind of powerful radar for morons."

— —

**Artifact: 1922b**

WIZARD REBUKES
TAR AND FEATHERS
AT KLANTAUQUA

[Exclusive Dispatch]

SHAFTER July 23—The charter of Klan No. 3 of the Shafter Knights of the Ku Klux Klan was suspended yesterday by Imperial Wizard William J. Simmons following the beating, tarring and feathering of Geoffrey Carmingler and Creighton Whitehead, growers from the nearby Rosedale Colony, on June 10. Carmingler is said to have been tortured from 9 o'clock in the morning until 10:30 at night. The two men, who are believed to be British citizens, were stripped, whipped, tarred, feathered, and dumped into the midst of revelers at a picnic and social event that was part of a 3-day Klantauqua in Shafter Park.

Yesterday a communication bearing the imprint of the Ku Klux Klan was received by two newspapers here, acknowledging the Carmingler and Whitehead beatings and justifying them by itemizing long lists of offenses supposedly committed by the two men, including "unspeakable acts against nature." On their chests were identical hand-lettered signs: "I foaut the Klan."

It was reported that following the conclusion of the speeches in the park, both men were carried in a torchlight parade through town and deposited in an unconscious condition on the jail steps. Whitehead was transported to Fresno County Hospital where he remains in critical condition. Carmingler died of his injuries at home July 1.

Simmons delivered his statement of suspension in a letter to the Los Angeles *Times*, reported yesterday in that newspaper.

—*Taft Daily Midway Driller*, July 24, 1922[5]

——

Pastor Dennis Kohlmeyer found himself in an odd mood, a troubled private respite from his duties. However, he did not like to think of moods at all. It was such a trick of the humanist psychologists to divert one's thoughts down secular pathways. Yet, clearly, his spirit was disturbed. He wondered if the devil might be hard at work already, slipping in via his inattention. He pulled a yellowing scrapbook out of his lower drawer, as if it might hold the answer to what he needed. He had not touched it in years, and he opened it to a washed out black-and-white photograph of his father, Bob-Don Kohlmeyer, standing in the back of a stake truck parked roughly where the church was now sited, though in the photo there were still rows of mature olive trees in ranks and spokes running off in all directions. Bob-Don was grinning and held a shepherd's crook, the old man's ministerial trademark in the early days, and seemed about to thrust it overhead in one of his genially triumphalist gestures. He had been a happy preacher and he had made his flock happy.

The next page showed the first church starting to rise on the cleared lot, just a foundation and lower frame, and a short distance away the raised platform where Pastor Bob-Don would orate through sound horns to the parked Plymouths and Nashes and Studebakers that gathered in the cleared grove every Sunday.

The first of the great postwar drive-in churches, he thought, with a mild clutch of embarrassment. He could hear his father's rude eloquence that had touched only the rarest note of disturbing religiosity. Bob-Don had been an includer and a forgiver and a bliss-bringer, with an Okie twang that did not hurt him at all in 1950s Bakersfield. *Think it and you half done it,* he had admonished his flock. *Smack your own back thanks. God don't mind hard work.*

Dennis didn't know where his dad had picked them all up, the endless, slightly off-center, slightly hoked-up aphorisms that had begat and multiplied in the man's ministry and given rise to endless sermons and pamphlets and a string of self-published books under the rubric *Goodness Spreads Like a Ripple.* In his teens, Dennis had grown embarrassed, even come to despise a little the whole shebang, in his own pious adolescent fervor. It was all bliss talk,

Jesus for the lazy. Gospel for dummies. But as far as he could tell, the elder son, Bob-Don, Jr. embraced every bit of his father's wide-eyed baloney with sincere admiration, and even did his best to emulate the old man's form, in a kind of second-team way, when he turned twenty-one and was invited to give guest sermons. Bob-Don Jr. came to assume that he was the heir apparent.

The phone's ring shook him, like an early awakening. "This is Pastor Kohmlmeyer."

"Pastor, it's Billy Rheinhart. You know, at the Starplex Seventeen."

"Yes, Billy. What is it?"

"Well, we got a movie you ought to know about, I think. They got it on four screens. I think it's at the Edwards, too. They must plan it's gonna be big."

He reined in his impatience with the boy.

"What's the title?"

"Oh, yeah. It's called *Exorcist*—let's see, what's a V sign mean, pastor? Is that five in Roman numerals? It's *Exorcist V Predator*."

The pastor almost laughed, but controlled the impulse. Really, you could not discount the effect, even of the most debased items of the Hollywood culture. "Thank you, Billy. By itself it may not mean anything, but we'll add it to our list. Bless and keep watch."

He set the phone down gently and made a meaningless tick mark at the top of a pad of paper. Maybe something was coming. Maybe it was all a trick. Then he pulled the memory book closer and turned a page. He saw the first Olive Grove church in the process of losing its roof and west wall to be incorporated as offices into the big new church, and he could see the radio antenna in the background, a great finger skyward. His dad had already been hosting the nightly *Good News Pioneers* on radio, before he'd moved into the TV studios in town and built up a syndication that gave him an hour over much of the San Joaquin Valley and later even parts of the midwest and deep south.

The next page hit Dennis with a chill that he didn't know could still affect him, and he almost flipped past. The massive funeral spreading around the new church, a sea of heads and bonnets over black clothing, all in the bright sun. It was said that over 50,000 souls had turned out to say good-bye to their beloved Pastor Bob-Don, who had died unexpectedly one autumn of a massive stroke. He flipped forward across the snapshots of Junior taking the reins with the hesitant blessing of their mother and the deacons' board.

Dennis Kohlmeyer stopped for a moment to eye an early photograph of Bob-Don Jr., at maybe twenty-four, talking earnestly with the elders, who appeared suspicious even then. It gave him such a mix of emotion that he was almost ashamed of himself. His brother's sad attempt to high step along in their dad's ingratiating footprints had led to sermons and homilies that were so pale a copy of the Big Ripple that some began to suspect they were parodies. But far worse, Bob-Don Jr. had little talent as an administrator and leader of men—even less as an empire-builder. The attendance at Olive Grove had tailed off disastrously, and with the worshippers went the finances.

*Goodness Spreads Like a Ripple* TV had dropped off the airwaves first in Modesto, then in Visalia and Merced. As things became dire, Dennis remembered offering modestly to help out. He'd made his approach through his mother as tentatively, and as full of brotherly love, as anyone could expect, and perhaps it had actually been that way. Still, Cain and Abel could not be ignored.

It worried him, that kind of pop psychology, the way it could affect the sheer complexity of religious faith. Two brothers: what do you expect, though? Anyway, he was no longer the person he'd been then. Now he knew God would always insist on absolute honesty, and he could acknowledge that there had been some underlying ambition in him—along with the sincere wish to save Olive Grove.

When he was given leave to speak at a service, he offered sermons that were of a different stripe altogether. Coherent, intelligent, piercing—they carried a far more solid message than his brother's or even his father's. The happy talk was gone. Maybe the congregation had needed an upbeat message in the 1950s, but times had changed. Quickly he preached his way around to questions of sin and retribution, fire and outer darkness, the importance of cleaving to the narrow rocky path—everything a Christian would actually need to resist the temptations of an increasingly material world. He'd felt himself touch a nerve, at a time and a place that demanded just such hardshell exhortations.

There was a photo of him in his first sky-blue vestment. Junior had eventually been voted out by the deacons, and in a rage he'd started a rival ministry a hundred miles to the north in Fresno. It had collapsed within a year. To show there were no hard feelings, Dennis had loaned him the money to buy his way into a Ford dealership and in this way Bob-Don Jr. became a local fixture on late-night movies on the town's NBC outlet, publicizing car bargains with a lively grin and his new trademark, a rotating collection of wild animals at his side.

One of the last photos in Dennis Kohlmeyer's memory book was of himself dedicating the school and youth center adjacent to the house of worship. He was smiling and cutting a ribbon with enormous mock scissors for the camera. Ridiculous, he thought. But a bit of innocent blarney carried nothing of brimstone, and he didn't think Jesus would mind at all as long as it furthered the work of Redemption.

He had not found in the photo album the kind of reassurance he'd sought there. Of some men, a great deal is expected, he knew. He could only hope that when his time came, he was up to the serious business of wielding the Sword of God.

And here they were, posing with him in their sweatshirts—the youth group he'd founded with Channing Pelt ten years earlier and that had gradually evolved into a men's group as well. A kind of Protestant Opus Dei, as far as he understood that vile popish organization. The Swords of God were the only crusading knights of the only realm of Christian struggle he knew, and there was little question in his mind that the devil seemed to be moving inexorably toward them. Offering a direct challenge.

—-—

"What did you and your dad come up with?" Gloria asked, as the two of them stood side by side in the kitchen so she could show Maeve how to make *chiles rellenos*. They hadn't been alone together, just the two of them, for ages.

"We finally went over to Ferndell for our heart-to-heart, since the landscape there was Dad's idea of a bucolic Rotarian heaven. The trouble was, the main park was too crowded with kids running all over the place so Dad showed me you just had to keep going upstream and you're into a wild canyon in Griffith Park, right below the planetarium. You know, where James Dean had his knife fight."

"You're as bad as your dad. You know that's not what I was asking about. I don't care *where* you talked."

"D'oh. Hey, here's one of those things that looks like a regular green pepper but's kind of triangular at the bottom." Maeve sniffed it.

"I've told you, that's a *poblano*, named for the town of Puebla, and it's very mild, perfect for *rellenos*. Stop changing the subject."

"It's one of the things I'm good at. Can I have a nibble?"

"If you agree to char the skin off later. Now. Report, young lady or I'll have you in an interview room under the hot lights."

"You're such a cop." Maeve decided against taking a nibble. She was overly sensitive to spiciness and hated that fact but could do nothing about it. "Dad and I sat down on some rocks and went around every angle of the thing. How it would interfere with college. How Mom disapproves like crazy. How it would burden me if I had the baby. And on the other hand, how it would hit me emotionally if I terminated it. We kind of decided on using that word as direct but not too horrific. Dad did his duty, on overdrive really, and he tried to be officially neutral. He's a pretty good guy, you know." She poked Gloria with a forefinger, as if the woman needed the reminder.

"Sure, he's just tops. Go on."

"I wish you acted like you felt that way, Glor. I'd like it if we could keep you."

"You get to keep me as a friend no matter what Jack and I do. I take it from all your hemming and hawing you didn't come to a decision."

Maeve made a face. "I keep making *both* decisions. They last about fifteen minutes. Dad insisted I talk to mom once more and he asked me as a favor—even if my mind was already made up—

to make it seem that I'm making my decision with her help. Of course that would be pretty hard to do if I decided to keep the baby. She's 150 percent for getting rid of it. Some of that has to do with it being Latino, I'm afraid. I'm sorry but it's true."

"You can't be sure she feels like that. By the way, does Beto know?"

"Your cop pals scared him so much about statutory rape charges that he won't come near me. It was my mistake, Glor. All that part is abundantly clear to me. Anyway, he's split for Mexico for now. All he wanted was a little gringa *chiquita* he could lord it over and fuck. *Guácala*, I was dumb."

"You *were* dumb, and you've got the flood of hormones to help out being dumb, and don't use bad Spanish just 'cause you hung with some bangers for a while." Gloria set down the whisk from beating the egg batter, slapped her hands a couple of times and turned to hug Maeve.

"Honey, after my first bad times, you know what I thought?"

Maeve was alert. Wow. Gloria seemed about to share something from her own blocked-off past. "Tell me."

"I was fifteen and I said to myself, Gloria girl, you're really something. You've got a past now."

Maeve smiled and hugged back. But she didn't quite believe her. "I bet you really thought that about a year later, after you got over him, didn't you?—not right then."

"You're too clever for your own good. When are you going to go see your mom?"

"I've got to go back there when school break's over. I'll go see her tomorrow. You haven't given me your advice yet."

"Hon, I can't. That time, when I was fifteen, and pregnant by a guy I loved a whole lot and really admired who'd saved me from heading down the delinquency road, I knew how it'd ruin him if it came out that we slipped up. Later he became my training officer when I joined the police. He's dead now and some of me still loves him a lot and misses him, and I don't have his kid to love because I got rid of it. The thing is, I honestly don't know what I feel about that."

"Ken Steelyard!" Maeve exclaimed. The man had been a childhood friend of her father's. And her father had been there with them on Terminal Island when an embittered and suicidal Japanese American had almost killed all of them but had ended up killing only Steelyard and then himself.

"Yeah. Now you know. Kenny and me."

"Well, I don't have any secret love for Beto. So that helps. Thanks for telling me your secret." And I have a secret, too, Maeve thought with satisfaction. I'm not going to go see my mom tomorrow. I'm driving up to Bakersfield to do my best to get Toxie out of the hell-hole.

—-—

"The pleasure is entirely mine, Mr. Liffey, and that is the Lord's own truth. I have made inquiries into some of your exploits in Los Angeles." For some reason, Sonny Theroux pronounced it Los ANG-uh-lees, with a hard 'g,' much the way that strange 1960s Mayor Sam Yorty had. "I believe a few years ago you were credited with terminating a diabolical plot to explode a radioactive bomb above that lovely city. And you paid a real sucker of a price for it."

"You do your research, all right."

Jenny Ezkiaga had arranged to have her investigator put Jack Liffey up for a few days. The man's house turned out to be an odd contraption just across the trickle of the Kern River in the ram-shackle slum called Oildale, and Jack Liffey was still having fun studying his host's accent, which he figured he could crank up, down, or sideways, at will.

"Actually I nearly got killed that time," Jack Liffey said. "I count it an excess of public spirit."

The small man in his tropical seersucker and Hush Puppies led Jack Liffey up the broad porch steps from the little Nissan that Jack Liffey had rented. The man's flame red hair and freckles over the white suit made him look a bit like a kitchen match. Which fit right in with the strange plasterwork Taralike Doric columns on a one-story house, the proportions all wrong, like Main street, Disneyland.

The inside of the house was more tasteful, with arts-and-crafts furniture and Turkish kilim rugs. Jack Liffey wondered what on earth it was all about.

"Consider this house, sir, your hotbed of tranquility for as long as you're domiciled here in Bako."

He opened the door into a Hollywood set-piece bedroom, possibly for *Midnight in the Garden of Good and Evil*, with silk wallpaper and varnished wood seats in the bay windows. White netting shimmered on the bed frame, presumably to keep out the tropical mosquitoes that the prop man had imported. Jack Liffey tried to ignore all the anomalies—not the least being the strange house's contrast to the surroundings that he'd just driven through, streets without curbs and real hovels with rusted Dodge hemis up on blocks.

"I know," he said, reacting to Jack Liffey's puzzled look. "A pre-vious owner had an odd sense of humor and you could say I bought into it cheap. I couldn't bring myself to plainify the premises."

"It all looks very comfortable."

"Unfortunately, Señora Hinojosa is off today. She's my house-keeper and cook. Normally you need only inform her of your least whim. Throw your wash in the wicker hamper."

Jack Liffey put his bag down on an ornate dresser.

"Mr. Theroux—"

"Sonny, please."

"May I ask you a question?"

"You certainly may."

"What the hell are you doing in Bakersfield?"

He laughed once. "I followed a bosom friend into the field of law enforcement. For reasons . . . well, let's say, for reasons, I chose to work in a number of black counties in the deepest south. I was the white man they kept around for those times when a white man was handy, if not essential, for instance in dealing with some of Dixie's tolerated eccentrics—old ladies who do not believe the War Between the States was ever lost. But one day my tenuous career as a fixer and deruffler went all asshole first." He smiled tightly. "That tale's meandery enough to require a comfortable evening with tall drinks."

"I don't drink, but I'll have a soda with you."

"The twelve steps?"

"Just ornery me," Jack Liffey said. "I quit smoking, too, just to prove to myself I could."

"Well—if it ain't chickens, it's feathers," Sonny Theroux said on his way to the door. "I'll order in some barbecue later tonight, if you've a mind for it. We're neck-deep in redneck here in Oil-dale and that's one thing they know how to do."

Jack Liffey was not particularly fond of sugary red sauces poured over meat, but he nodded. "Thank you kindly." It was difficult not to end up unconsciously parodying the speech mannerisms, even if Sonny was half putting them on himself. He liked what he had seen of the man so far.

Sonny was about to disappear from sight when he glanced back. "Remember, if you need something here concerning the police, you let me know. If I have to say so myself, you'll find I'm a pretty good man to tie up near in a storm."

—–

Teelee Greene couldn't make any of the early services because Catalin had been hiding in the back yard when she hollered for her, and a whole tizzy of a neighborhood hunt had ensued, with inevitable worries related to the dead infant on the news. However, it was only normal naughtiness, playing dog in the doghouse. Teelee had then telephoned and found out there were afternoon services, too.

She rounded up Catalin and decked them both in nice straw hats and they got to Olive Grove by three o'clock and found even the late service crowded. She had been going to Olive Grove since she was a kid, back when Bob-Don had run the place, but she had been feeling less and less welcome since Jenny had taken her in. It couldn't help but worry her, the things they said about the kind of feelings she had for Jenny. Still, she tried to keep it all separate.

"Mommie T," Catalin whispered as they sat near the back. "I can't see."

She was getting a little heavy for such spoiling, but Teelee boosted her onto her lap.

"Okay, honeybunch. Be good there."

The big organ roared as the choir burst into song, and she opened the hymnal to the number indicated on the annunciator.

Poor, weak and worthless though I am
I have a rich almighty Friend;
Jesus, the Savior, is His Name;
He freely loves, and without end.
He ransomed me from hell with blood,
And by His power my foes controlled;
He found me wandering far from God,
And brought me to His chosen fold.
But, ah! my inmost spirit mourns;
And well my eyes with tears may swim,
To think of my perverse returns:
I've been a faithless friend to Him.
Often my gracious Friend I grieve,
Neglect, distrust, and disobey;
And often Satan's lies believe
Sooner than all my Friend can say.

The hymn went on with its threats about the dire consequences of sin, but she didn't pay much attention, and after the singing, Pastor Kohlmeyer strode out of the wings and across the vast breadth of the building, looking unusually worked up. Instead of the normal service of professions and responses from the low altar, he climbed directly to the high pulpit that he rarely used.

"Would-be Christians," he thundered angrily, his deep voice booming on the powerful sound system. "We are called upon today for the utmost courage to engage in battle against the most terrifying of all our enemies. That would be Satan himself."

Teelee could hear the urgency in his voice and knew immediately that this wasn't one of his ordinary fire-and-brimstone sermons. Something was up. She held Catalin tight.

"It is right and good that every one of you should believe in the existence of the Father, the Son, and the Holy Spirit—the great triune God. *But that is not enough to save your souls today*! For James says, 'the devils also believe, and tremble.' No demon will be saved, of course, because they cannot be saved. They have been given up by God and they know they await the day of their consignment to the fires of Hell! But why did God say that?"

He went on like this, incensed and accusing. Soon Catalin was whispering, "I want to go home."

"Shhh. In a little."

"The trembling of demons when confronted with Christ actually shows that they have more faith than do you, my lost sisters and brothers! The trembling of the demons shows that they have full understanding of the awfulness of sin and their damnation—I tell you, more understanding than you have!

"Look into yourself. You have but a cold and mechanical belief in Jesus Christ and what he can do. But you have no *union* with Him. There is no emotion! There is no true fear of Hell, or terror of eternal punishment for your sins, no buckling on of armor for the immediate and present fight against the terrible Satan! This is no metaphor and no exaggeration, my friends! That fight is coming faster than any of us can predict! The fight may nearly be here! So I say again, your beliefs are *inferior* to those of the demons! You must examine yourselves!"

Around her, Teelee sensed distress in the air, as the congregants put down the hymnals they still held in their laps and a mutter of concern passed through the pews.

"In the great American spiritual revivals of the nineteenth century, many thousands of people trembled and were in such great fear that their souls would be damned to Hell for their sins that they sometimes screamed out loud, and grown men fell groaning on the floors of the churches!"

A young man with a crewcut many pews ahead of them shot to his feet. "I'm a sinner!" he shouted. Far up front a woman rose, "I want to be saved!"

"Feel it within yourselves!" the pastor shouted. "Feel you are lost in sin and must cleanse yourself *today* to gird for the battle that's coming! We have only days, maybe hours, to prepare—no more! Those who wish to declare themselves ready for the fight against the minions of Hell, come forward now! Now! Come forward, sinners!"

As he raged on about demons and faith and Godly decisions, first a few and then scores of people in the church fought their way along the pews and then rushed forward down the descending aisles to fall on their knees in the open floor before the pulpit, raising their arms toward the pastor as if reaching physically for sustenance.

"I want you to hear a personal witness," their leader cried out to them. "A young man who has begun his own crusade against the Devil. Raymond, come forward."

A boy who looked no more than fifteen rose out of the prostrate crowd and climbed quickly to the pulpit, and though the pulpit had never held two before, as far as she knew, it was ample enough for him to stand beside the pastor, who pushed the microphone toward him.

"Yesterday I was at Mike's Books." His voice broke a little and he turned his neck to cough and clear his throat. "You know, over next to the movies, and I don't know why I did it, but I picked up a book in the New Age section, and it was a pagan book called *Mother Goddess*, so I said something sarcastic to my wife. 'Can you believe how ignorant some people can be?' I asked Tiffany.

"Then, all of a sudden, before she could say anything, my head started to spin and it was like a heavy weight dropped on me. My hands started to burn where they'd touched the book. It was like some great beast had jumped on me. I tried to walk it off but I couldn't, I was filled with nausea and fear, and I told my wife I had to sit down. We missed our movie while I sat trembling and weeping. Only after two hours of sitting and praying for forgiveness for taking the demons so lightly—only then was I restored."

The boy shouted some words that sounded like a foreign language and the pastor repeated them, and then the pastor spread his arms to let his robe billow before pulling the microphone back to himself.

"Raymond learned a terrible lesson, you weak-kneed people. The demons of this world are extremely powerful, and we must not enter their arena lightly. We must not go there one by one, not now in the hour of our danger. Only after praying and only when we are ready to stand up to them together engirded by the Lord. The demons are preparing to do their wickedness right here in our town, right now—and we must prepare for war!"

"Help us!"

"The devils also believe and tremble. Remember: James says this—chapter 2:19. Who among you knows that he is lost? Tell Jesus now!"

"I'm lost!"

"Me!"

Teelee did not know exactly why, but she was becoming more

and more agitated. It was almost as if something had jumped on her, making her head felt light and dizzy. As more voices cried out around her, she set Catalin on her feet and then led her uphill away from the growing tumult behind her at the foot of the pulpit.

"Mommy, what's the matter?"

"I don't feel so good," she said. She pressed the crash bar on the blond wood door as gently as she could, and there was enough noise behind her, in the bawls and cries and the squawk of electronic feedback, so she doubted that anyone heard the door. Yet the sudden bright light washing in as the door came open could not have been missed, and she felt a chill as an amplified voice called in a threatening way, perhaps directly to her, but she was outside now, tugging Catalin along quickly across and down the vast plinth of steps as the building seemed to rumble behind her in the throes of an earthquake.

"Mommy, you're hurting me."

"I'm sorry but that's not a very nice place right now. I need to go home."

## Chapter Six

# DEATH SHAVES MY TEETH

The jail was a dark rectangle on the map right behind the courthouse, but Maeve wasn't interested in the jail per se. She just knew that somewhere in its vicinity was where the bail bondsmen would all be congregated. She'd never met one before, but she figured they'd probably be something like Robert De Niro in *Midnight Run*, running to leather jackets and super-macho get-it-done attitudes.

She parked on dead-end K Street across the railroad tracks from the jail and directly across from a clapboard bungalow with the screen door propped open by a brick and a sign that said BULLDOG BAILBONDS. What had once been a living room was a cluttered office with only one man in it who was watching a football game on a small flat-screen TV. He didn't look much like Robert De Niro. He was fat and the part of his upper body that wasn't covered by the half-open Hawaiian shirt was tattoo city. His hair was cut in a bushy mullet, which her friend Mina called a Camaro cut but Donnie said, no, it was called a Kentucky Waterfall. Whatever, it suggested some forgettable rock band of the 1980s.

He was chewing hard on a mouthful of something, and she waited patiently in the doorway until he noticed her. "Have a seat, sweetheart."

"I just have a question, sir."

"Just sit and be quiet for now. If I don't get to see this touchdown, the terrorists have won."

She didn't know what he meant, but she perched on the front edge of a stained green sofa that even the Goodwill wouldn't have taken. The animal noises of the game seemed to be building to some kind of climax. There was a big nameplate hung off the desk that said TONY "BULLDOG" DI STEFANO. She had no doubt that this man was the Bulldog. On the wall were a lot of photographs of him with various men and women. Some were signed but she couldn't recognize any of them from where she sat.

On the TV the crowd made a kind of anticlimactic noise, what amounted to a howl that died off into a groan of despair.

"Ah, crap!" the man blurted. He swung an empty wooden straight chair around easily with one immense hand for her, and rolled his own chair back behind the desk. "Come on over, girl. I am indeed the Bulldog, the one and only. You got a boyfriend in the jailhouse?"

Maeve sat down with her hands in her lap. She had rarely been so obviously undressed by a man's eyes, and she became self-conscious of her hormone-engorged breasts. She wondered if there was some way he could tell she was pregnant. But the important thing was to talk about Toxie, which she proceeded to do.

Until he interrupted. "Whoa there, girl. First off—what's your name?"

"Maeve. Maeve Liffey."

"Maeve Liffey, you can't bail nobody out of the juvie. It don't work that way. If they're not released pronto to their mom and dad, then there's what they call an adjudicatory hearing. If they say she's delinquent at the hearing, then there's a whole bunch of crap to deal with—social-work evaluations and school reports and things like that—before they give her a dispositional hearing. If you want to help her, then you gotta get her parents on the job."

He made a tepee of his hands.

"There's only her mom and I hear she's . . . got a problem with alcohol. And she—you know—brings men home. She won't be much good for this."

"Why so quick to judge? Nobody's hopeless."

"Sorry, that's just what Toxie told me."

"Uh-huh. And you don't know this Toxie's real name?"

"No, sir, I only know Toxic Shock. I'm sorry."

He chuckled. "Call me Bulldog. I know it's ridiculous, but I'm used to it and it's a damn sight better than Toxic Shock." He glanced wistfully at the TV that was still buzzing away. "Well, my workload's on the piss-poor side today so I'll tell you what. For a hundred bucks I'll find out this kid's real name and take you to her mom. Better to play real detective once in a while than always have some low-life waiting behind a door with an aluminum baseball bat."

"What happens if we find her mom?"

"That's up to you. You can either appeal to her material instincts or buy her a bottle of Ripple. Have you got a hundred bucks?"

Maeve wondered if she was getting in over her head, but she'd raided an ATM already and had more than enough money. She'd done so well finding him and engaging him that she felt she was getting a little of her spirit back. "You sure you wouldn't prefer the retainer in dogfood, Mr. Bulldog?" Maeve ventured. All at once a terrible shattering noise came out of his mouth, an aggressive braying that was nothing like the human laughter she was used to. It left her rather unhinged—it was that weird— but this was the guy she'd picked and she had to go with it now.

— —

Several hours earlier, deputies had taken Toxie and driven her to the Eastside Sheriff's Substation and marched her into a bilious green room to face more questioning. She was told she was privileged to be assisting the Cult Investigation Task Force. A video camera on a tripod caught her profile from the end of the table, but the sheriff's deputy seemed to be turning it on and off selectively as they questioned her. Though it wasn't exactly questioning either. Mostly, like before, they insisted that they *knew* things already and only wanted her to corroborate them. They refused to call her anything but Sue Ellen or Miss Crumm, names she loathed. Names seemed to be terribly important to them as each one sat behind a big paper nameplate canted toward the camera.

It seemed like the interrogation had been going on at least two hours and she was profoundly exhausted, a lot of it from having to stay alert for the tricks that she was sure were imbedded in the more outrageous allegations. She hoped that a clue here or there might tell her something about what was really going on, but their approach was so doggedly ridiculous that all she could do was repeat that she didn't know what on earth they were talking about. They were obsessed with what they referred to as the "Black Mass House." And now that she was tiring fast, she found herself giving in to sarcasm or groans of frustration.

"Young lady, we know for certain this vile ritual house is out there." The speaker was a fierce-looking woman with straight blonde hair whose nameplate identified her as Charletta Hudson from the D.A.'s office. "It's somewhere on the east edge of Old Town Kern. Don't bother denying it. Two of your friends who were picked up with you have already confirmed it. We know that Satanic rituals take place regularly there. Perhaps you started out thinking it was all just an innocent game. Did you ever take part in Dungeons and Dragons or any other role-playing games?"

"I hate that crap. Only dorks played D-and-D."

"Which dorks were those?"

"Maybe Lonnie Winokur." The old hag next to the blonde took a note—and more power to her, Toxie thought. Lonnie was the Highland High senior class president, a self-important jock and a relentless bully. She knew he'd have committed suicide in the lunch room before he'd hang with gamers.

Toxie recognized the note-taker from a previous run-in: she was Mrs. Orcutt from Social Services. With six sharpened pencils in front of her and a legal pad at the ready, she'd twist her mouth now and then as if responding to unheard jokes.

The deputy hadn't said a word, but a guy with a crew cut had regularly put in his two cents. Now he glared straight at her. "Miss Crumm, do you have a Ouija board at home?"

"Go check. If mom isn't drunk yet, she'll let you in."

His nameplate said CHANNING PELT, D.TH., M.S.C., and she was pretty sure he worked at that awful church where she'd once had to do community service cleaning the johns. Earlier, he'd announced to the camera that he had taken a special course on Satanism in Texas. He wasn't done yet, she could tell. "How about heavy metal music? Do you listen to Iron Maiden or Slayer or Black Sabbath?"

"Give me a break. They're all old and lame."

"If we check your room, will we find books on the occult?"

"I don't know. How do you classify *Wuthering Heights*?"

"I notice you like to wear black," Orcutt put in. "What does that signify to you?"

Toxie sighed. "It's in honor of my grandmother who died two years ago. I really loved her. And it tells people I prefer to be serious about life. Most people who wear bright clothes are dorks or golfers. Can I have something to eat?"

"Soon," the Hudson woman said. "We already know you've attended services at that house, Miss Crumm. And we have sworn testimony that you brought animal blood to at least one of the services."

"Puh-leeze. Somebody's lying and doesn't even know me. Blood makes me throw up."

The D.A. turned to Orcutt. "Has she had a work-up at the hall?"

"Not yet."

"Order one. See if the lab can find out if she's been ingesting blood."

"I'll have her place searched," the deputy contributed. "I

hope to God you didn't have any part in the murder of that baby, Sue Ellen."

"The devil is not always subtle or shy," Channing Pelt reminded them all. "But we may not recognize his every tendril. Look for candles, incense, especially pentagrams . . . ."

"I have sticks of sandalwood incense on my dresser," Toxie said quickly. "It's for a little ceramic Buddha that's a burner. I like the smell."

They all stared at her as if she'd just farted in church.

"You stupid fucking pigs," Toxie said. It was the best she could do in her exhaustion. "I suppose you're going to be arresting Buddhists now."

"Mind your tongue, you hooligan," the D.A. snapped at her.

"Look, if I had the Devil's private cell phone number, don't you think I'd call him up right now and tell him to hit this place with a bolt of lightning and fry all you assholes to charcoal?"

"I have it all on tape," the deputy said calmly.

— —

At the lunch break, Channing Pelt left the hearing with his own agenda in mind. He had to find Pastor Kohlmeyer and get him off the stick. The man often needed a little jump start, but he hadn't had much luck yet finding him. Dennis was not at the two-story sand-colored tract home with the big brass cross on the front door, not at the church offices nor in the nave where some hand-maids were putting out single white lilies for a funeral. He wasn't answering his cell, either.

Pelt took a chance and headed west out Fifth Standard Road toward I-5. This was the last section of farm fields close in to town that hadn't yet been subdivided. He guessed from the deep green floppy-ear leaves that he was driving past winter bush beans, though they weren't staked up so they were probably federal beans, the kind you got paid for not picking, and then got plowed under. A little farther, a big chugging diesel engine was pumping water into an ag ditch along the road where two dozen Latinos with their pants rolled up were hunched over placing siphons across the berm to carry water to the endless rows of expendable beans.

He saw the pastor's Porsche Cayenne at the base of the hillock ahead and knew he had guessed right. The hill itself was perfectly rectangular, maybe forty feet high and obviously quite artificial, dozed up long ago out of the alluvial flat for a reason that Channing Pelt simply could not guess. But Stinky Hill was the highest ground at that latitude anywhere between the Sierra foothills thirty miles due west and the Temblor Range fifty miles due east, both lost in the smog. All else for hundreds of miles to the north was as flat as thousands of years of erosion and a century or so of land graders could make it.

Pelt suppressed the disdain he felt automatically for the silver SUV. He drove a small Nissan himself, but it was only one of many private objections he had to Kohlmeyer.

His eye ran along the lip of the hill and he made out the backlit form of the pastor on his knees. Drama queen, Pelt thought. Dennis had always had something like a pagan gene in him. He'd caught the man praying here before, in moments of inner crisis, like a Roman seeking out the holy hill where the gods resided. From Kohlmeyer's fire-breathing sermons, based on the goofier fever dreams in the Book of Revelations, to his heartfelt insistence on every literal wrinkle of the King James Bible, mistranslations and all, Pelt had always felt that what the pastor really needed was a couple of years in a good theology school and a little Greek and Aramaic. But there were no suspect hermeneutics, no abstractions nor allegories in the pastor's worldview. Whale swallows man. God said it, I believe it, and kiss my Jerusalem ass.

Pelt trudged up the steep sideslope of Stinky Hill. It had no particular stench today, just the peaty tang of earth. Nary a hint of brimstone. Pelt held a doctorate from the Claremont Theological School, and ten years earlier he had signed on at Olive Grove as a kind of anthropologist slumming amongst the fundies, but in point of fact he had a rather mischievous taste for all the literalism. Why not stop the earth's rotation so a battle could play itself out? Why not a God who could scatter old bone fragments down through all the geological strata just to play a massive joke on the paleontologists? If I have a sense of humor, Pelt thought, why shouldn't God?

And in the end, even as a drama queen full of hellfire, Dennis Kohlmeyer was a decent enough man to work for, the gig at Olive Grove paid well, and the pastor was even amenable to suggestion as long as you led him to think some new idea had boiled up out of his own rather fevered psyche. To give himself his due, there were scores of children Pelt had been able to boost circumspectly across their literalist crises, children whose parents would never have let them go to a mainstream church.

"Pastor."

Kohlmeyer looked up from the bleached plank where he had knelt to save his trousers. "Channing."

"I hope I'm not interrupting something important."

"I felt a need to retreat here to prepare myself. I fear a battle is coming."

He offered to help the man up, but the pastor wasn't ready to

JOHN SHANNON

rise yet. "No one ever feels worthy, Dennis," Pelt offered. "Even Jesus doubted briefly on Gethsemane."

"I will always go the limit, with God's hand upon my shoulder. I'll push my limit if He asks it, you know that."

"Well, I think I've got what we need. We've got a girl just crying out to be . . . cleansed of her transgressions. With a rather plentiful collection of them, I've no doubt. Definitely in league with the Devil." Pelt was certain he had the pastor's best interests at heart. This challenge was what the man fervently wished for, and dealing with a pimply fifteen-year-old ought to be well within his powers.

"You mean do an *exorcism*? That's what Romans do. It's new territory for us."

"We have the materials from that seminar you sent me on. Perhaps it was Providence."

They looked at one another for a long time under the lowering cloudbank, and Channing Pelt wondered if the pastor might be doubting his sincerity, or his loyalty. "I saw a sandhill crane from up here," the pastor confided suddenly.

"That's a big bird. I have to get back to the committee. Do we go for it? It's the first step in something big that's going to develop here."

"The bird was as graceful as an angel. An omen." Pastor Dennis Kohlmeyer stood up easily now, like a gymnast, without using his hands for leverage. "I will take this cup of salvation and I will bruise the serpent's heel with it."

—–—

They rode Sonny's nondescript gray minivan north on truck-infested Highway 99 to Garces Avenue in Delano and then east

96

through a rough and largely Latino bit of the small town that Jack Liffey remembered as the heart of the United Farm Workers organizing drive back in the César Chávez days.

"What's become of the farmworkers' union?" Jack Liffey asked.

"You ever hear about bear baiting?"

"You mean when they'd tie up a bear and turn dogs loose on it?"

Sonny nodded. "That's the ticket. California's always had itself the biggest and most powerful agribusiness companies on earth. We don't even call them that: we just say *ag*. The average ag out there owns a hundred thousand acres. This valley never saw a golden era of family farms like Kansas or Iowa."

It was a California story they didn't tell much in the schools, Jack Liffey thought, or even in the papers down in L.A. Just guff about the Missions and Father Serra and the gold rush. "I guess it's too late for land reform."

Sonny chuckled. "As long as geese go barefoot. The California Water Project wetted the whole valley, all on the federal dime, and ninety-nine percent of that went to maybe fifty rich guys and a precious few corporations like Texaco. That's what I mean about bear baiting, the odds the union was up against. Give the bear an M-16 with a grenade launcher on it, he might have a chance against Texaco or big ag."

"You were in Nam?"

"Maybe. These days the union's mainly a social club for guys with long memories."

"That's too bad."

"Don't do no good to sull on it, amigo. That's our valley. The little man moved from Oklahoma and Sonora to Bakersfield to make himself over, and if he's lucky, his kids can now afford a beat-up Chevy."

The town of Delano petered out quickly to fields and then dry rolling hills. The van pulled off on a dirt road marked by a half dozen rural mailboxes perched on a single post. They clattered south on washboard toward nothing at all. At last a few cotton-woods and water willows rose up to mark a stream. It was little more than a trickle, and Sonny forded carefully at a patch of rocks.

"Five Dog Creek," Sonny announced with a smile. "*Ríachuelo de cinco perros*. One of the few geographical appellations that I prefer in English."

"It does have a nice rural, no-nonsense sound to it. I once saw a shooting range out in Owens with the restrooms labeled Pointers and Setters."

Sonny smiled. "This old cuss, Rubén Serna, he's a man I'd ride in and out of hell with. In the south long ago, when I was in L.E., I noticed that if colored people made it up into their eighties, even the grand old rascals, there was a kind of sainthood that set-tled on them. Not even the big growers pester Rubén any more, and he fought them tooth and nail all his life. Tough as a boot."

"He was union?"

He nodded. "Any union. First the old Commie cotton unions of the 1930s when he was a teenager and then the UFW. He chopped cotton all his hard life for the North Kern Land Company. When the farmworkers fell apart he finally accepted some money from his daughter, who's a lawyer over to Taft, and bought a little land out here, just a few acres. No electricity, he's completely off the grid, but after his wife died last year, Alejandra gave him a cell phone that he can charge up with his truck, when he remembers. I met him through the daughter on a case once. She's got manners but she can be mean as a settin' hen."

There was a tall stand of mature corn ahead protected by a rudimentary barbed wire fence. Crooked tree limbs and other found wood had been pounded into the ground as fenceposts. As they approached, the house appeared to creep out from behind the corn, a shack really, with walls made of old garage doors and a rusty tin roof held down with tractor tires.

"Looks like a good gust would bring that down," Jack Liffey said.

"I'll bet on Rubén. Some men the gods've just plumb give up trying to injure."

He parked in a wide spot of the road and they got out. Sonny worked a loop of barbed wire off a post to let them inside.

"¡*Viejo*!" Sonny yelled. "Where you at? It's Sonny!"

"¡*Aquí*, amigo!" A straw field hat waved in the air above the corn.

"I got a friend with me, knows something about mutilations." Softly he said, "You can pretend a bit of forensic wisdom about animal mutilations, I hope."

"Hell, yes."

The old Latino came slowly out of the corn, small and plump and sunburned to the color of an old leather jacket. Sonny introduced them.

"You're looking good, *hombre*," Sonny said.

The old man shook his head, but in a way that merely suggested unconcern. "*Hay más tiempo que vida.*"

"How's your Spanish?"

"Good enough for that," Jack Liffey said. There's more time than life. Which was as close to wisdom as anyone ever needed to get, he thought.

"I'm on the downhill side," Rubén went on in fluent English. "Can't get my breath for work no more. The doctor wants to make tests, but I won't end my days in no *pinche* hospital. You gentlemen for a beer?"

"No thanks."

"Can't keep it cold anyway. *Vengamos.*"

He took them around the far side of the house past a derelict International Harvester Scout, past a mound of car parts and other junk, then behind the shack to an enclosure where a small herd of skinny brown and black goats fretted. They looked skittish and there was a strong suggestion that something in the far corner of the yard drew their attention, equally torn between curiosity and fear. The goats started to speak softly when they saw Rubén Serna waddle toward them, but the tone of the baa-ing fell off when he went on past.

He knelt on his heels in the back corner of his enclosure, looking down at the ground just outside the goat pen. "*Mijo, ay.*"

What lay there may once have been a goat. It looked like it had burst open from within and most of the inner organs were gone. Its legs were spread-eagled in tidy display as if it had been dissected at some goat medical school.

"Coyotes," Sonny Theroux said. "Having a fiesta."

"*Sí, claro.* Maybe. But, Señor Toro, look here."

They all knelt to see where he pointed. A perfect circle had been cut around the goat's eye, and the flesh and eyeball were gone. It was a clean cut, as if by a scalpel. "No beast bites like that. And the ear."

One ear had been sliced off neatly. Sonny grunted. "Do you use Warbex? Any other insecticides?"

"—*Nada.*"

"Any animals have blackleg around here?"

Rubén shook his head. "*Señor, aquí.*" His rough-looking hand reached under the wire and patted in the dried weeds around the carcass. "There ain't no blood." He dug his fingers into the soil a little and let a handful sift dryly through. "Nothing. There should be—*¿quién sabe?*—three quarts?"

"Maybe it was killed somewhere else and tossed here."

"I looked around real good for tracks." He shrugged.

Sonny glanced at Jack Liffey. "Ideas?"

"Well, if several famished coyotes killed fast and ate fast there might not be much blood left. The eye and the ear sure look like trophies, though. Do you have enemies around here, Señor Serna? Maybe a grower with a long memory."

"I am nothing now. There's no reason to send me no message."

Jack Liffey considered his first impression—that of an operating table. "I'm just brainstorming. Does the government do any wildlife sampling, for—I don't know—anthrax or that deer-wasting disease that everybody's so worried about? Maybe some overzealous Fish and Game guy decided to take samples from a dead goat he found. For the good of all goats everywhere."

"Scrapie would be the thing that worries them," Sonny said. "But I don't think they swoop down in black helicopters to take samples."

Sonny got up and went to the fence and rested his hands carefully between the barbs. Quite nimbly he boosted over the wire without hooking himself. They watched him look around outside for a while, their eyes drawn back regularly to the flattened carcass right at the wire, little more than a goat skin with a skeleton and a mutilated head.

"Did it have a name?" Jack Liffey asked idly.

Rubén Serna shook his head. "You don't give a name to dinner, *señor.*"

Jack Liffey smiled. "My daughter is a soft-hearted vegetarian. She'd probably object if I started naming her carrots."

"How old is your girl?"

"Maeve is seventeen, eighteen in three months."

The old man shook his head. "*Ay.* I remember Alejandra at that age. She thought she knew every damn thing in the world just because she read a lot of books. So stubborn. I got a picture of her in my head that won't go away. She's ten and she stands in the door and she got her hands like this." He set his fists on his hips in a pose of high defiance.

Jack Liffey smiled and the old man lit a little dark cigarette with a wooden match.

Sonny Theroux came back over the fence. "Not a thing, not a track. You may as well go ahead and call the sheriff. Beware, *amigo.* In the present climate this will be interpreted as ritual mutilation by servants of the Devil."

On the way to the car Sonny had a thought and put his hand on the old man's shoulder. "Maybe before the sheriff, you should get your priest up here," he suggested. "Protect yourself. Just a witness to your character, you know."

"They can't hurt me, compa. *A mí la muerte me pela los dientes.*"

"You're the bossman, *viejito.* But take care."

In the car Sonny glanced at Jack Liffey, who shook his head slightly. "Not good enough for that."

"Death shaves my teeth," Sonny said with relish. "It's something like, Death can't do a thing to me. And you know, that tough old bugger is probably right. He may be the only one in this county who's safe in the shitstorm that's coming."

--

## Artifact: 1930

AVISO IMPORTANTE! CHANZA LIBRE

El representante del Agricultural Labor Bureau of the San
Joaquin Valley Inc., está aquí para informar a las familias y
hombres solos que quieran salir a la

PIZCA DE ALGODON

En los condados de Kern, Tulare, Kings, Fresno, Madera,
Merced, California. Este año las cosechas son muy buenas y

EL PAGO ES MAGNIFICO

Las condiciones inmejorables y la temporada de trabajo es muy
larga. Ocuran a la Oficina de Empleos Del Gobierno situada en
Bakersfield y pregunten por Don FRANCISCO PALOMARES,
Represente del AGRICULTURAL LABOR BUREAU of the SAN
JOAQUIN VALLEY; tendrá gusto en darles todos informes.

> —Circular printed in Spanish-Language newspapers
> and distributed all over California, early 1930.
> Basically—Come pick cotton.
> The pay is magnificent.[6]

——

The ridiculously tall truck joggled violently at every tiny bump
in the pavement, and Maeve was glad she'd strapped herself in
tight. It was a modified Ford four-wheeler that was so high off the
ground there'd been a two-rung ladder welded under the door to
help her clamber up.

Sue Ellen Crumm was the name, he'd told her back in his

office, after making only two phone calls. Two calls that had probably cost her the first half of her hundred. Sue Ellen Crumm, she thought. With a name like that, Maeve figured she'd have picked something else, too. Though probably not Toxic Shock. The mother's name was Tamara—Tammy—and he had the home address. They were on a long causeway now over a marsh and in the distance off to the right Maeve could see an immense field of oil wells and pipelines. The business street ahead was one of the rattiest looking places she had ever seen, with half the lots sitting empty like a denture with most of the teeth knocked out.

"You are now officially passing out of Bakersfield into Oildale," Bulldog announced, "the Okie capital of the entire universe. Right there, there used to be a sign that said NIGGER, DON'T LET THE SUN SET ON YOU HERE."

North Chester Avenue reminded her of the stretches on Vermont or Central back in L.A. that had been burned out in '92. A ramshackle beer-bar, then weedy dead space for most of a block, and across the four-lane road, a two-story boarded-up something that was surrounded by temporary fencing. Then a vacant lot with several sofas and a rusting fender truck where an old sign said LIMITED MOTORS: QUALITY VEHICLES ONLY. Eventually a McDonald's and a long glass-front Payday Liquor seemed to be trying to normalize the street.

He pulled left off Chester at another burger stand into a street that had no sidewalks and where all the bungalows needed paint or other attention. She recognized a Studebaker sitting in one yard though she wasn't sure she'd ever seen one in the flesh before. A couple of pit bulls ran hard after the truck as if they were sure they could run it down and dismantle it.

The bail bondsman did something under the dash and the

exhaust let out a deafening bang that made her jump and stopped the dogs in their tracks.

"Those were your namesakes," Maeve complained. She didn't quite approve, but she was glad the dogs had backed off.

"Huh? Oh, the pitters. Nah. I got me a good old-fashioned flat-face bulldog at home. *Mo*-hammed." He chuckled.

She didn't ask him about the name because she wasn't sure she wanted to know.

"Right there." He parked and they both looked across the scraggly lawn at a tiny clapboard cottage that had been mended long ago with a delaminating sheet of plywood nailed over one of its symmetrical windows. The effect was of a pirate with an eye patch. Bulldog seemed to consider the house for a few moments, and then he opened the glove compartment and took out a short length of black hose.

"It'd be good if her mom was conscious and cooperating," Maeve said quickly.

"You never know. You stay here, kid."

She watched him knock on the door, wait, call out, peer in the remaining window and then swagger around back. In less than a minute he came surprisingly out the front door and back to the truck.

"How'd you get in?" Maeve asked.

He ignored the question. "I bet I know where she is."

He drove back to Chester and parked in front of a long featureless building with a sign that said TROUT's lettered over a drawing of a fish, as if for the nonreaders. The blank door had a sign forbidding minors, suggesting it was a bar.

"Glad it's afternoon. Even I wouldn't go in that place at night. Tamara Crumm," he said thoughtfully, as if the words might mean something all by themselves. "Hold the fort, sweetheart. I got to rattle the cigar box. I might be a bit."

It was a bit of time all right, more than half an hour during which the only human being she saw was a toothless old man pushing a shopping cart full of refuse. His eyes just came to the lower edge of her window, and he stood there watching her, tilting his head back and forth and talking in what was probably a schizophrenic ramble. Luckily he moved on.

Then Bulldog came out the door, pushing a woman with dyed blonde hair ahead of him. She wore a denim miniskirt and a cowgirl blouse that was way too unbuttoned on a bright blue bra. Her face suggested Dorian Gray's picture just going into crisis. Bulldog had her hard by the upper arm and Maeve's heart dropped in her chest. If this was Tammy Crumm, she didn't look like she was volunteering to help.

Bulldog pushed her into the tiny back seat of the crew cab and Maeve could smell the beer immediately like a wave of fermentation breaking over her.

"Only had to hose her a couple times," Bulldog said before he slammed the door. It was hard to tell, but Maeve fervently hoped that he was joking.

"I'm Toxie's friend," Maeve said quickly as the man walked around the car and then, assailed by second thoughts, added, "Your daughter."

"You sure? Sue Ellen's friends mostly look like death warmed up."

"We were both arrested by accident and got put in the same room. I think she's great, really smart—and she needs our help."

The woman sat back and just stared at Maeve. Bulldog yanked the door open and climbed up.

"How come you're out of Bowles and she's in?" the woman asked suspiciously.

"My dad's from L.A.," Maeve said, and then realizing that wasn't quite enough, "I think they must have thought he was important." She realized for the first time that it was probably Gloria pulling strings who'd got her out, but it was too late to shift tack.

"Well, I'm nobody and there ain't nothing I can do for Sue Ellen. She's gone and dug her hole. Let her lay up in it."

"Mrs. Crumm, please. I really care for . . . Sue Ellen."

"Listen up," Bulldog announced all of a sudden. "This is good fucking deed day. The whole past is erased off the calendar like it's never been. Whatever kind of mom you've been and whatever failure I've been as a good-doer in this world are wiped out, just gone away in a puff of smoke. This girl here is the real deal. We both can see it." He stuck a fat index finger out at Tammy. "You and me are going to help Maeve help your daughter, or I'll knock your fucking block off."

## Chapter Seven

# SODBUSTERS HAVE RIGHTS, TOO

S onny juggled his cell phone dexterously as he drove down Highway 99, calling his own answering machine and thumbing in the code that made the machine talk to him. Then he spoke out of the side of his mouth like somebody in a George Raft movie: "The police called Jenny to try to speak to you. Polite as Alphonse they were, and she's passing on their good wishes. There's a callback number and a name, Lt. Saldivar."

"Later," Jack Liffey said. "He's no worse than a lot of others. What's all this worry about?"

Sonny shrugged. "The town's a bit like that. But you can bet there ain't no red-satin-suited Devil laying out all night with the dry cattle."

"What the hell's that supposed to mean?" Jack Liffey challenged him. He was beginning to get annoyed by the things around him that he didn't understand, and Sonny's willfully obtuse idiom wasn't helping.

Sonny made an apologetic face. "It means carousing with the willing gals. In plain talk—sure, we got a goat mutilation, but it's probably just a couple kids puffing themselves up. Couple of badasses got together and broke into an abandoned house somewhere and read some old book and recited some spells and saw if anything would happen. Then they caught an animal and had a roast. It's profoundly silly that a whiff of Lucifer gets this whole town's goat so easily. Ugh—no pun intended."

"There is a dead baby, Sonny, in addition to the goat," Jack Liffey reminded him. "That has to mean something."

"Babies pass on. Goats pass on. Without no devils popping up to dance in the hog trough. Trust me."

They approached a stretch of the highway where the thick oleanders that ran along the median had been smashed away for fifty yards, and he imagined an 18-wheeler skidding amok and bursting across into the oncoming traffic. It wasn't a pretty picture, but it was the kind of scene his imagination tended to come up with these days.

"Sonny, somebody severed that infant's hand, and it didn't throw itself into my pickup."

"Yeah, that's about the only rank happenstance in all this nonsense that can stand a second sniff. Any way you could have an enemy here in town? Did you cut somebody off changing lanes? Insult the clerk at the 7-Eleven?"

"I prefer to think my pickup was just convenient. And the back was unlocked. But why cut off the hand, for God's sake? They ID newborns with footprints."

"Got any bumper stickers on your vehicle?"

"I learned my lesson in the 'seventies when I put on a peace sticker and got three tickets in a month. There's times to stand up and make enemies, but not every single time you pass a cop."

Sonny nodded thoughtfully. "You know, I used to tell myself I could keep my head down, watch all the dumbshit acts on the part of the hardshell Baptists in this town and make them into a plus for me. It mostly worked, too. But it's a malignant kind of arithmetic. It just ain't worthy to live your life counting on others being burned-out bulbs. If this camp meeting goes out of control again, I might just remove myself to more sanguine parts."

"You lived through it once."

"Kindly my point."

"Can you tell me about that time? It might help."

"I'm too tuckered now and it'll just overwind my watch."

Sonny fell silent for a while, and Jack Liffey turned to observing the endless checkerboard of crops that drifted past. Here and there a corporate grower had thoughtfully provided a little explanation for the tourists: blue enamel signs on the roadside fence that said BEETS or KOHLRABI.

— —

Sunlight still streamed in the high frosted window of the interview room, but Toxie was so exhausted she kept drifting off, then popping awake with a jolt. They'd been talking to her in shifts for what seemed days. After a meal break, the regulars were joined by a skinny woman in a lavender housecoat. She had strange black-rimmed raccoon eyes and a way of tongue-wetting her lips for a split second like a snake. She didn't have a nameplate.

Hudson, the blonde D.A., was reading out loud the typed-up confession they'd prepared for her to sign—pages and pages of nonsensical confession that they'd culled and transcribed from the videotape. They'd edited out all the exclamations where she had sagged to one side and said "Oh, sure, why *not*?" or "Jesus, yes, put that down, too."

At some point it had all become a blurry joke and even though she knew it would probably return to haunt her, she felt she could always deny it and say she'd been putting them on. Who'd ever believe this stuff? It was like saying you'd seen pigs fly over City Hall. Somebody sensible would eventually give her a lie detector and set it all straight.

"'. . . and I was told of over a hundred human sacrifices conducted in the course of these Satanic worship rituals, though I did not see these in person . . . .'"

Hudson's voice went droning on. Toxie arrived at a kind of semidoze with her eyes open and her head rocking lightly, her mind in a near-trance state. She imagined she saw that girl from the first day—what was her name?—Megan or May or something—and she was wagging a finger at her, trying to tell her to be careful.

"'. . . And every word of what I have said is true, I swear it, though the fear of my coven may make me deny it tomorrow.' That's it."

"Not quite," raccoon eyes said. "We got to know where that house is. I'm sure it's built over some portal that gives access to the demons. We want that address, girl."

Toxie was sinking into exhaustion, unable any longer to focus.

"Sue Ellen!" Channing Pelt said sharply. He came round the long table and shook her shoulders once, then left his big comforting hands on her neck to support her lolling head.

"The Black House," the raccoon woman insisted. "Where is it? We have to know. Your confession is incomplete without it."

Go to hell, she thought.

"We need it now."

Yeah, great. That, too. Throw that in. Why not?

"Don't you want to sleep?" Pelt crooned behind her. This was the one, he thought. A rind of innocence and intelligence, almost attractive, and that terrible alien hostility to all authority at the core. Of all the adolescents they'd interrogated, something about this one's manner suggested she was the one who truly had evil inside, yet a strong enough self to help expel it. With the Lord's assistance, of course. That's what the seminar notes said to look for, and that was what would convince Kohlmeyer. "Just tell us where you and your friends met for your rituals, and you can go lie down and sleep all you want."

Sleep, echoed in her head. Such an amazing idea.

"Just an address," Hudson chimed in. "Then you can sign your statement and lie down."

Channing Pelt entertained no images of a literal fork-tailed devil hunkered down somewhere in the girl's belly. That was a boo-tale for children, and sometimes for men like Dennis Kohlmeyer. But Evil was real, and Evil could find its way inside you when you gave it leave. A spirit, maybe only an extreme manifestation of urges already harboring in you—anyone who had seen these children cavorting and laughing in their haunts late at night and heard their sarcasm and heartless scorn, anyone who had seen their mood turn from calm to insane fury in an instant, knew that some revolting energy worked there. And if there, in all humankind, too. But with help it could be driven out.

What the fuck, Toxie thought. I gotta sleep. She named the only address that came to mind, Lonnie's house in Highland. He'd taken her there one night when his mom was away. They'd watched some porn on cable and he'd tried to push her head down in his lap.

"That's it!" the raccoon lady said, pleased. "Finally!"

"Now just sign at the bottom here."

She gave in. "I'll print the name below, and we'll all sign as witnesses," Hudson said officiously.

Toxie looked around, sighed heavily, and let her head fall forward onto her arms.

—–—

Bulldog cruised along the diagonal parking lane in front of the juvenile detention center but there was nowhere to stop so he went on through and drove to the next block. Much had changed in the course of the five-mile drive. Bulldog had regaled them— mostly regaled Tammy Crumm—about some amusing bail cases he'd worked. In one he'd been sucker enough to consider taking a check from a woman who was charged with kiting checks.

"But she was a looker, like you, and I felt sorry for her."

He glanced over and Tammy preened a little. All at once Maeve was nervous. She realized they were flirting. Jeez.

"I'm not a complete dummy of course. I kept her in here right where you're sitting until we gone to the bank with her little 'to cash' paper. You'll find, by the way, you can't open that door from insides should you elect to skedaddle. And I went to the drive-through and asked the clerk to do me some process on that check right away and tell me if it's three feet up a bull's ass. He comes back pretty quick and says the account's been cleaned out and do I want to file a complaint.

"I just laughed and gave her a big squint, but you know what she said? Damn con woman didn't miss a beat, she said it must've been her evil twin. She was going to have to sue and could I help track her down?"

"What did you do then?" Tammy asked. She seemed truly curious.

"Here," he said, and he handed her an Altoid.

She took one from the tin he offered, popped it into her mouth, then said, "And, and . . .?"

"I took her straight back to jail. A year later you know how she ended up?"

Tammy waited. Maeve, too.

"She tried to rob a bank downtown. Left an old beater running in front, went in and flashed one of those notes that says 'I've got a bomb.' Of course the tellers are all taught not to resist, so one clears out her drawer into a lunchbag but slips a dye-pack in with the money and Joanie runs outside and finds somebody's driven off with her beater. And then the dye-pack blows up in her hand and she's standing there stunned on Truxtun in a big cloud of fluttering money and a mist of red dye. Cophouse was only a block away and the whole afternoon shift was just rolling out. No fucking evil twin that time, I guarantee you."

"What am I supposed to do over there?" Tammy now thought to ask.

"It's not so hard. I'll go in with you. Just tell them you're the girl's mom and you'd like her released to your custody."

"Would you say you're her stepdad?"

"I can't do that, but I can take some responsibility if I have to. You want to come too?" he asked Maeve.

She wanted to do her duty to Toxie, but she could see they'd rather she stay and they do it alone. "I'll wait here. But please come get me if you need me for anything."

Bulldog went around to help Tammy down, and she nearly fell into his arms from the high freeboard. The two walked back toward the building with Bulldog's muscled arm snaking around the woman's waist. Maeve wondered if she'd be quite so thrown by it if she weren't throbbing with all her pregnancy hormones. But they were just two lonely people, really. Why not get together?

She tried the radio but it didn't work with the key gone. Then she sat back and closed her eyes and thought about what she'd been avoiding for weeks. She had to look straight at it. She didn't really believe in a soul, but there was certainly a life force of some kind in there, revving its own engine and shooting her blood full of crazy urges.

They talked about viability, but wasn't that just some arbitrary point in the continuum? And to be selfish—how was it going to make her feel? People kept talking about whether or not she was ready for all the responsibility of raising a kid. But that could never be the true question. Go on, think the word—would she be able to deny that she was a killer? Stop it, stop it.

To distract herself she looked around. Sun slanted in low over a rooftop, red and feeble through smog. The premature evening of early winter. A tiny slice of a big street was visible two blocks away and cars whizzed past. There was life on the planet.

She closed her eyes and maybe dozed a little until a metallic clacking brought her half alert, wondering if she had heard it or only imagined it. Shock bolted her straight up as the barrel of a very short ugly rifle rapped against her window.

"Sheriff!" a voice called. "Open the door!"

He wore a black helmet and plexiglass face shield, and several other figures in dark uniforms moved about nervously in the background. Omigod! she thought. It was some kind of SWAT team!

She showed her open palms and reached very slowly to lift up the lock pin on the door.

The door was yanked open abruptly by several hands, and the man with the rifle tumbled backwards and shrieked, ripping off a burst of three or four deafening shots that mercifully seemed to go high and miss everything. She looked down and saw the blue plastic milk crate the SWAT officer had been standing on. He was making a terrible face behind his plexiglass and rubbing his butt.

"Now you get the sorry!" he yelled, but she wasn't sure whether it was to her or to the others who clustered around him. "I'm fine, dammit."

"Swell job, Tommy," one said. "You plugged that tree good. Hope it don't sue."

"Come down here," a voice said calmly to Maeve, though she wasn't sure which dark plastic mask it was emanating from. It was like being surrounded by giant ants.

"What have I done?"

"Just step down, young lady." And the nearest ant held out a helping hand in a fingerless glove.

——

116

**Artifact: 1933a**

WASCO MEETING PLEDGES
AID ON WAR ON STRIKE

WASCO, Oct 6 (Exclusive)—Five hundred cotton growers and local Legion members crowded into American Legion Hall at noon today to discuss the strike situation.

A resolution was passed to support the Kern County Committee composed of directors of the Farm Bureau and the executive committee of the Chamber of Commerce who are working on a plan to rid the county of strike agitators.

The discussion was spirited, but opinion was unanimous in standing for the protection of the growers.

It was announced that the county welfare department wanted car numbers and names of strikers for their records so as to refer to them when help is asked this winter.

—Los Angeles *Times*, October 7, 1933

——

Lonnie Winokur and his mother sat at their card table, playing the tattered Monopoly game that she'd brought back from London before he was born. It always seemed too weird to him with its properties like Picadilly and Whitehall, but it was her birthday and he knew she loved to dig the game out. Edith Winokur was an Anglophile, even if her son didn't know the word.

"Get Out of Gaol Free," he said, flashing the card. He pronounced it GAY-ohl, knowing she'd correct him.

"It's jail. They just spell it that way."

"It's dumb. What's wrong with the American game? We're Americans."

"Don't you find it interesting to see how another culture reinterprets our common things?"

"No. When I hear the world culture I reach for my pistol." He made a pistol of his finger and shot the offending boardgame a few times. She glared at him. It was she who'd told him the supposed Hermann Göring aphorism, too.

Edith Winokur folded her arms in defeat. Every kid now seemed to need to establish before every adult that they already fully grasped everything worth knowing in the world, thank you very much.

"Do I roll again?" He tried to appease her.

But Lonnie would never learn the answer to his question as at that moment a voice bellowed incomprehensibly from the front porch. An instant after that the door crashed open so hard it tipped over a lamp and the bulb shattered on the wood floor. All of which nearly stopped Edith Winokur's fragile heart. Lonnie leapt up to confront a stocky man wearing a face mask and a flak vest. He pushed Lonnie back down hard.

"Stay there, kid. SWAT. We have a warrant to search 5041 Crown Crest Avenue."

Mrs. Winokur, sitting at the table in shock, had her fingers opened by force and the warrant pressed into her hand as the house began to fill with more of the dark creatures. Behind them came a tall man in a crew cut, dressed in street clothes. With him was a woman with rings shadowing her eyes.

"What are you looking for?" Edith Winokur choked out.

"Signs of Devil worship."

Her eyes popped out uncomprehendingly. "Devil what?"

One of the police team rested his hand on her shoulder. "Read the warrant, ma'am. And stay right there."

"Don't we have no rights?" Lonnie thought to challenge.

"Judge Stone has declared abetting the Devil a form of terrorism, and all this comes under the Patriot Act. You do have the right to remain silent, kid. Use it."

——

The sunset lit up the southwestern sky in horizontal bars of unlikely ruby and crimson, backlighting the ugly shotgun houses across the street. Jack Liffey and Sonny Theroux were sitting in wicker chairs on what Sonny called his "great verandah," to differentiate it from the "one-dog porch" in back.

"Pretty sunset. Smog, of course," Sonny noted. "If you look real close at some things, there turns out to be a skunk in the sack. They tell us we got worse air quality these days than L.A."

"It's still pretty," Jack Liffey protested. Sometimes even pollution needed a friend.

They'd settled in with lemonades, and Sonny was just telling him about his people being chased out of Vermillion Parrish by the flood surge of Hurricane Audrey in 1957 when the phone rang. The screen door banged hard when he went inside to get it.

Jack Liffey wondered why he was being dogged by this feeling of apprehension. No matter how bad things were here, it had nothing to do with him, as he'd told Jenny Ezkiaga. Maeve was safe in L.A, and he would be, too, as soon as he got his truck back from the cops. He wished poor Toxic Shock well, but he'd never even met her, and she was in Jenny's hands now. He liked Jenny and her partner, and Sonny, too, and he hoped whatever was going down here wouldn't bring them any great grief. He hoped to read about it all in a short squib on the deep inside pages of the *Times*, and in a year or so he could look back fondly and think good thoughts about all those interesting folks he'd met here.

Yet, he still worried. Sometimes he wished he could be more accepting of whatever came, more Buddhist. But that meant a kind of submissiveness to fate that had never really appealed to him, even if it granted peace of mind. He knew he'd always been prone to pushing against the grain of things. It was a kind of primal craving to set the world right. Even when all you really had to set right was a big rock of Sisyphus that had to be rolled back up a hill again.

But I can still damn well choose which hill, he thought. And this town was not it.

"Jack, we've got to go."

"You've got that ah-shit look."

"Ah, shit," Sonny said. "Jenny's been right as usual."

He wouldn't tell him any more because Jack simply would not have believed him, or so he said. When they'd gotten onto 99 south from Oildale, they turned right off again onto one of the roads that sloped into the southwest suburbs of Bakersfield.

Suddenly Jack Liffey noticed the impressive pillar of smoke up ahead, like a small nuclear blast, and a chill took his scalp. "Is somebody out here going to need help?"

"Nobody stocks that kind of help these days," Sonny said.

"Did they ever?"

"Probably only when it wasn't needed."

They pulled into the parking lot of an upscale open-air mall and right away they could see a massive crowd on the far side.

The smoke column issued from the center of the throng, as if they had all come together to worship at a volcanic vent. Now and again flames licked high up into the dark smoke, flashing animal shapes. Here and there aisles opened reluctantly in the crowd and people pushed shopping carts toward a blinding glow that the parting revealed at the center of things, like a rip through the firebox of a furnace.

"Jenny said something about burning witches," Jack Liffey said. "I hope that was hyperbole."

"It's not witches. Look there. That's Mike's bookstore, where the staff is forming a Maginot line."

"Jesus."

Across the front of the bookstore a number of people had linked arms to form a human wall. A handful of jumpy town cops stood several feet in front of them, holding out their batons as a first line of defense.

Sonny parked back from the crowd and as they got out, some kind of chant or cheer could be heard. It was rendered indistinct by distance, though it got louder as he and Sonny made their way slowly toward the conflagration.

"Looks like a homecoming bonfire," Jack Liffey said.

"Depends on how you look at it," Sonny said.

A boy with one of the silver SWORD OF GOD T-shirts overtook them at speed and pounded past with a fat book in each hand. Jack Liffey wasn't sure but he thought one was Howard Zinn's *A People's History of the United States*. He'd given Maeve a copy and thought he recognized the cover. Three girls hurried by them wearing oversized white TRY GOD T-shirts.

He was picking out individual voices now, the ones with good pitch, and the song was clearer:

*I have the joy! Joy! Joy! Joy!*
*Down in my heart!*
*WHERE?*
*Down in my heart!*
*Down in my heart! Heart! Heart! Heart!*
*I have the joy! . . .*

He could see that the crowd was young, mostly teenagers with a sprinkling of young adults. But just about all unruly crowds were kids, he thought. No matter what the provocation, adults guarded their homes first and the elderly weren't up to the excitement. A girl with a plastic laundry basket full of paperbacks ran past them toward the fire. This time he clearly saw *When God Was a Woman* and various Harry Potters. The crowd around the fire was thin enough to allow newcomers to pass among them and push forward. The singing built all around them now.

*I have the joy! Joy! Joy! Joy!*
*Down in my heart,*
*WHERE?*
*Down in my heart! Heart! Heart! Heart!*

He lost track of Sonny but kept edging forward, noting the silver shirts all around. Whenever anyone looked at him, he smiled as brainlessly as he could and nodded. A big teen grabbed for his jacket in a menacing way. Jack Liffey stared hard at him. "I'm with the pastor," he said, and the boy let go.

The forward edge of the mob had formed where the searing heat from the bonfire exactly counteracted the urge to see better.

Many of those who ran forward to hurl a book, had to shield their faces with their hands and retreated immediately.

Now and again he could hear phrases of the song, but toward the front, the howl of the fire had taken over, a ravenous ugly sound that was alarming in its suggestion of something living and malign. Fireshapes leapt far up into the smoke, dancing. Now and then he heard a happy shout and thought sadly of the innocence implied by the camp song.

In a few places, boys, their faces wrapped in wet towels, wound up like baseball pitchers to hurl books into the fire. Jack Liffey edged into the buffeting heat toward one of the satellite piles of books waiting to be immolated. He saw *The Chalice and the Blade*, a DVD of *The Chronicles of Narnia*, even a *Communist Manifesto*.

A girl arrived to drop a big colorful paperback of *The Grapes of Wrath*.

"Hey!" he shouted over the din. "Why Steinbeck?"

"He hated Bakersfield and good people!" she yelled. He smiled maniacally and nodded.

Like a living thing, the flames coughed and billowed up all at once. What must have been an unbalanced stack of books within the fire collapsed and puffed out a geyser of sparks. The sudden burst gave off a sound like an animal exhalation of great pain and a freshened wave of heat that pressed the whole mob back.

"The Devil is here!" someone cried out.

Jack Liffey noticed two boys nearby who did not look like they belonged to the clean-cut legions of Jesus. They had tattoos and long greasy hair and one was carrying a black cat. They seemed to be stealing toward the bonfire with the animal. Instantly Jack Liffey started toward them.

"Give me that cat!" he shouted.

"Cats are servants of the Devil," one boy insisted, but with a sly grin.

"Not that one." Jack Liffey got the kid's thumb in a compliance grip that a policeman had once used on him.

"Oww!" Immediately the boy loosened his grip.

Jack Liffey wrenched the cat away from him, and in the same motion gave the terrified animal a low heave away from the fire. "Go home!"

The dark streak flashed through the loose crowd who mostly shied back as if terrified of the cat's touch.

"We'll remember you," the other boy snarled.

"You're in the shit now, man!" The first boy was rubbing his sore thumb as he began cursing Jack Liffey.

Honest sodbusters have rights, too, Jack Liffey thought, as he stared furiously at the boys, who were not backing down. He had no idea from what woozy recesses of *Shane*-land that thought had emerged, or how his psyche had come to equate cats or cat-lovers with honest sodbusters, but he knew decency would always and forever demand a defense of small helpless creatures.

— —

Eventually he met Sonny back at the van. He was trembling a little with the terrible images of auto-da-fé—their real glee in destroying books—that he knew he'd probably never be able to forget. It didn't improve things when Sonny handed him a note he said he'd found under the windshield wiper.

You and your girl better vacuate fast. Devill-lover

How does this person know I have a girl? Jack Liffey wondered.

124

Chapter Eight

# GRUNT LOGIC

His first thought was that the Devil wouldn't last the first round at a spelling bee, and then he realized he could relax because Maeve had been back in L.A. for a long time. She was probably snugged up in her bed in Boyle Heights tapping on her laptop, or even over in Redondo having a heart-to-heart with her mom. He wondered who the hell around here wished him harm. And why?

"Beats me," Jack Liffey said. "The only people I know in this town are you and Jenny and a couple of cops."

"Somebody knows *you*," Sonny said. "Somebody out of your past who moved up from L.A.?"

Jack Liffey laughed softly. "I'll just go through your phone book then. What's the population?"

"City: three hundred thousand or so. Metro is getting on five. Some say eight."

"No problem."

They watched disconsolately as the bonfire surged again in the distance. He never saw Pastor Kohlmeyer there, but a sizeable number of the bonfiristas he'd run into had been wearing the distinctive silver sweatshirts. Sirens announced the arrival of more police cars and some fire engines, their light bars flickering colors off the shop windows like a carnival, and cops got out to add to the defense of the bookstore. The fire engines just waited. They made no attempt to break up the massive crowd or put out the fire, probably prudently.

"Let's go," Jack Liffey said. "I want to talk to Jenny."

"A second," Sonny said. He rested a hand on the side of his van, bent over for a moment as if to heave, then inhaled slowly several times. "Sorry. I get spells."

"Take your time." They got in and Jack Liffey watched the man rest his head on the headrest and close his eyes.

"I'm sorry. Thought I was tough as old fishhooks, but mobs get to me down deep. I seen Klan stuff I wouldn't repeat."

"And such clean-cut children," Jack Liffey said.

"Praise the Lord."

Still, Jack Liffey knew what the man meant. He'd felt it after the '92 riots in L.A. It was the sensation of utter dislocation, seeing ordinary shops being torched and ordinary people doing it, like some tectonic plate had shifted under the city. Whatever else the fires back then had been, they were an announcement that a lot of people were hurting and angry, and nobody with the power to fix it was doing a damn thing. Something very different from what was going on here.

"You know, a lot of this just isn't very damn interesting," Jack Liffey said sourly.

"What do you mean?"

"These aren't poor people acting out of their own deprivation or their hunger or exclusion. This is just ugliness. They're nursing some festering grievances, all right—but it's all Looney Tunes. The Jewish bankers or the illegal Mexicans. They'd like to lynch J. K. Rowling or burn Rosie O'Donnell at the stake or find some hapless lesbian and beat her to death. Their grievances would be pathetic if there wasn't so much ash in the air."

Two nearby teenagers turned to glare at the truck in the dusk as if the occupants were deserters, enemies.

"True," Sonny said softly. "These are some of the most privileged kids on the planet. What is it that's eating them?"

Neither man looked back as they drove off.

——

A group of girls in dark tank tops leaned together to sing the enduring anthem of the Goths—"Bela Lugosi's Dead." They were lavishly accessorized by metal piercings, and Maeve kept her distance.

The teens were all locked inside a huge echoey space—one of the most creepy buildings Maeve had ever been in. Rows of gas outlets suspended overhead would have shocked anyone with a sense of history. Apparently the police had overfilled the town's jail and were now detaining their round-up of street kids and freaks and prostitutes in this warehouse. A girl had told her it was an abandoned degreening shed for oranges. The rows of white cones were for spraying ethylene gas over crates of citrus that had been picked green. The gas neutralized the chlorophyll and turned the fruit bright orange for market. But fruit tampering was the least of her worries right now.

A hastily-built hurricane fence down the middle bisected the warehouse to segregate the sexes. Port-a-potties were available against one wall. A new influx of a half dozen boys was pushed in a door at the far end of the room with a momentary glare of light, and they didn't look freaked up at all. Apparently the dragnet had spread even wider.

The SWAT team had taken just about everything from her and given her in exchange a stiff numbered card on a plastic lanyard, which most of the street freaks had instantly swapped around or mutilated or discarded. Eventually Maeve found Toxie's mother sitting wearily on a cot near the wire barrier, just across the wire in fact from Bulldog, who sat on his own cot with his fists on his knees.

"Mrs. Crumm, I looked all around but I couldn't find . . . Sue Ellen."

The woman looked up blearily as if trying to place Maeve and then started to manage it. "You were in the car. Sue Ellen's friend, aren't you?"

A dark silhouette of a man stood backlit in the doorway. "One-oh-seven-twenty-one!" his voice bawled into the room with a bullhorn.

She realized that the man at the door had no way of knowing that the teens in the room had already defeated the ID system.

"Let me make this real clear! Female 1-0-7-2-1. Come up here now! This will be your only chance."

Maeve finally glanced down at her necklace. It wasn't the one.

—‒

**Artifact: 1933b**

THE GOVERNOR SENDS
AID TO PIXLEY
24 Deputy Sheriffs
11 Highway Patrolmen
WE WANT
FOOD!

— Sign on a farmworker truck, 1933.[6]

—‒

As Jack Liffey and Sonny came into Jenny Ezkiaga's living room, she and Teelee were sitting there having tea with two men Jack Liffey had never seen before, one wearing the dog collar of a priest. In the corner, a TV was tuned to local news, showing the book burning but with the sound off. He didn't remember seeing any TV trucks at the shopping center but they must have been there.

"Gentlemen," Sonny announced. "This is a good friend of mine from L.A. who's gotten himself mixed up in our embarrassing town—Jack Liffey. From St. John's, Father Brogan O'Shea, and Rector James Hood of St. Adrian's Episcopal. The two most respected and obstinately conventional Christian leaders in town. No one need worry about so much as a whisper of too much fervor from them."

Rector Hood glared at him.

"Sorry, I'm on your side, really. I grew up with the Jimsonweed preachers, and enthusiasm gives me the creeps."

"Be nice now, Sonny," Jenny said. "You two sit down and stay polite and you can have tea."

They all shook hands cordially. "I'll skip the tea," Sonny said.

"Me, too," Jack Liffey seconded.

Sonny had a look of anticipation. There was a history here Jack Liffey knew nothing about. "I assume you were all talking about sending out a search party to find a *very* long spoon to sup with the new arrival in town," Sonny said.

"They don't come that long," Jenny said. "Father O'Shea was just saying that there are plenty of good people who could be mobilized to offer a calming influence, but right now they're keeping their heads down."

"We just came from the Nuremberg Rally." Sonny hooked his thumb at the TV.

"Were the police there?" Adrian Hood asked.

"There and doing little," Sonny said. "Just the way they did when the white mobs went after the black college kids who sat down at the Woolworth's back in the day."

"It might have been a politic move on their part to go easy right now," the priest offered. "Look at it. The police are vastly outnumbered, and the crowd appears to be burning mainly their own books, plus some that they actually purchased at Mike's. The TV quoted Chief Williams a while ago. He said that sometimes it's best not to risk riling up a crowd and let it simmer down on its own. He said he's instructed his officers to protect property and let the unruly kids shout themselves out. The only thing singed so far is asphalt."

"How do you know all this?" Jack Liffey asked quickly.

"From my Kiwanis and Rotary contacts. Obviously I have friends in the police, as well as other places," Father O'Shea replied. "There's very little that happens in this town that I don't know about." He held up his cell phone as some kind of evidence.

Jack Liffey took the note out of his pocket and slapped it in front of him. "Okay, you know it all. Who left this on our car tonight, and who threw the baby's hand in my truck last week?"

The priest frowned at the note.

Sonny was about to say something to the priest when Jenny hushed him.

"I'm not grinding any axes," Jack Liffey said. "It's personal. I have nothing to do with this town, but someone here seems to be threatening me and my daughter."

The priest looked at the note again, as if he might find a hidden code if he tried harder. "I don't know anything about this, Mr. Liffey. It's really quite perplexing." He thought for a moment, then spoke carefully. "I can talk to the police chief if you like. He's a friend."

"I've asked around about the cops here," Jack Liffey said. "Let's just say they're not at the top of the league," he added, trying to stay diplomatic. Gloria had told him that the skinny on the Bakersfield P.D. was that they were aggressive past the point where aggressive got usable results, they jumped to conclusions too fast, their forensics were second-rate, and they relied far too much on pressured confessions.

It was Adrian Hood's turn. "Chief Williams and his wife have been attending Olive Grove for almost a year now, Brogan. While his men are avoiding arresting any of Kohlmeyer's squeaky clean teens at that book-burning, they're detaining hundreds of inoffensive street kids from downtown and Old Town. Did your Rotarian connections tell you about that?"

"James, I'm so sorry."

"They're holding them without warrants in the jail and in some warehouse they've set up for the overflow. It's all at the behest of that wretched cult committee they've got going again—with the blessings of the D.A. and the sheriff, I might add. They're all cronies of Kohlmeyer, too, even if they don't attend Olive Grove. I have my own ideas about what's unholy around here, may I say."

The priest's face seemed to sag a little. "Holy Mother of God," he said. He looked down at his cell phone as if that was what had betrayed him. "Nobody told me they were picking up kids wholesale."

— —

They'd set a hospital bed up in a largely empty room, and Toxie's wrists had been strapped to the railings. To be kind they'd used the kind of sheepskin-lined restraints you saw in nursing homes and psych wards. She was also gagged with duct tape and since she'd had a deviated septum from birth, she was having trouble breathing. For all she knew, she was about to be raped for Jesus.

In fact, though, she knew where she was. From her days of forced community service, she recognized Olive Grove's child observation room, where parents and approved psychologists could witness the behavior of the problem children at the preschool through a one-way mirror.

One other person was there with her. It was a pleasant-looking gray haired old woman knitting something powder-blue. Toxie was reminded of *A Tale of Two Cities*, another of her favorite novels. The woman witnessing all the rebels, but Toxie had no illusions she would be witnessed.

After a while, the man who had brought her here came back in, saying to the old woman, "I'm going to remove the tape. Don't listen to her. It may be quite disturbing, but you can console yourself with the thought that it won't be the girl speaking. It'll just be the Evil inside her trying to disturb us."

"I understand," the woman replied placidly.

"Hello, Sue Ellen. Whoever is present, I'm only speaking to Sue Ellen," Pelt said to her. Then he stripped the tape off her mouth in one yank.

"Oww! You fuckhead! That *hurt!*"

He leaned forward gravely to peer into her eyes, wrinkling his broad flat brow, the way you'd stare searchingly into a shallow stream for the sunglasses you'd accidentally dropped in. "Who are we now? Are we Sue Ellen or are we Toxic Shock or are we someone new?"

"Kiss my asshole."

"*Kako ti je ime?*" he said.

"*Je ne razumijem.*"

"Ah, you speak Croatian. Without any record of language classes. We have all your school records. A clear sign of possession by Evil."

"My best cousin is a Serb, you buttlick."

"The devil is quick on the uptake. I want you to do something for me, Sue Ellen. Trust me now. I'm speaking only to Sue Ellen, not anyone else inhabiting Sue Ellen. I want you to think back to anything you may have done in recent memory that involved taking in arcane knowledge. You may only have meant to enhance your knowledge, but you may have been contacting powerful sources of the occult. Without knowing it."

"You mean like reading *Macbeth*?" Toxie said. "'Bubble, bubble, toil and trouble.' How about that?"

"Rest for now." He backed off, then abruptly came right back, his face hovering a few inches from hers. *"Evil One, leave this girl's body*! I charge you in the name of Jesus Christ!"

It was just too absurd, she thought. She'd stored up a good goober and spit it in his face.

"Ow!" He pulled back as if her saliva were burning him.

"Eat shit and die."

—-—

Channing Pelt withdrew to the observation room, wiping his face obsessively with a handkerchief. Pastor Kohlmeyer stood with his hands clasped behind his back, watching the girl sadly.

"Have you no fear for your own soul if we undertake this?" he asked mildly.

Pelt was already immensely enjoying the spectacle of the undertaking. He realized he was probably approaching the task rather differently than the pastor, but he figured they had the same end in mind. He was tense with excitement and felt that he should be speaking every third word with a special stress, as if there were a camera and a spotlight trained upon them. Everything now was special, important. And he didn't even believe in devils per se. But he believed in Evil.

"It isn't for me to perform the rite, Dennis. I know I went to the seminar and I collected the materials, but an exorcism can only be performed by an ordained minister."

"Aren't things like this really the province of the Romans?"

"Not any more. You know, they're unwitting servants of the

Antichrist. We certainly can't trust them. Do you want to turn her over to that drunken idiot O'Shea? I'll bring you the pages that contain the words of the rite. The people in Laredo told me they'd carefully purged it of all Roman Catholic heterodoxy."

The pastor blew out a slow breath. "It's just such unfamiliar ground. It worries me."

"Dennis, Evil is here in town, right now. We've had so many signs. You know that. We're already at war for the good of the Church and the thousands of believers that your ministry protects. Maybe all of Christendom. You prayed your Gethsemane out there on Fifth Standard Road. When your father died, I know you didn't just sign on for the easy times. This girl may be a portal of access for Evil to enter our world. She just spoke to me in a tongue she can have no way of knowing. That's the final proof. We cannot shirk our duty now."

"I suppose we must do the Lord's work. But we'll give her a night's sleep. I want her body strong enough for what's coming."

"I disagree, I think we want to catch her with her body weakened—but you must do what you feel is best, Den. You're the vicar of Christ."

— —

A big undistinguished statue of a padre issuing a blessing stood in the traffic circle being ignored by all who whirled around him, so very California.

Nothing had been decided, though their Episcopal and Catholic eminences had promised faithfully to begin marshaling the saner influences in town. Teelee had gone off to bed with a worried look on her face, Jenny had walked them outside with the news that she was going to try to find exactly where they were holding the rounded-up kids, and Sonny was now driving Jack Liffey home to Oildale.

"You never went to see the cops," Sonny said.

"It can wait," Jack Liffey said.

"And it can wait because . . ?"

"There's a kind of rule of life I have about only challenging things that can hurt you. I like to make cops dance a little. It sounds nuts, but it makes sense to me."

"Just be glad that you can hightail it out of this town," Sonny said. "For me it's all just another tour in-country with a crazy officer in the command tent. And since I'm stuck in it, I got to live with Grunt Logic. You know Grunt Logic, don't you?"

"No."

"Grunt Logic says there's only win or lose. If you win, the other guy is dead. You're alive—it's all good. If you lose, *you're* dead and you don't have to worry any more. And that's cool, too. Grunt logic."

"That's the army, all right. We had a sign over the radar trailer where we worked, IF IT'S STUPID AND IT WORKS, IT'S NOT STUPID. The captain made us take it down. He said it was stupid."

Sonny laughed.

When they got back to Sonny's southern manor, Jack Liffey phoned Gloria. "I miss you," he said and meant it.

"Uh-huh." Her voice coming back was flat and hurt a little. Not even a "Me, too," he thought. At her end, the TV was going softly in the background. He could tell she wasn't in a great mood. She probably had her shoes off, her feet up and a beer in one hand. It wasn't all that easy to wind down from a lousy day "on the job," as the cops called it. He'd tried often enough to help her.

"And how's Maeve coming with her decision making?"

"She's at her mom's. I guess on your advice."

"Can I get back to you, Glor?" He wanted to talk to Maeve and make sure she was okay. Find out what she was up to.

"Of course. It's just me here with all the single guys in the Harbor Division. Nothing serious."

Jokes like that made him feel awful. He wondered why she felt she had to needle him. "I'll talk to you later."

"Okay. Whenever."

That made him feel even worse. But when he called Kathy, she told him that she hadn't seen Maeve in more than a week. So he begged off with the lie that it must have been a misunderstanding. Christ, he knew in the pit of his stomach that Maeve was getting herself into some kind of a fix. Either she had gone off somewhere on her own to brood over her pregnancy, or—his stomach dropped several floors fast—*of course.* She'd scurried back to Bakersfield to try to rescue Toxie.

"Sonny, I've got a problem."

Chapter Nine

# MORAL CHOICE IN MINIATURE

Señora Hinojosa seemed to be back on duty because by the time he was up and showered, the table had been laid with little pots of jams and butter, and a platoon of toast stood at attention in a rococo ceramic rack the like of which he'd only seen in movies. A short round woman came in from the kitchen with sweet rolls and a double-deck French coffee pot, also ceramic.

"Mr. Theroux go for newspapers. Revolve soon."

"I'm Jack Liffey," he said and stuck out his hand, which startled her no end, but she juggled the tray and took it deferentially. "*Buenos días*," he tried out. "You must be Señora Hinojosa."

"*Sí,*" she said. She poured him coffee. It had chicory in it and would take some getting used to.

He nibbled on a sweet roll and soon Sonny was back carrying the *New York Times,* the *L.A. Times,* the *Bakersfield Bee,* the *Oildale Gusher* and a one-page flyer of some sort. "Good morning to you, Jack. This first." He left the flyer beside Jack Liffey's plate.

Devil-Worshippers are among us!

Teenagers running wild! Dead babies! Mutilated animals!
    Can you recognize the evil one by his signs? Come join us for the Lord's Show of Strength! Meet in Centennial Plaza tomorrow, Tuesday, at 3 pm! March with your neighbors in the name of righteousness! We will demand City Hall take action!

We must stamp out all signs of his dominion!
* Devil-literature and devil-music
* Hooliganism, blasphemy, free-thinking
* Animal mutilation and sacrifice
* Tattoos, piercings, leather garments, unnatural hair
* Sexual immodesty, homosexual marriage, public displays of affection

Report any signs of deviant behavior or secular humanism.
Covens will not be tolerated in our Christian city.
Remember, Satan hides in plain sight!
You must learn his disguises! They are legion!

Join us! Join all right-thinking Christians!

Banish Satan!

"At least this thing is literate," Jack Liffey said. "No relation to the vac-u-ate note. Are they really proposing to outlaw tattoos and rock music and leather jackets?"

"The city attorney will explain the Constitution to them. I hope. On the other hand, who knows how far this might go?"

Jack Liffey thought about the flyer. From what he kept hearing, Bakersfield had a bad track record in business like this, but it was all so hard to believe. He just couldn't imagine an anti-Devil parade in L.A.

"I looked through quickly," Sonny said. "There's nothing in the *Bee* about rounding up street kids. Let's hope Rector Hood was just passing on a rumor."

"Yes, let's hope," Jack Liffey said. "If a kid anywhere is in trouble, there Maeve will be."

"Tom Joad," Sonny said. "This is Mr. Steinbeck's town, you know, Jack. He lived in a small bungalow just up the road while he was writing *The Grapes of Wrath*."

"Good for him."

"The book was banned in Bakersfield for many years so, of course, everybody here knows it well."

"Sorry, Sonny, I can't think about anything but Maeve."

He could picture her so clearly—loose limbed, big eyed, utterly present, fragile—that he did not want to torment his imagination with images of her sitting rigid in the back of a police car. It was true that she had a tendency to dreaminess, he thought, and there was that indomitable will to do good at all times. But she had a practical side, too, and could be as down-to-earth as Huck Finn. It was amazing how difficult it was to pin down a consistent picture of a complex person that you loved so much.

"You're sure she's here?"

"No, but I dreamed it and it's amazing what my unconscious knows. Sometimes I'll watch her drive off in her little car, all thrumming with intensity, and I'll think, how could that fantastic bundle of positive energies have come from me?"

"I never had kids," Sonny said with regret. The cook came in and hovered. "Would you like eggs?" Sonny asked. "Pancakes? Señora Hinojosa is a superb cook."

"I'm not much of a breakfast person."

"Well, I'm having the works. Maria, *quiero todo. Nada más para Señor Liffey.*"

He was still thinking of his daughter, worrying it, hoping that saying her name aloud hadn't jinxed her in some way. "She's almost eighteen. As you can tell, I know the time is coming. I'm working hard on letting go," he said. "Or at least running out a whole lot of line so it looks the same."

"You aren't very well armored," Sonny observed.

He nodded. "There it is. Indifference is not one of my options."

Sonny opened the *Bee* again to the local section and searched it carefully. "Why isn't there a follow-up on the dead infant? I ask myself. I guess it's the fifth day, and the news cycle has just exhausted itself. And not a word on the bonfire. Very strange. Maybe they have an early deadline."

"Can you take me to the cophouse later?" Jack Liffey asked. "I need to see if they'll give me my car back." He reached across the table for the *Oildale Gusher*, which looked to be mostly ads, a local throwaway.

"No problem. Oh, *here's* the bonfire," Sonny said. "I missed it. A little box right on the front page of the *Bee*. Jones is downplaying, but keeping his options open."

Jack Liffey searched every page of the *Gusher* but there was nothing but supermarket ads and cheerful feature articles. And recipes, anachronistically featuring cans of mushroom soup, diced Velveeta and crushed potato chips. There was a cake that involved several cups of fruit cocktail, too, the kind with the bright red cherries.

"Thus begin the hallucinations," Sonny said. He started reading aloud: "'Several teenagers insist that they saw the devil rise dramatically out of the pyre and hurl a black cat into the crowd.'"

Jack Liffey sat straight up. "Jesus Christ. That was *me*."

—-—

"Sombitch showed up at last." Etcheverry was in his accustomed posture, tipped back against the wall, staring at Jack Liffey with heavy-lidded eyes.

"Where you guys keeping all the kids you picked up?" Jack Liffey asked casually. There was no harm in trying it on.

"Lose your sense of humor and this job could be a real pain in the ass, you know that? Guys come in here from out of town acting like King Tut. Guys who want everything done just like the way they always done it down in the big *El Lay*."

Jack Liffey gave up on the idea of getting any information. "Could I have my car?"

"Back in the day, a guy was polite to officers of the law or he'd pay the price. Even in *El Lay*, I hear."

"Pretty please," Jack Liffey said.

"I could tell you to go fuck yourself and you couldn't do a damn thing about it."

Jack Liffey was starting to get angry, and he knew it was a very bad idea. The thing was, beyond a point, he had little control over his temper. "There it is. You know what the L.A.P.D. said about you guys?"

Etcheverry looked suspicious, but mildly curious, and Jack Liffey almost stopped himself, but he'd had a bad night and it tipped the scales. Somewhere around 4:00 he'd had an anxiety attack, not quite the full panic experience, but he'd come awake gasping repeatedly for oxygen and feeling displaced and vexed by some imminent danger that he couldn't identify. He didn't get back to sleep for two hours.

"What do our betters say?" The big cop was like a cobra coiling up for the lunge.

"They say up here they've got to send you guys out in threes to bust somebody. One of you can read, for the warrant, and one can write, for the report later, and the other one to watch the two dangerous intellectuals."

He'd actually heard the slur about Mexican cops, but it seemed a fine time to use it.

Etcheverry came to his feet. "Are you looking for trouble?"

"I'm almost sixty years old, *pendejo*," Jack Liffey said, "and I know more about trouble than you'll ever know. Take your shot."

"Tommy!" The call came sharply from across the room and Lt. Efren Saldivar hurried over. "We got a development."

Jack Liffey watched him come, curious to see how the man would rein in his partner without seeming to rebuke him—if he chose to go that way. He'd calmed down enough himself that he decided to give them both a break, and he sat on the edge of an empty desk to suggest nonbelligerence.

"I just want my pickup."

"You wonder why we called you in?" Etcheverry said.

Not really, but I'm about to find out, Jack Liffey thought. The only thing he really cared to know was if they had his daughter locked up somewhere, but he didn't want to ask directly and stir them in that direction. And he didn't want to ask about Toxie, either, which might lead back to Maeve, too.

"Stay there," Saldivar said to Jack Liffey. "Sit down, Tommy. You'll like this."

Etcheverry took a final glare at Jack Liffey and returned to his chair. Jack Liffey noticed the oil stain on the wall immediately behind his head.

"Benny, send him in," Saldivar called out.

A glass door came open across the big room and a boy wearing a small cardboard box over his head was ushered in. The box said SUNUP DISH SOAP upside down, and it had an eyeslit cut into it.

"Son, walk to the metal desk with the trophy on it—right in front of you—stop. Okay, look around the room."

"That's *him*!" a squeaky voice cried, and the boy pointed straight at Jack Liffey. It was heartbreaking to hear a voice teetering on adolescence like that—like listening to one of those excruciating junior high embarrassments of your own that you were certain would torment you forever.

"When did you see him?"

"At the Lord's fire last night."

"And what did you see him do?"

"I saw this man here accept Satan's familiar directly from the devil and throw it at the people around him. He had a big grin on his face like he was sending them all to hell . . . ."

Interesting assumptions regarding my motives, Jack Liffey thought. He decided not to interrupt the boy or appear perturbed. This was all getting nuttier by the minute, but he couldn't believe that these men, actual trained police officers on the city payroll, no matter what Kool-Aid they'd been drinking, would go for the devil stuff.

"What else did the man do?"

"I followed him but his evil work had been done. He pushed some people hard to get away. Then he drove toward town with a confederate."

"What did the confederate look like?"

"He was short and wore a white suit. They drove a Ford Aerostar."

"Okay, son. He doesn't know who you are, and he won't. Thank you."

"Boo," Jack Liffey said softly. What if I can see right through cardboard? he thought, but decided not to spook the poor kid.

The boy clutched the box to his head with both hands and ran out the glass door.

"Actually," Jack Liffey said, "I took the cat away from a couple of young thugs who were about to throw it into the bonfire. Pure meanness. Then I let the cat go. But, hell, let's assume I did everything the mystery kid reported, just as he described it. Maybe Old Nick himself reared up in the fire and winked at me and tossed me his very best black cat. Remind me, what's the California Penal Code for aiding an evil spirit?"

"Don't get cocky, Liffey. The D.A. has invoked the Patriot Act, and the whole town is under emergency procedures. A child is dead, with Satanist implications, and we're told to consider devil-worship in all its forms acts of terrorism."

"There's no such thing as emergency *procedures*, lieutenant. If we're under martial law, you're not in charge, the National Guard is. None of this is going to stick. You're not stupid."

"We have our own shrink look at you, we could probably find you're disturbed as hell. That would do to hold you for a time that you wouldn't like."

"You know, there's a person out there somewhere who killed an infant," Jack Liffey said. "That's my idea of disturbed. Is anyone looking for the perp, or are you incompetents all too busy sauteeing witches?"

Saldivar turned to his partner. "Call Dunne and . . . No, go up and see him. Tell him what's up."

Etcheverry levered himself slowly to his feet. "Can I take this asshole into the cage for a few minutes?"

Saldivar just inclined his head ambiguously and Etcheverry jostled Jack Liffey's chair hard as he walked past.

"*I don't have to wonder,*" the cop sang with a twang, on his way out.

*Who she's had.*
*No it's not love.*
*But it's not bad.*"

—-—

"Merle Haggard?" Jack Liffey asked Saldivar when the man had gone.

"How would I know?" Saldivar said. "I hate that hillbilly shit. The boss is probably going to tell us to cut you loose. If I was you, I'd get in your vehicle and keep right on going south. The county line ends at the top of the Grapevine. When you hit Gorman up there in the pass, you can exhale."

Jack Liffey nodded. "You know, I'd do that, but I have a bad feeling my daughter is in town, which means she's probably in that bunch of hapless kids that I hear you've picked up. You wouldn't feel like checking that out for me?"

The man stared at him impassively.

"Before I have to get the Feds in. Don't think my wife and I don't know some Feds."

"Oh, noo, not the *Feds*. Hey, you really pitch hardball."

For a moment Jack Liffey was afraid he'd overplayed it, but he could see a little doubt peeking through Saldivar's assumed disdain. So he clung to all the confidence he could muster and stayed silent. In fact, now that he'd brought her up, he was quite frightened for his daughter, alone and pregnant, wherever she was.

"What's your daughter's name?" Saldivar asked finally.

He was reluctant to offer it, but if she wasn't in town it wouldn't matter, and if she was and was being held somewhere, it was probably best that the cops knew that he knew. "Maeve. M-A-E-V-E. It's Irish."

Saldivar wrote it down. "You still better drive fast to the south, Liffey. If I find out anything I'll tell your *bocona* lawyer friend."

Jack Liffey thought the word was slang for big-mouth, but it equally might have been a nasty reference to Jenny Ezkiaga's sexual preference, and he wasn't going to ask.

The two men watched one another warily. It seemed to Jack Liffey that the cop had just softened his attitude toward him, and he wondered if he should acknowledge it as a kindness. It occurred to him then that life was chock-full of these miniature moments of moral choice, and what to do in even the smallest and most inconsequential ones was rarely self-evident. It made it all the worse when you were powerless, of course.

"Thank you, lieutenant."

JOHN SHANNON

— —

**Artifact: 1933c**

FOUR DEAD AND SCORES
HURT IN COTTON STRIKE

*Two Pitched Battles Result When
Pickers and Ranchers Clash in
Kern and Tulare Counties*

Bakersfield, October 10. (Exclusive)—Four men were killed
and scores were injured, at least one of them probably fatally, in
two pitched battles waged today when striking cotton pickers
clashed with ranchers and their supporters in Kern and Tulare
counties.

Apparently the more sanguinary of the two battles was
waged at Pixley but only meager reports of it had been received
tonight by telephone. The dead at Pixley were: Eltrea Fernandez,
Delfino Dabila and Felipe Estrada, all Mexicans.

The other battle raged in the Arvin district, about twenty-two
miles from here. In this encounter, Pete Subia, 40, a picker,
whose home was in Arvin, was killed by a charge of buckshot.
Sheriff Cas Walser of Bakersfield took a force of thirty men to
the scene which culminated a series of disturbances growing out
of a cotton pickers' strike in which 10,000 pickers refused to
work. Many volunteers from the Agriculture Labor Bureau
arrived in a caravan of trucks to support the growers.

Deputy sheriffs were using tear gas bombs in quelling the
rioting, it was reported here. Merced Velos, a picker, was shot

through the left arm, and Bud Ledbetter, also a picker or union organizer, was beaten about the head during the fight. Both were taken to hospital.

—*Daily Midway Driller*, Taft, October 11, 1933[7]

——

"I've wet the bed," she shrieked, taunting them. "Must make you feel powerful!"

Pastor Kohlmeyer turned to Channing Pelt. The Pastor wore a billowy pale blue robe, as befitted an important ritual, though he did not look very comfortable in it. "We have to let her up to use the necessaries."

"She never asked." Pelt was in fact observing her distress and relishing it.

"Better make it fast," the girl challenged. "I feel a big dump on the way."

"Mrs. Barkdale, would you take her down the hall, please."

"Yes, sir." Mrs. Barkdale was the wife of one of their most respected parishioners, a developer of minimalls who had grown up in town and never left it, and who read lay lessons regularly at the church. As Pelt's Laredo material explained, it was essential to have at least one respectable woman of the community present when dealing with a female subject so there could be no question of indecent or immoral acts.

Mrs. Barkdale lowered the bedrails, slowly pried free the Velcro restraints with what looked like arthritic fingers and led Toxie out of the room.

Channing Pelt admitted to himself that he was having the time of his life here, standing back a little, metaphorically as well

149

as physically, while at the same time urging the rite forward. There were, of course, difficult religious questions involved. Were those persons inhabited by demons—or inhabited simply by the spirit of Evil, as he preferred—still to be counted within the providence of God? If so, how much concern did you grant their physical comforts as you were trying to release their souls? The girl's curses were hard to take. *The* curses, rather, of her resident demons/Evil, which was certainly the true source.

He knew the ignominy of any failure would fall in the long run on the pastor's head so it released him to fold his arms and watch the difficult business with a certain equanimity and detached righteousness. He could see the girl barely listening to the import of the ritual words that the pastor uttered. She seemed to respond only to his tone, whether he was hostile or kindly. Or the thing inside her responded. He wondered if, should the ordeal ever become too painful—like Isaac ordered to sacrifice his son on the altar—if an angel would intervene in some way to stop it. He even wondered if, in fact, *he* had been given that role. But he had no intention of intervening on the side of mercy. The girl annoyed him no end. He wanted the Beast/spirit of rebellion crushed utterly and expelled. Winning is everything.

"Are you sure I can do this?" the pastor asked during the awkward silence. "I called Bob Shawdon last night, and he said he'd never heard of an evangelical pastor performing rites like this."

"Dennis, look here." Pelt began to read aloud from the stapled document they both held: "'You must never underestimate the demon. He can be very subtle. You need to be wary of anything that seems to undermine your self-esteem or your right to perform an exorcism.'"

"Oh, dear. This is all such strange ground."

"This is the manual, remember? It's been approved by a committee of evangelical leaders. And it's been thoroughly de-Romanized. We can use our grape juice in place of the communion wine, but it says you should bless some pure water, too, since we don't use holy water, of course. Apparently the devil really does know the difference." Pelt handed him a plastic bottle of Trader Joe's distilled water. "You'd better say a heartfelt prayer over the water, Denny."

The pastor took the plastic bottle dubiously in two hands. Eventually he carried it to a small oak altar that he had had brought into the room, then knelt before it and began to pray silently.

—–

The battle-axe kept a firm grip on her arm. The woman was stronger than she looked, and a couple of younger acolytes trailed behind so there wasn't much chance for her to make a break for it. Toxie was of two minds. She could just ignore the whole dumb procedure and roll her eyes at everything, or she could give them a real arm-flapping show. After telling them all the shit that they wanted to hear to get the damn interrogation over with, she probably didn't have much to lose. After all, she'd seen that old movie on TV, the one with the little girl barfing green, and she knew what was expected, though without the special-effects guys, she'd have a hell of a time spinning her head all the way around. She might have trouble with the green vomit, too.

"No funny stuff in there," her keeper warned Toxie, as she released her into a toilet stall.

Perhaps she should get started, she thought in a sudden rush of resentment, maybe whack this old bitch with some soggy human shit.

—-—

The pastor decanted a little of the water into a metal cup so it would be handy to dip his fingers into. Abruptly there was a scream from down the hall, more a bellow of outrage, and then the slam of a door.

In a moment, the two guardians who'd followed Mrs. Barkdale and Toxie to the restroom were dragging the girl back into the room.

"She threw her . . . BM at Mrs. Barkdale. The poor woman will be back here after she cleans up."

"Sue Ellen, there was no call for that," Channing Pelt said calmly.

"How'd you like a blow job?" Toxie asked, flicking her tongue at him.

"Is that the way it has to be?" the pastor said.

"I can do a two-fer. It'd be fun."

The youth leader handed the mimeographed booklet back to the pastor, pointing to where he'd marked the restart point. Dipping his finger into grape juice, Kohlmeyer painted it across the girl's forehead and down her nose in the shape of a cross.

"In the name of the Father, the Son, and the Holy Spirit."

She screwed up her face to lick some of it off her upper lip.

"*Welch's*! Can't you pathetic assholes even use *wine*!?"

The pastor sprinkled some of the Trader Joe's distilled water over her. Enjoying herself now, Toxie screeched. "It burns! It burns!"

The pastor began to read in a sonorous voice: "I command you, unclean spirit, whoever you are, along with all your minions now imprisoning this poor servant of God, by the mysteries of the incarnation, passion, resurrection, and ascension of our Lord Jesus Christ, by the descent of the Holy Spirit, by the coming of our Lord for judgment—that you tell me by some sign your name, and the day and hour of your departure. I command you, moreover, to obey me to the letter, I who am a minister of God despite my unworthiness; nor shall you be emboldened to harm in any way this creature of God you inhabit, or the bystanders, or any of their possessions."

"My name is Beelzebub Hugh Jass!" Toxie succeeded in making her voice guttural and male. "I will depart this girl when you stand on your hands and repeat my name fifteen times!" It was hard not to giggle.

The pastor was doing his best to cling to the conventional, as the printed sheets had commanded him, but he kept eying the astonishing number of pieces of metal piercing the girl's ears, nose, lip, and even her eyebrow.

—-

"Only thing I ever liked in school was the 4-H," Tammy Crumm said.

Maeve wondered how long she'd been estranged from Toxie.

"I liked combing the sheep but I didn't like the showing. It's so weird and shit. The whole rest of going to school just made me sad and scared. It was like I was stuck there to be made a fool every day. Words kept wiggling when I tried to read them. I was so ashamed."

"Raise your right hand," Maeve suggested, with a sudden idea. She tapped the woman's left hand as she said it, and Tammy raised the left without thinking. Maeve had read that this could be a tell-tale sign of dyslexia.

There was a thick layer of dust on the concrete floor. Maeve found an undisturbed patch and used her finger to write R-E-C-O-G-N-I-T-I-O-N in big capitals in the dust. "What's that say?"

"Rrr. Ree. Ree. Rrrr."

"Don't worry about it. It's not important." Maeve slashed the word away with her foot. "I'm no expert, but I'll bet you've got a thing called dyslexia."

The woman looked terrified.

"It's not so bad. Maybe it's even a gift. I've read that a lot of geniuses have dyslexia. It's just a different way of seeing things, and you have to learn to read in a different way."

The woman still looked worried, almost panicky.

"When we get out of here, if you promise to try to be friends with your daughter again, I'll take you to somewhere they can teach you to read."

"Naw."

"I'll bet you've been smart all your life, and people just made you feel you weren't."

The woman grabbed Maeve's wrist. "Nobody's ever said nothing so sweet to me."

"But you got to try with Sue Ellen, too."

Tears showed in Tammy's eyes, and she slapped her arms around Maeve so hard that she felt she'd suffocate in the woman's baggy beer-smelling cardigan.

—-—

They drove up to Jenny's office just as she came out into the parking lot that had once been the back garden to pile a tall arm-load of blue-bound writs into her Passat. The cops hadn't given Jack Liffey's car back after all, claiming somebody in the motor pool had misplaced the keys. He had no idea whether it was a ploy to keep him in town or just general incompetence. It occurred to him they might be planning to arrest him for aiding and abetting the devil. But he almost looked forward to it. He could get the ACLU in and it'd look great on his resumé, if he'd only had one.

"Jenny," Sonny called out from the van. "Jack's got a problem. He thinks his daughter might've come back to town on her own."

"Check the juvenile hall again. If she's not there, you can take heart that I'm engaged right now in getting her freed. The sheriff's about to get his apple cart upset. These are John Doe habeas corpus writs that I'm taking up to Judge Kentner in Sacramento. I can't trust a single judge in this town."

"Can we help you?"

"Find out where they've taken the overflow detainees. You know my cell number, Sonny." She slammed her car door and started up.

They watched her swing recklessly out onto Twenty-fourth Street, setting off a couple of angry honks and a screech of brakes.

"Some day she's going to get creamed," Sonny said.

"You know what we have to do," Jack Liffey said.

"Like she said."

"More important. We've got to find out who killed that infant. Nobody else is even looking. Whoever it was, he knew just how to bamboozle the whole town."

Chapter Ten

# WITH US OR WITH THE DEVIL

T he pastor flicked a fingerful of distilled water on the girl's forehead as she yanked hard against the restraints. The water that he had done his best to bless was the only thing that seemed to have an effect on her.

"Owww! It's burning me!"

"'I cast you out, unclean spirit,'" he read, "'along with every Satanic power of the enemy, every specter from hell, and all your fell companions. Begone and stay far from this creature of God, in the name of our Lord Jesus Christ. It is God who commands you, who flung you headlong from the heights of heaven into the burning depths of hell!'"

"We've got air-conditioning down here now!" Toxie shouted. "It's cool as a brass tit!"

Channing Pelt noticed that the women standing guard across the room recoiled at the suggestion of A.C. in Hell, as if that were a particularly blasphemous assertion. He thought it pretty funny, actually, but managed not to smile. He was fascinated and occasionally frustrated by the ritual, and he suspected the girl of being much brighter than anyone supposed and making up a lot of her offensive responses, though maybe not all of them. Mrs. Barkdale had changed into a shapeless cleaning lady's housecoat that she'd found somewhere and had rejoined them.

"You there, flat top. You want my pussy, don't you?"

"Your body doesn't interest us. It's your eternal soul that's in danger," Pelt said.

"Who dares insult my host body?" the girl intoned dramatically. *"Gle kurtsa ti na biciklu!"*

"I charge you, demon, to speak only in American!" Kohlmeyer commanded tremulously.

Channing Pelt knew she wasn't making the language up, and it worried him. He was from an old ag family near Chico, and three generations back, long before a privileged son had been sent off to Stanford and Claremont Theological Seminary, the name on all those peach crates had been Peletich. Even he tended to forget. But the devil would know, of course, if there really was a devil here.

"Do you know what she said?" the pastor asked.

"Just a curse," Pelt replied, reluctant to translate the insult that had been hurled good-naturedly out screen doors so often by his uncles: There goes your dick on a bicycle!

"Fuck you all!" the girl cried.

157

The youth leader showed a restless little shuffle of impatience, and abruptly Pelt found himself grabbing Toxie's right wrist with both hands. Crushing it against the mattress in frustration, he snapped, "Shut up! Obey the Lord! You're nothing but an insolent girl!"

"'God commands you!'" the pastor barked, growing impatient himself, his eyes flicking from the thrashing girl to the photocopied script. "'Tremble in fear, Satan, you enemy of the faith, you foe of the human race, you begetter of death—'"

He had to stop to catch his breath and the girl spat out: "Lick my holy pussy. *Kuja ti javo!*"

Pelt had been leaning over the bed to study her eyes, wondering if anything could be discerned in their depths. Almost reflexively reacting to the ugly phrase, he found himself slapping her across the cheek. The physical blow sounded like a gunshot in the room, and it shocked and stilled them all. Even the girl went quiet. Her dark eyes bored into him, and he could have sworn then that there was something deeper, within her, watching him.

"Oh, you've done it now, shithead," she said slowly. Her voice wailed upward and became so shrill that it ripped away into a cough. "Be afraid of me now! Assaulting a girl in restraints! I have witnesses."

"I'm not afraid of you, demon. Never!" But Channing Pelt could hear no conviction in his own voice.

She smiled evilly at him. "*Bog te jebo*, you big fucking Serb asshole!"

—-

Sonny parked his van up the street from the newspaper office, and the two of them watched a small picket line walking an oval out front with homemade signs. BEE MORE FOR JESUS. WITH US OR WITH THE DEVIL. WARNING: ATHEISTS WITHIN.

"What do you think the *Bee* did to upset them?" Jack Liffey asked.

"I suppose the paper hasn't been stern enough against Old Nick. Wait here and I'll go upstairs and love up some of these news fellers." Sonny got out and came around to the window. "First, I got a quick confession to make to you, Jack Liffey. I'm about to do a back-bayou shapeshift and turn myself into a cop for a while, unworthy as I am. I been letting some of these reporters think I was just a good ol' boy, dumber'n a barrel of hair, but it's a new day now."

"You never did tell me why you quit being a cop."

"Let's say, anything I was alleged to have done would have been done in furtherance of justice."

"And a higher law."

"Exactly my point. There's something about where I grew up that always makes one reach for the law of the special case. But nothing is known for certain against this gentleman's character, as we say."

Sonny had had four beers in quick succession, and Jack Liffey realized he was probably a cheap date. His companion was unraveling a little, in a number of ways, including a kind of glaze over his eyes. But he'd seen plenty of people function that way.

"Go do what you're going to do," Jack Liffey said, ready, after three days of the man's hospitality, to give Sonny Theroux the benefit of the doubt.

Jack Liffey, after Sonny left, began working himself up to call Gloria and ask her to come help. He knew she was a first-rate investigator. Maeve was all that mattered here, and for better or for worse, they both agreed on that.

——

## Artifact: 1937

"Air: This is your country dont let the big men take it away from you."
—Photograph of sign above air pump in gas station, Kern County, 1937. Dorothea Lange, for the California State Emergency Relief Administration. One of the more famous photographs of the Depression, reprinted many times.

——

Bulldog was back at the wire screen, obviously smitten by Tammy, and the two of them were twining fingers through the wire and whispering. Maeve looked away discreetly.

All around her girls were holding singing sessions, flipping ID cards at the base of the wall and claiming winners as if they were pogs or baseball cards, or disagreeing vehemently about their favorite bands.

There was a fistfight on the boys' side and Maeve saw Bulldog pull himself reluctantly away from Tammy and lumber off toward the clash, the default peacemaker in the room. His presence alone quickly stopped the struggle. One riot, one Ranger, Maeve thought, remembering reading somewhere about the motto of the Texas Rangers.

"Is that big guy with you?"

A skinny girl who looked about thirteen had sidled up next to Maeve. She had a bad complexion and silver rings in both eyebrows.

"Kind of," Maeve said. "My name's Maeve."

"I'm Little Hazard," she said. She said it pugnaciously, without a hint of irony, as if daring Maeve to deny it. "I go by Hazzie."

"Do you know Toxie?" After all, it seemed logical.

"Everybody knows Toxie."

"Why isn't she here?" Maeve asked.

"Don't you know?"

Just then the roll-up door clattered. "Food call!" a cop yelled through cupped mitts. "One bag per mouth."

Hazzie tried to run for her food, but Maeve grabbed the straps of her black overalls.

"Tell me about Toxie."

"Leggo! They took her away for special doctoring. They said her mind was sick by the Devil."

"Where did they take her?"

"Leggo, jerk-in-the-box!" The little girl flailed wildly, and Maeve let go.

Just as a food fight started up, with balls of Velveeta and compressed bread filling the air, Maeve finally got up to obtain whatever food the cops were begrudging them.

— —

"They didn't know? Or wouldn't tell you?"

"Epistemologically, down where the water hits the wheel, Jack, there may not be much difference," Sonny replied. After their mission to the newspaper and then to several other reliable sources had yielded no results, Sonny had driven a reluctant Jack Liffey back home. He was now sipping a gin-and-tonic on the verandah, while his guest worked on a ginger ale. Outside, an irregular scatter of toothless old men and big-armed women made their way home from work or wherever they had been for the day. Jack Liffey had never been so unquestionably on Tobacco Road and he found it fascinating.

Now and again a Harley pa-tooted along the cracked street or a '70s Buick. It wasn't quite sunset by the clock, but the light was murky and foreboding. A solid cloudbank pressed down oppressively, so low that Jack Liffey felt a man with very long arms could jump up and touch it. Sonny suggested that the people they saw were trying to beat home one of Bakersfield's dreaded tule fogs.

"The *Bee* knows damn well there's a devil-worship hysteria going on. Some of their best reporters are looking into it. I know the pattern. The D.A. will have interrogators working on the most impressionable kids, or the angriest kids. Before the night's out they'll have tapes full of kids admitting they danced to Beelzebub's music."

"Half of them will finger me as his pal," Jack Liffey said.

"But no one I talked to seemed to have a clue where they're holding the kids. And, as far as I could tell, knowing that crew well, they actually didn't know." Sonny shook his head.

Jack Liffey had already called Gloria at work. He'd told her what he could, especially his fears about Maeve, and she'd already phoned back after double-checking several places in L.A. and finding no trace of her. She loved Maeve, too, certainly enough to drop everything and claim emergency leave.

"This woman of yours," Sonny now said. "You sure she'll be any use here?"

"I'm not sure the sun will rise tomorrow, Sonny, but I'm still going to set my little travel-alarm. Gloria's a pro and she's tough. Put her in a room alone with Saldivar *and* Etcheverry and a clutch of wolverines, and I know who comes out alive." He glanced over. "Speak of women. Where's Jenny with her writs?"

"I don't know," he said glumly. "Her cell isn't answering. Jack, I been triangulating on this, and I think it's coming on pretty bad. There's too many omens. I think we're entering a dark parable and we're not going to like it."

"Then let's find out who killed the damn baby and put paid to all the crazies before anybody actually gets burned at the stake— including me."

—–—

Pastor Kohlmeyer and Channing Pelt sat exhausted in the pastor's study sipping a chamomile tea that was guaranteed to be free of stimulants. For years Dennis Kohlmeyer had innocently sipped what was called Mormon tea. He'd chosen it on the grounds that, with a name like that, it couldn't possibly contain anything ill advised. Then a naturalist in his congregation had pointed out that it was made from a desert ephedra, second kin to an amphetamine. The man couldn't resist adding that the stuff had been used by pioneers for generations as a stimulant and had been served in bawdy houses all over Nevada as "whorehouse tea." From that simple blunder that he'd persisted in for years, the pastor had learned a profound lesson about the nature of innocent error. He even used the tale as a joke on himself from time to time, but Pelt noticed that it was a moral leeway Kohlmeyer never seemed to offer anyone but himself.

"Who's on board for the march?" Pelt asked.

"I'd say just about everyone." The pastor's answer wasn't good enough, so Pelt waited.

"Two council members have promised to join us. For starters."

Alas, only two meant that their crusade was still confined to the usual suspects, Pelt thought with disappointment. Poppy Bumpers from the Southwest of town, one of their own parishioners, and Duncan Bundy, who was still chairman of what remained of the Kern County John Birch Society, and who firmly believed that many thousands of chanting African troops waited in the hills for the U.N. helicopters that would ferry them in to city hall to take over. It would have been good to have some of the machine Republicans on their side, even the lone Democrat from Ward 1 on the east side.

"The mayor sends his regrets," the pastor admitted.

"I suppose it would have been . . . a bit strange for the mayor to join a march that's going to present demands to the mayor. Any other pastors?"

"Mike Olin, from Silver Creek. He'll be okay if he doesn't try to grab the spotlight."

"He will."

Kohlmeyer shrugged. "You're good at dealing with the practical matters. I think when the time comes, Jesus will move a lot of others to join us."

Pelt wasn't quite so sure Jesus was out recruiting, but he nodded to maintain the peace. He recalled the enraged Methodist minister he'd spoken to that morning on the phone. "Is Kohlmeyer that *demented*?" He'd tried to ring off politely, but the man just went on railing about fanaticism. Then he'd approached the history professor from the community college who sometimes worked with them, but the prof had said he was backed up with schoolwork. Pelt didn't really mind if they were out there on their own. It would be juicy, no matter what. He looked over at Kohlmeyer's long face and thought he ought to lob the man a bit of sympathy.

"This girl's a tough nut," he commiserated. After a long day of repeated readings, chantings, hymns and sprays of grape juice and distilled water, she had sagged a bit in her pugnacity, but not before they'd been pretty exhausted, too. Toward the end, they'd been forced to wake her again and again, and finally Kohlmeyer had called it quits.

"What on earth is the paschal lamb?" the pastor asked abruptly, a bit exasperated. It was one of the phrases he had incanted aloud from the photocopied rituals.

"I'm not sure." Pelt took a 4-by-5 card out of his shirt pocket. "But the cult team already has another girl lined up. Over in Shafter, they have a girl who's admitted she fornicated directly with the Beast. Carmela Silva, a Pentecostal family."

The image of fornicating with the devil seemed to be a little too vivid for Kohlmeyer who held up protective hands and closed his eyes. The man muttered, "In the name of the Father and the Son and the Holy Spirit. Protect us now and guide us in what we do in Jesus' name. Amen. If it be Your will, take this cup from us."

Pelt was surprised.

"I know you think I'm imperturbable, Channing, but I've had my own tests in life."

Pelt looked at the man, obviously very tired. "Of course."

"Oh, I can put on the full armor of God, all right, and I've been resilient, as the situation called for it. But I wasn't always that way.

When I was thirteen, my mom and dad sent me to relatives in Arkansas for the summer. They were Missouri Synod Lutherans, and mom figured that was fundamental enough to keep me safe from bad influence. I was a fan of the *Reader's Digest*, and I was always hoping somebody I'd run into would qualify for 'My Most Unforgettable Character.' So I figured it might just be my uncle Rainey who'd had polio and was in a wheelchair. He took me bass fishing one day out on a dock at Bull Shoals Lake. What a day."

He seemed to run down for a bit. Channing Pelt felt the need to stand up and leave the room, but he knew he was trapped. He peered into the teapot and managed to scavenge a little more chamomile tea.

The pastor went on with his story. "I did everything he asked that afternoon, because you can't be mean to a cripple man, can you? Oh, oh. Later, I needed to get angry at somebody. For a long time after I got home, I think I went into what you'd call a depression. To me, I felt I was angry at God.

"I scorned God for a long time, and it just made me resent my older brother more. Bob-Don Jr., who was always given all the Easter eggs and always dropped them."

Dennis Kohlmeyer stared off into the middle distance, and Channing Pelt had no idea what to say. He didn't want to hear any more.

"A couple years later Uncle Rainey wheeled himself out into the garage and put his duck gun in his mouth."

Pelt tightened his lips.

"I demanded that if God wanted me to believe in Him and serve Him, He could change that horrible day on the dock and make it come out different, and if he left it the same, I'd just worship trees and rocks instead of Him."

"Did God give you a sign?" Channing asked quickly.

"Yes, he did, and He's got my full heart now. Channing—that girl today. . . . She regarded me just the way Uncle Rainey did—for no more than an instant, but I saw it clearly. That's got to be the Devil inside her, doesn't it? How else would she be able to mimic Uncle Rainey?" There were tears in the man's eyes. Pelt looked away.

—–

The pizza was gone by the time he heard Gloria's RAV-4 slowing outside so she could read the house numbers. She parked half off the asphalt, and the fog was getting lower, with wisps almost touching the rooftops. She glanced around a little at the dilapidated houses nearby and came up the walk. Jack Liffey, waiting, could see her thinking, What a dump this area is. Not with disdain necessarily, just one of her frank observations, a cop's quick note. She carried a small canvas bag. At the door she ran her finger down his cheek and kissed him softly, as lascivious a moment as he needed. He'd also needed a sign she wasn't angry at him for dragging her up there. So now he could relax. He never knew for sure.

"It's wonderful to see you, Glor. I've missed you. This is Sonny Theroux, he's the investigator for the lawyer I contacted last time I was here. Sonny—Gloria."

"Ma'am." They shook hands like old colleagues. "Hard drive up?"

"Yeah. There was terrible fog on the Grapevine and the Highway Patrol ran a break at Gorman and started escorting groups down in convoys at about fifteen MPH. Pretty eerie. We came out of the fog bank just before we hit the valley floor, and suddenly we were driving through this thin low slice of visible world."

"It may settle to the ground later tonight, if the dew point's fixin' to drop. It might not. You can't count on tule fog any which way. You'll hear the hush if it comes down."

"Little cat feet," Jack Liffey said.

"Pepperoni?" she asked, eying the empty flat boxes.

"We finished it off," Jack Liffey said with chagrin. "Sorry. We didn't know if you were coming tonight for sure. We'll get some more."

"No. I ate before I left, but I wouldn't say no to a beer."

Sonny grinned as he gathered up the mess on the table. "I'll get you a pilsner, if that's all right. I could also nuke some biscuits and slow gravy from this morning, just to take the edge off?"

"I'm not hungry. Honest."

Jack Liffey took the bag from her and pointedly carried it to his room and set it on the half-made bed, an act that stirred him a little by its suggestion that he'd soon be bedding the bag's owner. It had been a long time since he'd been this sexually aroused, and he wasn't sure why, but he gave her a big hug when he came back and ran his hand over her bottom and whispered that he wanted her.

"Sure," she said. "It's not the impossible dream, guy."

Sonny brought out two beers and another ginger ale and they sat around the table. She finished off almost half of hers in one go, and Jack Liffey picked up a slight sulfury smell that reminded him what drinking used to be all about. "I got thirsty," Gloria said. "I should carry water in the car. Have either of you private investigators thought to put Maeve's car on the police hot list?"

"Uh-oh," Jack Liffey said. "I told you she'd take charge."

She looked from one to the other of them, obviously trying not to be too critical. "Fill me in."

Half an hour later she said, "Here's what we're going to do. Tomorrow morning, you show me the spot where the dead infant was found. Then all three of us will go door-to door through the area and see if anybody remembers a couple with a baby who all of a sudden didn't have a baby any more. Most of these dead and missing infants turn out to be crib death or shaken-baby syndrome, and the parents just panic."

"You don't think the Bakersfield PD's done this canvas already?" Sonny said.

"Even if they have . . . ," she said, shrugging. "Not the best cops around. What I hear, when they're on stakeout and it's a hot day, they all follow the shade around the house. I trust what I do myself on this case."

— —

"Have I told you recently enough that you've got the biggest clitoris I've ever seen."

"Oh, oh. Now's fine. *Oh.*"

"I love you, Gloria, and I'm going to stalk you and keep doing this, and *this*. Until you give in."

"Oh, God, right there. *Jack.* Right there. Why are you so good to me?"

"You know why."

"Yes yes yes. Now now. Harder."

Chapter Eleven

# SERVANT OF THE ANTICHRIST

I t wasn't hard to find the exact spot. Alongside the walking path that ran along the bottom of the bluff adjacent to the wide boggy bed of the much depleted Kern River, spiky with reeds and water willows, there were four lengths of rebar driven into a patch of bare mud to define a quadrangle about six feet by four. The metal rods were enwrapped with the predictable yellow ribbon saying POLICE LINE DO NOT ENTER over and over. The ground all around had been heavily trampled. There was even a potato chip bag plus recent cigarette butts. A scene that Jack Liffey assumed would at this point be unlikely to yield up any information.

Gloria squatted down anyway in the morning mists to read sign, like an Indian scout—an observation he would never have made out loud in a million years. He did study her generous bottom for a moment, wanting to fondle it. Over the night, they might not have entirely patched up all that seemed to be going wrong between them, but it had been a lot of fun trying.

Morning vapors wisped up off the trickle of river, but the main body of the fog had never settled in the night and it had withdrawn now well above the cliff behind them. The day was gloomy and surprisingly chilly, maybe in the low 40s.

She took her time while Jack Liffey and Sonny Theroux looked on.

"What does the fog do next?" Jack Liffey asked.

"It breaks up about noon," Sonny said. "Or it doesn't."

"There aren't a lot of houses down here the baby could have come from."

"There's some big trailer parks downstream, right along this path. And you know what it's like across the river in my neighborhood. Several hundred folks who sit way below the salt, as the saying goes."

"All poor whites?" Jack Liffey asked.

"In the past, but there's some Mexicans now."

"The baby was Anglo?" Gloria put in.

"So I hear."

Jack Liffey thought of other child deaths he'd run across in a ten-year career hunting for missing children, one eight-year-old in particular he could never get out of his mind. A stubborn boy who'd been beaten to death by a wannabe gang of twelve-year-olds for refusing to surrender his nerf football. Imponderable, how much more violent the world had become since his own youth.

"Look there," she said, pointing to a spot within the tape. Then, in frustration, she tore the tape away and went into the no-go zone.

"You're kidding."

But she wasn't. They came forward and squatted gingerly beside her.

"Cop, cop, cop," she said, pointing to distinct flat-soled imprints. "EMT, or ME, or CSI." That was a ripple tread imprint, from something more comfortable than a brogue, and another similar one that was smaller. "And here and here. But *here*."

It was little more than the size of a thumb, obviously older because the other shoeprints overlay and obliterated most of it—not much more than a square inch of pock marks. There was just enough remaining to suggest V's of tiny octopus suckers.

"That's an L.A. Gear Luscious Gibbs' In the Paint. The ridiculous shoe is silver and red, has fins and portholes, and looks a lot like a 1958 Buick."

"How do you know these things?" Jack Liffey asked. He always asked that, knowing it pleased her.

"It's my job. Nobody connected to the law—not on this planet, anyway—would wear a Gibbs to work."

"So we're looking for a guy running around in 1958 Buicks," Jack Liffey said.

"No, we're looking for a busybody who remembers there was a baby in the neighborhood and then there wasn't. The shoe is a plus for the follow-up."

She stood and slapped a bit of mud off her fingertips. "The locals should have beat us to all this, but maybe they've been too busy looking for a guy with horns and a pitchfork. We'll know soon enough if we're walking in their tracks. You two go ask across the river. You know the neighborhood, Sonny.

"You say there's trailer parks up that way? I'll take them. I'll work better alone, and I can always flash a badge. Nobody looks close at a badge."

Jack Liffey had one, too, from a mail order detective school in New Jersey, and he'd used it for several years on exactly the same theory. But he didn't use it much any more because the silver was wearing off and orange plastic showed through.

As they stood, he could feel a chilly exhalation that seemed to drift very slowly downriver, but it must have been his imagination because tatters of fog hung absolutely motionless among the willows.

"Thanks for coming to town, Gloria," Sonny offered. He and Jack Liffey made their way up the cliff trail to head for the bridge.

"I like her," Sonny said. "Very impressive."

"Right," Jack Liffey agreed.

—-—

"And how come you're not taking this to a judge in Bakersfield?"

After a half dozen false leads that had wasted the whole day previous, she'd gone where she knew she'd get a hearing. Though even Judge Thomas Wilder was now striding rapidly along the main corridor to his chambers in the Sacramento courthouse, and she knew she wouldn't have long to make her case. The word was obviously out to duck the whole Bako devil-worship business.

"Eat me," Jennie Ezkiaga said.

"Pardon?"

"Come on, Tommy. I don't have to tell you that a public prosecutor answers to no power except his own discretion. Padget is leading that big-eyed deer of a grand jury down this nutty trail, and you know perfectly well no judge in Kern dare say else. They've already got indefinite internment and indefinite interrogation of innocent children."

"Let's not go hysterical, Miss Ezkiaga. An infant was actually killed in Bakersfield. I even hear that there have been several confessions to membership in devil clubs."

"Judge, they're grilling those kids day and night. They're suggesting, they're demanding. The Ninth Circuit finally threw out all those phony confessions back in the 'eighties. Why not be an early hero on this one?"

He stopped long enough to take the paperwork from her and glance at it.

"Ms Ezkiaga, if you rewrite this for any minors that idiot Padget is holding, I'll release them to their parents." He handed back the writ. "With the Patriot Act what it is, I'm afraid he can keep the adults for now."

"Can we at least be told where they are? They're not in any of the normal jails."

"Talk to J.J. at the *Bee*. His nose is pretty good. If he sniffs it out and they try to prior suppress, he can ask me for an order to print."

"Judge—"

"I've got to go."

"Just one word, and it's heartfelt. I'm not being paranoid on this. There's already been a book burning. I'm only trying to head off worse."

He sighed and watched her for a moment. "Jenny, you want

me to take sides publicly with an attorney who is, let's say, unconventional, and against all the massed ladies and gentlemen of Jesus?"

She just regarded him steadily, not letting him off the hook for an instant.

He sighed again. "You've got the whole bite of my tiny morsel of divine courage."

— —

### Artifact: late 1930s

Dear Odessa,

You and Coy must try and come to California this fall. We've got everything we want now. We get our relief checks for forty dollars every two weeks and we've bought a new car. We go into town every two weeks and we get commodities. That helps a heap on our grocery bill and the case worker comes out and gives the children clothes so that they can keep in school. You sure want to come out.

Your sister, Bessie

—Bogus letter widely distributed by Associated Farmers and widely reprinted, supposedly written by an Okie family in California, 1938[8]

— —

Maeve woke abruptly on her cot after a terrible dream of throwing up all over her dad's apartment. She was tormented with the guilt of it. He still carried the condo on the books for storage—and of course, as a retreat if he ever needed respite from Gloria. She wondered what the dream meant. Part of what it meant, though, was obvious: she was abruptly wracked by real nausea.

She sat up on the edge of the cot and put her head between her knees as the big dim warehouse did a Tilt-A-Whirl. It frightened her, and she thought of waking Toxie's mom who was snoring softly beside her, as other throats in the echoey space were coughing, snorting, blubbering and talking softly. A few kids were still awake and astir.

Of course, she thought, after she'd come fully awake. The pregnancy. She retched back the rising bile and ran for the row of port-a-potties along the wall, dreading the stench she knew she would find inside.

—-—

"They's one about two, terrible two, next door there. Snivels all day. Ain't been no other in years. All our kids is raised and gone."

The woman was missing most of her front teeth and had a bad scar from the corner of her lip up her cheek. Her forearm showed a tattoo of a butterfly with part of its wing torn away. Jack Liffey and Sonny Theroux were going door-to-door together now, by choice, after a block of making their inquiries separately.

"You sure you don't know of any kids you saw around for a while and then they disappeared?" Sonny tried again.

"Huh-uh. An old broom knows where the dirt is."

"Thank you, ma'am. You've been helpful."

They walked the bare path worn through the dead lawn to the next house. "It's all DNA here, I'm afraid," Sonny said.

"That's a bit politically incorrect of you."

"Trust me. I know broken chromosomes. This is ground zero of the bitter end of the Okie migration trail, and those with anything on the ball got themselves out."

"Moved on to become aerospace engineers and French teachers."

"Sure. But fifteen years ago, you could drop out of high school in Oildale and get a damn good job roughnecking in the oilfields. Some still can. I don't mean to put anybody down, but let's not pretend the fridge belongs on the side porch."

They had to squeeze between a rusty panel truck that looked dead and a possibly still functioning 1959 Impala.

Jack Liffey took his turn and knocked. A woman in a flowered muumuu opened suspiciously and he repeated their standard approach. Her brows furrowed up. "Dix!" she bellowed.

A toddler came toward her in that wonderful bowlegged Frankenstein lurch. He was pretty late walking if he was the two he looked, Jack Liffey thought, but, looking more closely, he guessed there was some physical disability.

"Dix, where-at was that damn baby threw his bottle atchou?"

"Nuh."

"Useless little twerp. Get your noggin in gear. Baby. Throw. Bottle."

The toddler's eyes went wide, as if he were being threatened.

"*Where?*" she bellowed.

The little boy started to sniffle and she slapped him.

"Hold on a moment, ma'am," Jack Liffey said calmly. He squatted down facing the boy who was holding his slapped cheek and snuffling. "Shhh. Your name is Dix?"

He didn't respond.

"Did a baby throw a milk bottle at you?"

The child finally nodded feebly.

"Did it happen near here?" he asked softly.

Another timorous nod.

"I'm going to point to different houses. Just like *this*. I'll do it very slowly and when I'm pointing to the right place, where that baby was, I want you to say something or just touch me. Will you do that for me?"

He nodded, doing his best not to catch the mother's eye.

Jack Liffey began making careful pointing gestures at the houses along the block. At each one, he gave the boy a few moments to consider, then he retracted his finger and re-aimed at the next one. Finally, the boy gave his arm a light pat. Jack Liffey smiled in reward. It was actually a court of tiny stucco bungalows, facing one another, but he doubted the boy could get any more specific.

"Why, thank you, Dix. That was just perfect. Here's some coins for you." Jack Liffey handed him some loose change out of his pocket, and he squealed and ran off with it.

"Dix, you gimme that!" the woman howled and slammed the door on them without another word.

"Jesus," Jack Liffey said.

"No one to root for there," Sonny said. "He's doomed. Oh, I've seen saints and I've seen sinners and plenty in between. That's the first time I've seen rickets in years. Osteomalacia they call it now."

They headed across the road toward the stucco court.

"I wonder if that boy has even a ghost of a chance," Jack Liffey said.

"With that mom? The only good luck would be if she keeled over and he got fostered out."

"How many foster parents want a handicapped kid?"

"You'd be surprised. I know a family that has a dozen of them from a Down syndrome to a quadriplegic. They're happy as clams."

"So the world is full of hope, except right here," Jack Liffey said. "If I don't find Maeve soon, I'm going to put a curse on this town."

"With your friends still in it?"

Jack Liffey cracked a tiny smile. "I'll give a few a chance to get out, but don't look back."

Not one of the doors answered their knock in the ramshackle court of nine tiny dwellings. Pots of dead geraniums and plastic chairs were set out everywhere in the courtyard—what Sonny called "Okie air-conditioning." There were no cars in the alley or on the street. He wrote down the names from the bank of mailboxes, including PIPER GRIT. He wondered if it could possibly be a real name.

—–—

"I had one possible, too," Gloria said. "Nobody was home but a neighbor thinks he saw the wife carrying a baby in her arms two weeks ago. A young couple, just moved in a few months back, that's what my informant said." She had met up with Sonny and Jack where they'd arranged, on a bench atop the cliff that overlooked the river and the oil fields beyond. From somewhere, she'd picked up a big foam cup of coffe, and Jack Liffey slid it out of her fist and had a sip, even though he figured it would have some horrible flavoring, and it did—hazelnut.

"We don't even know that much about ours," Sonny said. "Our informant was probably mildly retarded and about two years old. The mother was *definitely* retarded."

The day was growing a little brighter as the cloudbank started thinning and you could almost tell where a pale sun would eventually burn through.

"I bet the preferred term is mentally challenged," Jack Liffey said.

Gloria took her coffee back. "The Department encourages us to use *special* or *exceptional* in our reports when it refers to a whole group or a facility, and something about *developmental needs*, I can't remember, for a person. Unless of course somebody might need to know what the *hell* we're talking about. Then we just say it."

"It's too bad I was laid off too long ago to be *right-sized*," Jack Liffey said. "I would have felt so much better about it."

"What's that!" Gloria cried abruptly, and she stood up and pointed straight out over the river.

"Jesus Christ," Jack Liffey said. "It's a flying dump truck." It was in fact an extremely large gray bird with its neck and legs stretched out in a straight line to maybe six feet long, beating immense wings with a quick upthrust and then a slow graceful down.

"Ladies and gents," Sonny said, "behold the famous sandhill crane. Probably wintering over at Buena Vista or the Carrizo Plain. Notice the way the neck is stretched out. That's how you know it's not a blue heron, which flies with its neck tucked back."

"I only know them from reading Aldo Leopold," Jack Liffey said. "Do these come from Nebraska?"

"No, sir. Most likely they come straight down the coast from British Columbia or Alaska."

There was one bleat of complaint on the air as the great bird turned and headed cumbrously away, as if it would rather not be talked about, and they all watched it fade slowly into the mist, flapping, flapping, until it dimmed away into the cloud, a ghost that had never been.

Sonny smiled as if he had had a private thought. "Sandhills mate for life."

Jack Liffey reached out for Gloria's free hand. She allowed him to take it but didn't squeeze back.

—-—

The elderly doctor in the golf sweater knelt beside the sofa where Sue Ellen Crumm slept so deeply she would not wake up. When he peeled back an eyelid, only white showed. He wrapped up his stethoscope and stuck it back into the old Gladstone bag, then turned to the two sheepish-looking men.

"Pastor, has anyone drugged or molested this girl?"

"Absolutely not."

"Why is she here?"

Channing Pelt could see that the pastor was at a loss for words, for once in his life, and still overcome with weariness. It was fortunate Dr. Schuman's wife was an occasional member of their congregation. "We were entrusted by the Emergency Cult Rescue Board with drawing the devil out of her. She's been extremely resistant. I mean the devil has."

"For how long has she been resistant?"

"Most of two days."

"Frankly, I think right now she's exhausted beyond exhaustion. I don't know anything about exorcism and I doubt if anyone else in this town does, either, but I'd suggest letting the devil sleep a bit right now. In fact I'm going to give the girl and her devil a sedative."

"Don't belittle what we're doing, doctor," Pelt cautioned.

"And you two, perhaps you should spend some time now

trying to find a way to reconfigure this girl's physical collapse to your advantage."

"Collapse?"

"I'll be sending a discreet private ambulance to collect her and take her to a discreet nursing home, and, before too long, Olive Grove will get a discreet bill."

"Remember that Satan is everywhere," Channing Pelt accused.

The doctor straightened to face him, almost nose to nose though he was inches shorter, furious. "When he's not crowded out by assholes," the doctor said.

Chapter Twelve

# SATAN-KILLERS, BAKO

They drove to the station so Gloria could ask the one
friendly source she'd found in the local police if the
hotlist had produced any results on Maeve's car. Jack
Liffey and Sonny stayed in the van, each having various and suf-
ficient reasons for not going into the cophouse. The fogbank was
hovering a few hundred feet overhead, still murking the light so
that greeting the day was a little like sitting five feet down in a
swimming pool.

Sonny leaned over and opened his glove compartment to
reveal a long thin radio with a row of LEDs on it. "We'll get a hel-
luva signal here." He flipped a tiny switch on the emergency

scanner and a green light stepped along the LEDs twice and then stopped about a third of the way along.

"Two-william-thirteen, disregard." It was a woman's voice, harsh and overpowering.

"Allrighty. Hey, Sandy, what's the status of the big dig? Over." This was a much weaker male voice, presumably some distance away.

Strong female: "We got us two now, thirteen. You mean the Winokur house at Crown Crest?"

Weak male: "Come back?"

Strong female: "You mean at Crown Crest?"

Weak male: "Affirmative. That's our area, but what else you got going? This is new."

Strong female: "Nowhere you at. Way south Union."

Second weak male: "Hey, that's gotta be slopes. Sandy, tell them to lasso me one. He's probably got the Bulova they grabbed off my wrist in Saigon and I want it back."

First weak male: "Go ahead on the status at Crown Crest."

Strong female: "No bodies yet. Negative. They digging up the whole yard."

Jack Liffey looked at Sonny. "You think there's other dead babies?"

"*They* seem to think so."

Sonny's eyes wandered the big paved lot behind the police station as if he were hunting for snipers. "Amazing. *Slopes.* Anybody can hear the dispatcher's black."

"Only color they've got is blue, so they say," Jack Liffey said.

"Yeah. I remember."

"Hey, not much on that route surprises me, my friend. My own dad writes some pretty foul articles, in strange little magazines dedicated to proving the scientific inferiority of other races."

Sonny shrugged. "I know they's all kinds. Some parts of the south is more live-and-let-live these days than the north. But, it's still best to avoid anyplace that sells Cokes out of a wet bottle machine. A lot of the good ol' boys out there have switched over to hating you and me."

"Who are we?"

"Cosmopolitans," Sonny said.

"Funny word," Jack Liffey said. Before he could say more, he saw Gloria steaming out the glass doors as if somebody'd helped her along with a cattle-prod. "I think Stalin used to use it to mean Jews."

Sonny reached over to push the Mute button on the scanner and shut the glove compartment. "Us Cajuns are the Lost Tribe, some say."

Gloria yanked the door open.

"Any word on Maeve's car?" Jack Liffey put in quickly. He hoped to find out before Gloria could roar off into whatever was eating her.

"It's parked a block from here as the crow flies," she said.

"And what was so upsetting?"

"What *wasn't*? It's a zoo in there. I got hit on about twelve times, and my ass felt up. I had to hurt that one to stop him." She calmed enough to explain to Sonny where Maeve's car was parked across the railroad tracks. The tracks looked thoroughly fenced off and apparently it would require the long way 'round.

"I'm on it," Sonny said.

"I wonder what's put all the cops in heat," Jack Liffey said.

"I've seen this stuff before—all the aggression oozing out. It's when something really big is going down in town. I saw it in the '92 riots. And after the '94 earthquake. I heard they're digging all over the place for bodies. And they think national news is going to fly in here any minute to make them famous."

"We heard some of it on the scanner," Jack Liffey said. He accessed the radio again and unmuted it.

Male voice: "Will copy. The kid in black is on foot north. Can someone set up a perimeter at the edge of that factory? Uh . . . the paint place. He was eyeballing us pretty hard when we rolled up."

Strong female: "Bike-W-18, can you respond?"

Second Male Voice: "Come again?"

Strong Female: "They's a young male in black running north on foot on Mt. Vernon. Cut him off at—"

Male Voice: "The alley behind the Ralphs, Tom. He was on a cell and he dimed us to his pals."

Gloria had slid across the short seat in back and she rested her head against the window as Sonny started up the van. "If I hadn't idolized a cop when I was a teenager, maybe I'd have done something else."

Male Voice: "Fuck this kid, Tom. He just grabbed a banana bike from a little girl and went down the tracks there."

Second Male Voice: "I'll get him. You can run but you can't run from me, Jesse James. You're going *down*."

Male Voice: "Take the little punk down."

Sonny pointed at the radio with disdain and Jack Liffey turned off the scanner as they came around a corner into a short dead-end street.

"My God, that's it," Jack Liffey said. There was no question: a white Toyota Echo with a bumper sticker saying POWERED BY TOFU.

It was a dead-end half block of cottages that had all been converted into bail bond offices. It took the three of them only a few minutes of asking around to discover that one of the offices, locked up and dark, was normally inhabited by a bond agent named Tony Bulldog Di Stefano whom nobody had seen for twenty-four hours.

"Well, we know for sure she's in town," Gloria said. "Do you know anything about this Bulldog?"

"I've worked with him," Sonny said. "He's a standup guy. If your girl's with him it's a stroke of luck. He'll watch over her."

"When's that damn Jesus march?" Jack Liffey asked. He found himself getting exasperated, and he wasn't sure why. Maybe it was the emotions unleashed by seeing Maeve's car. "And where's Jenny and her writs? Everything in this place is starting to piss me off."

"You got yourself wound too tight," Sonny said. "Gloria, did you pick up any sense where they're holding the kids?"

She shook her head. "I don't think the cops that I ran into knew."

"Twenty years ago the whole child-molestation campaign was run by a special detail from the DA's office and Child Protective Services. Most cops were kept out of the loop. The people at the *Bee* think as many as three hundred kids have been picked up, but nobody's saying a word." He thought for a moment. "I suppose they've got to feed them. Let's see what I can do with catering services."

He glanced over at Jack Liffey who was thinking hard.

"Whoa! I know that look, man," Sonny said. "That's the face of a guy who's working himself up to go to war. *Don't* do it."

Gloria reached over from the back and put two hands firmly on his shoulders. He liked her touch.

"It makes me nuts when Maeve is in trouble," Jack Liffey

said, trying not to grit his teeth. "I can't help it. I just want to knock somebody's head off."

"Jack, calm down. We'll get this sorted out."

— —

Tammy was absent-mindedly filing her long red nails as Maeve sat beside her on the cot, holding both their allotted cans of Nehi Orange Soda. Maeve's stomach was settling down after another wave of nausea.

Their fellow internees had apparently tired of protesting and throwing food and banging on things, and little groups had collected to entertain themselves like at summer camp.

"Ow! A split," Tammy complained.

Maeve became aware suddenly of the metal nail file Tammy Crum was using. She wore it on a chain around her neck, where anyone else would wear a crucifix or a Saint Anthony. This was the kind of contraband tool they were always coming up with in POW movies to dig their way out of German camps.

"Could I see that nail file?" Maeve asked.

"Sure. You got a ways to go, hon, with *them* nails." She rolled her neck to help the chain off and handed the whole thing to Maeve.

"Not for me. I think this is our ticket." She'd taken a good look at a gash in the wall where something had run into it and it seemed to be made up of a thick layer of metal foil over about an inch of Styrofoam and then the outer structure itself, just aluminum sheeting. She was pretty sure she could find a secluded spot behind the toilets and carve off the foil and foam then wait for dark and have somebody big kick out the outer structure.

She'd try out a small spot of the wall first and see what happened if she tried to cut through it.

Nausea came over her again, all of a sudden, and then retreated to leave her lightheaded. Gradually her escape plan became a blaze of exultant melodrama in her head. "We're bustin' out of here," she whispered to Tammy. "And they'll never get us back alive."

—–

### Artifact: late 1930s

No greater invasion by the destitute has ever been recorded in the history of mankind. Okies come from the impoverished sub-marginal stratum.

—Thomas McManus, California Citizens Association, a well-financed front for California business, late 1939.[8]

—–

After seeing the doctor off, Kohlmeyer nervously headed out to the parking lot to wait for the ambulance, the asphalt at his feet flickeringly lit by the electronic crawl sign that he had always detested—at the moment offering a looping rant against *The Lord of the Rings* and *Harry Potter*.

He had finally given in to Channing's wish. He tried to imagine Jesus ordering up the sermon on the mount in chase lights. *Fishes and Loaves—endless supply!*

Channing had demanded it in the end because Grace Maranatha had one. Pelt's enthusiasm for the shiny and the new sometimes needed to be restrained. The problem was, in the end, Kohlmeyer was having a hard time resisting when there was no real objection.

It wasn't long before the ambulance appeared in the distance. Not a city ambulance, of course, it was one of the private ambulances that made their thirty pieces of silver by transporting patients in no medical danger.

He could see it almost overrun the turnoff and brake hard. PROTECH MEDICAL TRANSPORT it said on the big square box. He waved the vehicle down as it came up the slope and signaled to open the driver's window.

"I'm sorry, gentlemen. You were summoned by mistake." He handed the driver a folded $100 bill, trying to make it as casual as tipping a parking valet.

The man took it, but only after a protest. "Doc Schuman called us. There must be a patient somewhere."

"I'm Pastor Kohlmeyer and I'm in charge here. Thank you for your time. If that's not enough, you may bill the church."

The driver and his helper glanced at one another. "They're expecting a girl at Rosedale Rez Care. What do we tell them?"

"Tell them a mistake was made, and the girl is fine now. I'll call them myself. Good day, gentlemen."

The ambulance did a turn around the flashing signboard with a little squeal and headed back to town. Dennis Kohlmeyer watched it carefully until it was definitely gone.

—-—

Several hundred people seemed keyed up for something as they milled around the cement foreplain in front of the convention center. They applauded Pastor Kohlmeyer as he stepped out of the big SUV with Pelt. Several town luminaries were already waiting. Bucky West in his Stetson and full fringed plumage waved happily to the crowd. The Bakersfield Sound was represented. Nearby was Poppy Bumpers with her gold hair piled straight up. She had coat-tailed onto the city council only after her much older husband, Fleecy Bumpers, had died of a massive stroke.

A buzz of expectation and something close to aggravation rested on the air like a fever. Channing Pelt drew himself erect and noted some of the hand-lettered picket signs surrounding them and spilling into the street: DEATH TO SATAN, JOHN 1:13, PUT ON THE FULL ARMOR OF GOD. He rounded up the elders of Sword of God and sent them off to organize the youth group into a calming picket out at the peripheries.

"Mrs. Bumpers, is the mayor coming?" Kohlmeyer asked.

"He can't walk very dang far. His weight, you know. He said he'll meet us at City Hall."

Apostle Olin from the Pentecostals, in a powder blue wide-lapel leisure suit that seemed to fluoresce, arrived with his entourage. "Howdy, pastor," Olin boomed in that voice that could nail you to a wall. His eyes went skyward, as if expecting a plummeting dove, but finding instead a fog bank that was only about 100 feet overhead.

Duncan Bundy, in a banker's suit and waistcoat, was surrounded by his little honor guard of upscale Birchers. A small group of blacks led by two black preachers kept to themselves, and elsewhere a few Latinos followed Sanchez Ford of the *Iglesia de Dios de la profecía y el fuego eterno*. They had brought their own marimba band, just discernible through the tumult.

Pelt noticed a half dozen police cars up and down the street and a couple of unmarked Crown Vics, keeping a careful eye on things. A policeman in a gray suit got out of one of the unmarked cars and sauntered toward them. Pelt recognized Lt. Efren Saldivar immediately, a man he'd always found confident and efficient.

"Gentlemen, your attention," Saldivar announced. "I need your full and alert minds." His eyes were on Pastor Kohlmeyer, knowing where the authority lay.

"Go ahead, officer," Kohlmeyer said.

"If you're planning to march along Truxton or Seventeenth to city hall, there's something you should consider. That is roughly the boundary between the Beale Sonoras and the Lakeview Pirus. In case you don't know, the Sonoras are affiliated with *la Eme*, or the Mexican Mafia—you'll see the '13s' on all their grafitti. That's M if you have trouble counting that high. And the Pirus are a set of the Bloods, the natural enemies of the Sonoras. Has anyone thought to ask their permission to make this march, just as a courtesy? We don't concede that they control the territory, of course, but we don't want any misunderstandings with women and children involved."

"What would you have us do now?" Kohlmeyer asked. "We're set to start."

"It's a bit late, but I'll talk to any of the bangers I can scare up and try to get you a free pass. Next time, call me. Go forth and express your constitutional rights, gentlemen."

He sauntered away, and Pelt could see what the policeman's intervention had been about, just making sure everybody acknowledged that he was on top of things, the go-to cop in town.

Just then, a large contingent of veterans marched raggedly across Truxton into the irregular public space, following an elderly man who was bearing aloft an oversized flag on a pole that rested in a parade harness in his groin. Some of the older vets were in full military parade uniform, medals and all, but the younger men straggled along in fatigue jackets or camo pants. One geezer had what looked like an old Cavalry bugle with red tassels, and now and again he brought it to his lips and blew a few bars of some ancient call to arms that gave Pelt a strange chill. He was beginning to sense that the portents for the march may have been far less favorable than he had hoped.

An increase in the rumble that he'd heard growing for some time didn't help. Maybe thirty Harleys and V-twin Japanese bikes snarled down the street in a long spectacle. The riders and their passengers all wore sleeveless denim jackets, and as they passed, Pelt saw SATAN-KILLERS in an arc on the back of each. Most of the insignia said BAKO, though a few read OIL-DALE. Pelt wasn't very confident of his security dealing with such dubious allies. He just hoped nobody got in their faces and set them off.

Pelt whispered to Pastor Kohlmeyer, urging him to make use of the flatbed truck—a vehicle Pelt had ordered for just this reason—to deliver an emotional kickoff, something he was good at. And, not incidentally, to remind one and all of the way his father had founded Bakersfield's first mega-evangelical congregation from the back of a truck.

But before he could shoo Dennis onto it, a marching choir from Olive Grove's rival, Grace Maranatha, strutted dramatically down Truxton, bawling out in song:

"I'll climb from out the Wilderness! and trust Jehovah's might!

I want that mountain, it belongs to me!

"I want that mountain! I want that mountain!
Where the milk and honey flow, where the grapes of Eshcol grow,

I want that mountain! I want that mountain!
The mountain that my Lord has given me."

Chapter Thirteen

# THE BIG MARCH

P arked above the oil fields, Sonny told them the sad tale of his dad's decline from ALS, then still called Lou Gehrig's disease. "Pop said he was just having an early sundown. And he kept making his crazy schemes to get us rich. I hope I'm as brave."

His words dumped them all into a funk, and Jack Liffey craned his neck out the window of the van. The fogbank had gotten perceptibly lower.

"That's awful," Gloria said.

"The point is not pathos," Sonny said. "The point I was getting to is kids are resilient as hell. I was tough as an old deer. It sounds like Maeve is, too."

Eventually they intended to head back to the places they'd visited that morning, but as long as they had to wait until quitting time, Sonny owned that it might be a good idea to detour downtown and have a peek at the Olive Grove march.

"Maeve had part of her gut shot out last year and wore a shitbag for six months and never complained," Jack Liffey said. "In the midst of our last riot, she walked me to the hospital in a wheelbarrow when I was shot up and unconscious. She was—I don't know—fourteen. But she still weeps at rumors of a dead squirrel. It's hard to say what 'tough' is."

Gloria frowned. "She's also an underage girl who let herself get pregnant. I can assure you that's scaring her to death inside."

"And she drove right back into this hellstorm to help out a friend," Jack Liffey said. He tried to read Gloria's eyes, which were spiky with something angry. "We're both experiencing some displacement, aren't we?"

Sonny started the car. "Let's go see the show. I can guarantee it'll be worth the admission."

— —

They parked about as close as they could without suggesting they were taking part in the event. Looking out the window, Jack Liffey kept thinking of the jubilant mob at the book burning, which made him look away from the crowd now and then to keep his senses free of those memory whiffs of soot and ash. Looking above the people milling around, he could just discern a man standing tall in the back of a flatbed truck, as if about to address them. He thought it might be the silver-haired minister from Olive Grove. He carried a mike and his voice boomed suddenly across the afternoon, maybe even echoing back from the low cloud cover. They could just make out his words through the echoes and distortion.

"Since his defeat and his exile from heaven—for high treason—Satan has delighted in deceiving and confusing the children that he catches up in his vast network of games and cults."

To Jack Liffey, it seemed there was the same awful hearty insincerity in the pastor's voice that had ruined every president of his grown-up life. He couldn't figure out why almost no one else seemed to notice.

"Lucifer has a score to settle," Kohlmeyer went on. "And he's on a final mission to bring down every innocent who stumbles within his grasp. Make no mistake—his grasp is wide and it's strong, and it's clenched around our homes, our children, our town. Right this minute."

A kind of eager rumble rolled through the crowd as Kohlmeyer ranted on. Jack Liffey let his eyes drift over them, some in their Sunday best, young people in the silver T-shirts from Olive Grove, dodgy-looking bikers out on the periphery, war veterans in oddments of uniforms. A man in a golf sweater with a large family around him carried a strange polite picket sign that said SATAN HAS NO LEGAL RIGHTS.

"Sergeant Jacobs of the Cult Committee said to me just this morning, 'If I were to tell you everything I've heard listening to these misguided kids, your congregation just would not believe it. We've got children who confess to eating the raw flesh of animals, drinking blood, even the blood of human babies. Cats and dogs are killed every week in backyards in this town.'"

"Do you think any of it's real?" Jack Liffey whispered.

"A few kids might have been trying to seem important to

themselves, you know," Sonny said. "Acting out the most shocking things they could. In L.A., they'd get swastika tattoos. This is a religious town, so they give Jesus the finger."

"The good news!" the pastor called out, a whole register louder, "is so many of us have come together to fight back against the devil! And there's still plenty of time for the good people of Jesus to triumph! We come here today to demand that our town fathers side *with* us—and *against* Satan. You're either on one side or the other! We insist that they write new laws to support the struggle against evil. By what right do our libraries offer children step-by-step references on how to practice Devil worship? By what insane right do we allow teachers to indoctrinate our children in godless collectivism? By what right do we allow our youth, wearing the Devil's own black, to show off their Devil piercings and Devil tattoos in the pizza parlors and theater lobbies and music clubs where other children, still innocent, gather?"

"I'd like to see them try to outlaw black down in L.A.," Jack Liffey said.

"Let us heed the call of first John 5:19—'And we know that we are of God, and the whole world lieth in wickedness.' Satan is on the loose *right* here *right* now and we must gather all our forces against him! Come with us now and demand that our elected representatives show themselves to be on our side. They're either with *us* or they're with the Devil!"

—–

Now the march was under way. Crows rose spooked from the trees ahead of the front guard, and the birds complained bitterly as they flew off. The fog did not seem any lower but the afternoon had darkened noticeably. The choir sang as they marched and bikers revved and thundered along the sidewalks.

Sonny, watching intently, was starting to look a bit jittery, prepared to start up the van at any moment as the crowd engulfed them. Jack Liffey had seen edgy crowds before, but none quite like this. There was no discernible collegial spirit at all. Groups were going out of their way to define their boundaries, exclusive and petulant, and out at the edges people challenged bystanders for no apparent reason. There was something irrational in the ferocity that hung over the march, like a pampered and exhausted child who felt unfairly used and needed a nap. Here and there somebody leapt into the air and shouted. A scuffle broke out among those carrying a church banner, but it soon simmered down.

"Weird mood," Jack Liffey commented.

"Jack, look over there." Gloria pointed.

A handful of what appeared to be counterprotestors were filtering down the side street opposite them, a motley troop of teens all wearing orange sashes that read FREE SPEECH.

"Uh-oh."

The newcomers carried their own signs, waving and bobbing them on their sticks to draw attention: CHRISTIAN NAZIS = AMERICAN TALIBAN. JESUS WAS A FREETHINKER! REPRESSION IS THE REAL WORK OF SATAN! Jack Liffey was surprised there were enough dissidents left on the loose to make up a counter demonstration, though these kids looked clean cut enough to have eluded the dragnet of Goths and punks.

When the counterdemonstrators reached the main street, they formed a line along the crosswalk, enduring shouts and waved fists. They were brave enough, Jack Liffey would give them that.

A police car was parked behind them, and abruptly its light bar came on with a burst of flashing color. It U-turned and scooted away—like an open invitation to mayhem.

"Nervy kiddies," Sonny said. "Wonder what they hope to accomplish."

"Everybody out there needs a good squirt of pepper spray," Gloria said. "But that car shouldn't be *leaving*."

A group in the now-familiar silver T-shirts were taking their peacekeeping role seriously. They got between the angrier marchers and the handful of counterdemonstrators and held hands, remaining sternly interposed.

"Bless their little hearts," Sonny said. "Who amongst us relishes guarding our opponents?"

"Look." Gloria pointed upward. The tops of the streetlamps were being decapitated by the settling underside of the fogbank. The taller buildings along the street faded out of existence above the first story. Long gouts of heavy mist sank slowly out of the mass, and a damp chill invaded the open windows of the van.

A Satan-killer bike cut behind the Free Speechers and revved a few times just to announce that he was there. Two of them turned to face him, but he offered only a feral grin and accelerated away in a wheelie.

Sonny started the van and let it idle forward among the marchers after tapping his horn to give warning. He gave the paraders plenty of time to clear a path. A cop car was parked slantwise in the next cross street to block the road and Sonny honked again, making an urgent turning motion in the windshield to tell the cop he wanted out. The officer glowered at him but started his car and pulled forward a few feet, maybe an inch more than Sonny needed to get through. By the time the van was edging off the main drag whole sheets of fog were descending, blurring the vista and seemingly towing the fogbank itself down.

"It's here, folks." Sonny flicked on the bank of fog lights beneath his bumper and they threw a wash of orange light out under the descending mists. In a moment, he stopped on the side street, turned off his engine and opened all the power windows with a master switch.

"It's chilly," Gloria complained.

"Hush."

"Stay together, Christians! This is another trick of the devil!" The voice came out of a megaphone. Was it Kohlmeyer? Jack Liffey thought so.

Somebody screamed.

"The Devil is over there!"

Glass broke somewhere and one of the motorcycles exploded past their van with a howl, escaping the parade. Two gunshots went off somewhere, but where?

"Stay calm, everyone!" the pastor's voice bellowed, competing with the squawk of his own feedback.

A whooping police siren blotted every other sound for a moment, and then a new male voice could be heard, on a clearer amplifier. "Everyone stop where you are. Now! Move to the curbs and stand still. We will give you instructions. This is the police."

There was another scream and the shattering of a much bigger sheet of glass. A voice nearby began to sob, and the sounds of feet running in every direction suggested a descent into chaos. The fog obscured almost everything behind a veil of white.

More gunshots crackled, seemingly from all directions. One of the weapons was clearly on automatic fire, pumping away. Upward, Jack Liffey hoped.

"That's an AK," Sonny said evenly. "Some gun nut."

"Maybe the Devil's sent his very own SWAT team."

They could no longer see even the bumper of the police car that should have been twenty yards behind them. Their own fog lights did nothing but set up an eerie orange incandescence ahead of them.

Two young silver-shirts, arm in arm, materialized, high-knee jogging, then vanished again.

"Could you get us out of here and over to the suspect's apartment?" Gloria asked.

"I can drive a tule fog—just about as well as anyone."

"How do you drive when you can't see?" Jack Liffey asked dubiously.

"Damn carefully."

—–

Clustered together in the midst of the riotous din all around, Kohlmeyer, Pelt, and Lt. Saldivar were conferring. They could barely see the ghostly shapes of others around them.

"Just walk this group slowly to City Hall," Kohlmeyer suggested to the officer. "Get us inside first, then go out and bring in another group."

"My idea," Lt. Saldivar said sarcastically, "is how about we keep *you* out here with the megaphone as a kind of sonic beacon for all the lost souls." He grinned unpleasantly. "You got the hundred-dollar voice, Pastor. How about calling your flock?"

A pistol went off nearby and they all flinched.

"Lay it back!" Lt. Saldivar shouted. "There's women and children here."

A male voice off in the murk bellowed with laughter. "And scared cops!"

Once again Kohlmeyer lifted his megaphone and spoke, his baritone booming out into the fog. "Christians, please stay calm! This is Pastor Kohlmeyer. A little fog is no cause for alarm. We've all seen it before. We're within a short walk of Truxton and Chester, and I propose to bring you all to the steps of City Hall without further incident. Don't let anyone among you incite panic or violence. Do *not* use weapons. Anyone breaking the peace here is acting in the interests of the devil. Any nearby musicians, would you please strike up a Christian hymn and we can all gather around you."

An invisible band seemed to be coalescing, a few instruments bleating together, trying to find a key, and Pastor Kohlmeyer went on calming and drawing others toward himself.

"Come close to the music! Let's stay together. Hold on to the person in front of you."

A gigantic plate glass window smashed just out of sight, and the skitter of glass shards chased across their feet like tiny rodents.

"Invisible, all men are disorderly," Saldivar stated.

— —

### Artifacts: late 1930s

No Niggers or Okies
    —Sign in many Bakersfield restaurant windows, late 1930s[1]

Niggers and Okies upstairs
        —Sign in Bakersfield movie theater, late 1930s[8]

— —

Sonny drove with almost painful slowness toward the north. It was the only sensible way to drive. Gloria had her sliding door open a foot and watched the pavement for the lane lines. She called, "Left some more!"

"Just calm down, both of you. I have to do this every year," Sonny said. "If somebody doesn't run up my ass, I'm fine. I know the town, this is a one-stripe-ahead fog, and I can tell when we pass cross streets. This isn't the worst it gets."

"I got caught in peasoup like this on the Blue Ridge Parkway," Jack Liffey said, holding tight to his armrest. "I think I got permanent white knuckles."

They were heading for Gloria's suspect, since his house was nearest and neither of the men had much faith in their own suspect, at the apartment court the rickets-child had pointed out.

"Here we go."

He parked carefully and lay his arm on the seatback to turn around to Gloria.

"The street's only a block long if you remember. Do you think you can find your way? I figure you want to do it alone."

"Count on it. Can you gentlemen entertain yourselves for a while?"

"If we're smooching, rap three times," Jack Liffey said.

She cracked a smile. "Don't get any ideas. Those lips are mine."

Chapter Fourteen

# DEATH ON THE RIDGE ROAD

They watched Gloria turn ghostly and then disappear within a few paces. Sonny ran his window down but the only thing to be heard outside was a kind of eventful hush, like a thousand house cats padding along on alert.

"If she ever wears you out, my brother, let me know," Sonny said. "A good woman who can take charge is like a whole keg of soaped nails when you're trying to build a house."

Jack Liffey stared at him. "Man, that's about the strangest simile I've ever heard."

Sonny laughed. "I like it."

"You never told me the full story of how you got into this line of work. I told you I just fell into it after I got laid off."

Sonny glanced around, as if there might be witnesses lurking near the van. "You said for you it was a way of going sober."

"Sure," Jack Liffey said. "But in the scheme of things, it's not such a bad job, you know. Trying to save kids who get themselves out there too far. It's so easy as a teenager to work yourself into a rage or maybe just a bad loneliness and flip out."

"Me," Sonny said. "I'm just a dick, peeping through windows, pointing a shotgun mike. I do only work for the defense, though. That's on my side."

"Come on, Sonny. There's good reasons for leaving the cops, and there's bad. I've heard most of them."

"Why don't we say I had a slew of reasons. I even moved around to new departments to find extra ones."

They sat until the silence became unbearable.

"Well, okay," he said abruptly. "First, my wife went daffydil, the whole eleven yards with voices and shit, and I had to put her in Greenwell. It's a kind of Southern belle occupational hazard. She was always a troubled soul. It was dumb of me trying to save a beautiful wingbroke bird, and all that shit. Anyway, it seemed like a good idea at the time but, man, it wounds you in the heart. Bad."

Jack Liffey watched him, recognizing that there were always degrees of trouble far beyond his.

"It just leaves a mark on everything about you. That was in Louisiana. Opelousas. Later, in a little Alabama town, what happened was I caught the deputy chief pilfering drug-bust money from the cage, and we made a little deal for him to retire early and me to move on. In Tennessee, not far from the first nuke-u-lar reactor—that's, believe it or not, a tourist spot now and I used to point out to people as the most evil place on earth—I tumbled another cop's wife. I just didn't care, you know, and I got caught. The whole situation went comical with the laugh meter spiking. Loners should never become police officers. We've got all the wrong inclinations."

Jack Liffey figured there was more so he waited for it.

"I was born short, as you can see, and I thought I was doing okay with it, but I got slapped down hard."

"One more," Jack Liffey said. "There was another one, wasn't there?"

"Wait for it, mister. All this time I seem to have been wending northward from the Gulf through little Podunk P.D.s and then I decided to try my busted luck to the west. I'd got to the fine town of Eagle, a far-flung suburb of Lincoln, Nebraska, and one lovely spring day I was at a residence taking a death report, sitting on the sofa, my clipboard on my knees. Facing me was the very new widow showing far too much cleavage, so I was having me a hard time trying not to stare at what Mother Nature grew her. It was a suicide, the guy still warm, but I wasn't such a sensitive fucker then, so we just watched as he was carried out by the EMTs. The minute they drove off, that young woman plunked herself down beside me and said, 'Officer, do you have any questions I haven't answered?'"

Sonny puffed out a big breath. "Later, with my gunbelt hanging over the chair upstairs, that widow got into teaching me just how far you can go with your shoes off. Right in the midst there was a vexing outburst of noise down below in the house. 'Oh, shit on a shingle!' the widow woman declared."

Sonny described a pause in the action then, lying quiet, during which the bed-crawling cop could not learn a thing about who might be making all the noise. The husband was out of the picture, of course, and no secondary lover had the kind of entitlement that would bring about the panic he saw on the widow's face.

"In a whipstitch that bedroom door slammed open and one honking big silhouette stood there, and we all waited for maybe a second or two that seemed like forever, and then there were gunshots all over God's earth. My police reflexes saved me. The widow bought one in the leg right off, but I rolled and grabbed my piece on the way to the floor. It was the only time I ever fired a weapon in emotion. The pertinent emotion here being scared-to-fucking-death.

"Who had I plugged? Why, my hostess's fourteen-year-old six-foot-three son, who was somehow strapped with a big ugly Glock."

"Shit on a shingle," Jack Liffey said after a while. It seemed worth repeating.

"All survived the day, in fact, but the son will always be a little gimpy. After that I kinda lost my nerve for police work," Sonny said.

"Sounds right," Jack Liffey said. He liked Sonny and wanted to find some words that would soothe. But life wasn't like that.

"I don't rely much on luck no more. In fact, I consider a belief in luck a kind of addled rapture, not unlike the snake throwers and catchers I saw in my youth."

"I guess so."

They waited in what seemed a mutual funk until Gloria coalesced out of the fog, about ten feet offline toward the center of the road, then corrected course toward the car.

She looked soaked through.

"Did you get your man?" he asked.

She shook her head. "I don't think so. It was a couple who told me they'd been putting up a granddaughter from L.A. They admitted she was taking one of those discreet plump vacations so she could deliver far from home. She's Catholic, planned all along to give the baby away. The granddaughter stayed for a few days afterwards, and then they drove her home to the city. I called a friend who'll check it out for us, but it sounded legit. Could we have a little heat back here?"

Sonny started the engine. "I need a drink. I guess that only leaves our suspect."

"There's always a few more than you know," Gloria said.

— —

Outside City Hall, Pelt was having a rare cigarette away from the TV cameras and the hubbub within. He'd already had his insider report and was feeling exasperated. Thumper Harris and his Good Ol' Boys were about to chop Olive Grove off at the knees. It was an efficient political machine, he thought. If anybody built a juggernaut in their town, they'd keep the keys, thank you.

Pelt blamed himself a bit for not seeing it coming. He'd seen much the same three years earlier when the local Republican Party had outmaneuvered an evangelical run for an open state assembly seat. What in fact his spy Ellen Boggs, the city clerk's secretary, had just told him was that the city establishment was about to propose its own legislation to ban all depraved behavior. They would recast the Olive Grove religious campaign as a less extreme moral one and set up neighborhood antidelinquency committees. They'd look perfectly righteous, but skip all the hymn singing.

Pelt admired the plan, as he admired any effective political gambit. And the evangelical churches—always the bridesmaids. . . . Pelt flipped his butt high out into the fog.

He strolled back inside the big lobby and found his arm clutched at once by a worried-looking Pastor Kohlmeyer. "What on earth are they doing?"

"Thumper is beating us like a drum, Den. They're going to steal our campaign and wrap it up tight in their secular blather. But don't attack them right now—it won't serve us. Anyway, we're not tapped out completely, just finessed for now. I'm sure they'll give us a small but noticeable role. You know, holding their hats." Kohlmeyer seemed nonplussed, and Pelt felt like slapping him to wake him up. "Wolves eat dogs, Denny, especially when the dogs aren't prepared."

"What are you going on about?"

"We've been outmaneuvered. It's simple. They're going to legislate most of what we were asking for, but make it all secular. We're out of the loop."

"I'm not playing some political game here! I'm trying to fight the devil!"

"Then we'll have to fight on our own. And by the way, it's probably best if you sent that girl on to rehab. I mean, quick."

Pelt could see his colleague's mind going a fiery stubborn blank. Kohlmeyer had almost no sense of political retreat and maneuver. The man was going to dig in his heels in some futile way that only he could understand.

If only he could learn that it's always about power, Channing Pelt thought, pure and simple. Next time he wouldn't let Olive Grove play its hand until he knew they could win, until Thumper and his political machine had been outmaneuvered, strapped down, every one of them, and gagged and counted, and he'd sprinkled salt on their tails. He would never again let himself get sandbagged like this.

--

Their bumper had grated lightly against the guardrail in getting across the Chester Street Bridge in the all-obscuring fog, and Sonny had cursed once, too unimaginatively to remember. He became very careful turning up the street in Riverview that held the little court where the bowlegged boy had pointed that morning. Piper Grit was the name Jack Liffey remembered from the mailboxes, though it seemed implausible that a name as delightful as that could have anything to do with this incident.

Gloria didn't quite trust the men so she trailed along as they made their way on foot into the courtyard. It was hard to tell time by the light, a kind of dirty radiance that oozed out of the solid fog. One door toward the front of the court was open, but the screen was shut. A woman's voice skirled out the door in rage, interrupting faint music in the background, something '50s and romantic, Sinatra.

"God damn you! God *damn* you! You're just a fucking turtle. Oww! Stop it. Get away!"

Jack Liffey and Sonny Theroux glanced at one another, a few feet apart in the mist, expressing in some way a mutual query whether they wanted to know more about this woman—and possibly a turtle—and both of them shook their heads, deciding they didn't. It was that very domicile that belonged to Piper Grit, Jack Liffey recalled. Though perhaps the name belonged to the turtle. Gloria just kept walking toward the back, pressed the indecisive men apart with her hands and thrust between them.

No one answered at the next bungalow where a big note was affixed to the door with a white pushpin: CABLE GUY. THE ANSWER IS ALL WAYS *NOOO*.

Gloria was already walking away to the bungalow in the back corner. Instead of knocking, she squatted all at once and stared at the moist earth beside the cement walkway. When the men came up, she pointed to a small impression of tiny circles arrayed in a herringbone pattern.

"'Luscious Gibbs's In the Paint.'"

"Damn," Jack Liffey said. "It really is. An honest-to-god forensic clue."

She pointed at Sonny and said softly, with urgency, "Cover the back."

He nodded and made his way up a path that had been trod bare in the colorless grass. The little houses were only a few feet apart and the shrubs planted near windows for privacy had long ago shriveled to skeletons.

Gloria knocked with that unmistakable cop manner of confident prerogative. No matter how hard Jack Liffey tried, his knock was always either more tentative or just plain strident.

"My husband says we don't do no business at the door." It was a young woman's voice through the wood.

"We just have some questions, ma'am."

"Are you the church police?"

Jack Liffey exchanged a glance with Gloria.

"City police," Gloria said. "Open up, ma'am."

The door cracked, but on a chain, and Gloria showed her badge wallet briefly.

"You sure you're not those other ones?"

"What makes you think that?"

"They been all over this place, asking 'bout the Devil and if folk here be holding Devil-rites and shit."

"That's not our concern. We just need to know if you or someone else staying in this courtyard has a small baby."

"No. 6 there got a five-year-old, a real terror-pants."

"What's your name, hon?" The girl hadn't moved much, but there was something strange about the way she was swaying in the small opening.

"Rhea Jane."

"Rhea Jane what?"

"Sparks. *Mrs.* Sparks. There ain't no kid here, like I tell you. I think you got to talk to my old man, Roy. He works nights. He'll be back in the morning."

"Where does he work? Maybe we can catch him at his break."

"They don't like him to be disturbed any at work."

"Have you got a phone number?"

"I can't give it out."

"Now listen, Rhea Jane, either you give us the number or you come downtown with us for more questions right now. One of you has to help us clear some things up. And don't shut that door or we'll bust it wide." Gloria quickly stuck her foot into the gap.

"I got to get some paper. To copy it down."

"I think I saw your husband," Gloria suggested innocently. "Doesn't he have a pair of those crazy tennis shoes, the red ones with the metal holes? My boy's got some just like it. You just can't stop young people and funny shoes."

"No," the girl said. She pressed her face to the crack with what appeared to be a kind of fearful cunning. "He ain't got no such thing."

She handed out a scrap of paper. The minute Gloria withdrew her foot, the door shut hard and they heard two dead-bolts slam home. Jack Liffey leaned forward to look at the phone number.

"Something familiar," he said. They'd know soon enough. Gloria called out to Sonny, and he emerged from his duty out back. On the way out of the courtyard, they nearly tripped over a big desert tortoise on the cracked cement path. It had a red heart painted on a shell that was the size of a serving platter. The huge animal appeared extraordinarily aggressive: it lowered its neck and plodded straight for them as they paused to look at it.

Sonny was just catching up when the tortoise spurted forward with surprising speed and drove the neck edge of its shell hard into Sonny's ankle. "Ow! You *shitbag*!"

"Ten-ninety-eight," Jack Liffey said, stepping far around the tortoise. It was the LAPD's ten-code for: Business completed here and we're about to saddle up again.

"Don't you use that crap," Gloria said.

— —

The first layer had been easy, just a kind of thick soft aluminum foil attached to the Styrofoam to protect it and then about an inch of white foam insulation. Hacking away with the nail file behind the port-a-potties she had attracted quite an audience and cheering section, which was just what she didn't want, but the cops all seemed to have retreated outside.

"You *go*, girl!"

"Tell us if you get tired."

She cleared away a human-sized portion of the plastic foam but on the other side of the foam was some fairly substantial rippled metal that none of them could budge. She cut some more insulation away and uncovered a seam but it seemed to have been bent over itself and then riveted. By this time Bulldog and several others on the male side had rammed a bench through the hastily erected wire partition separating the sexes.

When they noticed what Maeve had done, Bulldog's crew picked up their bench again and cleared everyone away.

"Sing, kids. Sing loud!" Bulldog cried out.

Girls began drumming on the benches and two African-American boys shuttled back and forth shouting out a hip-hop song that others gradually picked up. Several boys sledded one of the potties out of the way.

"Heave-ho!"

The second impact put a bulge in the metal at the seam. Before they could take another run at the bulge, a deputy looked in the far door and blew a whistle against all the noise. He called out, "Pipe down, all of you!"

When the response was a near unanimous roar of, "*Fuck you!*" the deputy retreated and slammed the door to a burst of derisive booing and hooting. The next thrust of the bench tore right through the skin of the building, and kids were immediately shouldering the opening wider as they squeezed their way out.

"Scatter!" Bulldog shouted. He took Maeve and Tammy by the hand and led them out into the damp blindness. From inside, they'd had little warning of the fog.

"Left," he said. "Stay left. I know where we are."

--

## Artifact: 1938

The three-year-old child has a gunny sack tied about his middle for clothing. He has the swollen belly caused by malnutrition.

He sits on the ground in the sun in front of the house, and the

little black fruit flies buzz in circles and land on his closed eyes
and crawl up his nose until he weakly brushes them away. . . .
The first year he had a little milk, but he has had none since.
He will die in a very short time.
—John Steinbeck, *Their Blood is Strong*, Simon J. Lubin Society
of California, 1938: the nearly forgotten and never reprinted
nonfiction report on the plight of Okie farmworkers that inspired
Steinbeck to go on to write *The Grapes of Wrath*.

——

There is a nondescript place just north of Delano where
Highway 99 jogs sharply east maybe twenty yards to become an
overpass set in the flat plains strangely offline from the highway.
The northbound on- and off-ramps at this misplaced overpass
make a straight shot from the right lane of the highway, a con-
tinuation of the arrow-straight line of 99, and one assumes the
ramps were in fact the original road. These days the off-ramp has
a stop sign where it crosses a small highway. On certain dull and
boozy nights, local kids dare one another to take this "shortcut"
at freeway speed, risking collision with the extremely rare cross-
traffic below.

Jenny Ezkiaga knew the anomaly well and had steered left-
then-right through it thousands of times in her life. She was
running ridiculously late with her writs beside her—late
because the Fresno police had stopped her and questioned her,
she suspected at the behest of the Bakersfield D.A., and then
just to gild the lily, the California Highway Patrol had halted
all traffic for an hour at Pixley fifty miles north of Bakersfield
because of the fog.

At first the patrolman had seemed set to convoy them prudently south, as often happened in the fog, but his radio had called him away to an eleven-car pileup in the fog just north of Pixley and he let them all go with a serious slowdown caution.

His timing was almost perfect, as far as Jenny was concerned, since she was at the front of the pack and the long delay meant there would be virtually no traffic ahead of her to worry about. For once she could let out the Passat's powerful V-6 engine, all 280 horsepower, five valves per cylinder, and run fast on the ultra-bright fog lamps that would at least light up the cat's-eye lane markers ahead. With the only plausible danger being someone with an even faster car overtaking her. She'd had a quick look around and the only more capable car she saw was a BMW M3 that she immediately deferred to with a wave. It sliced past her with a growl and disappeared into the fog, while the rest of the cars started up slowly as if running under a caution flag.

She'd lived in the valley long enough not to sweat the details. Nothing was immediately ahead of her but that hell-bent M-3, so she ran her speedometer up and up to eighty and even more. Nothing was going to catch her from behind, and the fences would keep off any errant cows or elk. No locals would be out. What could go wrong, fog or no fog? She settled in for the last thirty miles and punched an old Doors album up on her CD deck for just the right twist of angry irony to accompany her crusade against the bastards who, if they could, would criminalize her love. I'm coming, kids. I'm coming, all of you.

"This is the end, beautiful friend, the end," Jim Morrison crooned as she sailed straight off Highway 99 at the off-center overpass near Pixley and abruptly saw the flat slow-moving bulk of the Wal-Mart eighteen-wheeler materialize out of the fog. Always . . . Low Prices.

What occurred to her in that instant as she crammed on the antilock brakes and the car began to yaw, was not a flash of her past, nor her immediate duty to deliver the writs, nor even her love for Teelee and the child, but a glimpse of a painting she had seen in an art book back in college: Grant Wood's "Death on the Ridge Road," with a wriggling speeding sedan, almost Disneyesque in its exuberance as it was about to crest a hill and ram straight into a bright red truck coming a-leap the other way.

— —

There was no working cell in the van so Sonny had driven them carefully back to his house, only three blocks away. The lights on Chester had been flashing red all directions, a standard fog precaution. The only traffic they'd seen was a prudent motorcyclist creeping along on the sidewalk.

"Let me call," Jack Liffey said when they got there. "I somehow know this number. Something about it . . . ."

"Go ahead."

"Rancho Bakersfield Motel," a voice said. "Special rates. May I help you?"

Jack Liffey hung up. "Son of a bitch."

## Chapter Fifteen

# SLICK

Bulldog hadn't guessed quite right. The degreening shed was out in East Bakersfield all right, but a lot farther out than he'd thought, actually in the foothills of the Sierras, and probably slated to be torn down for housing development because survey markers kept grabbing at their shins as they worked downhill over the damp chaparral in the fog. Maeve could hear busy whitewater off to their right so they had to be following the river down. As far as she knew, there was only the one, the Kern.

There were cries and shouts behind them, some of which had the despairing note of rearrests. Bulldog held grimly to Tammy's hand, and Maeve grasped the long tail of his untucked shirt so they would stay together. Big chunks of the fog glowed eerily overhead with what must have been security light, but most of the world was dead blind and punctuated by hoarse police challenges, short bleats of sirens and shouts of distress that sounded like trips and falls. Fortunately they were leaving most of the noise behind.

Then they were forcing a passage through a hedge onto the secure footing of asphalt. Bright lights up a ways revealed a hint of a big building where two very old semi cabs were backed against the building. The nearest truck door said GOOD NEWS CARROT CO-OP.

The cab door was locked but Bulldog climbed up and smashed a window. He balanced precariously on some part of the truck to swing the door open and then helped them up onto a long hard bench seat.

"Still got that nail file?" he asked.

Tammy stripped it now from around her neck and handed it to him. The little implement looked absurdly small in his palm.

He fussed under the dash for a while, bent uncomfortably, and then he went outside and opened the hood, which folded up from the side. He went to work underneath, belly to the fender with his feet stuck straight out in the air.

"He always knows what to do," Tammy said. "I truly admire that in a man."

"Me, too. Man or woman," Maeve said, thinking of Gloria.

Bulldog climbed back into the cab and ducked under the steering wheel. "These old trucks are child's play," he said. "The new ones got armored cables and stuff."

"You can get it going?" Maeve asked.

"That's affirmative."

Tammy watched him with a funny little smile on her face.

——

Pastor Kohlmeyer drove very slowly back toward Olive Grove through the ghastly fog, clasping to his faith, but in a state of unendurable tension. He had invested everything in the battle to come. Bakersfield was to be the field of sacred war. A lake of fire. Perhaps he had put too much faith in his allies. Was that to be God's way of testing him? Was he to be tempted by the conceit that he was going into battle with moral strength *and* numbers on his side—only now to find that he was facing the devil nearly alone?

Suddenly a sedan that had drifted across the centerline loomed, and he yanked the wheel of his big Cayenne as a horn blared and a terrified woman's face filled the windshield of her car. But a traffic accident was not to be his fate—he knew that much. It would be nothing random. His fate, one way or another, lay on the titanic battlefield ahead. Who was to say what combats had to be waged before the great one at Armageddon? Each would be crucial in the eye of God, a testing in its own way, pitting ancient foes against one another and revealing the strengths, hesitations, failings, open wounds and earthly panics of all of God's allies.

He saw Olive Grove's cycling electric sign, remarkably comforting now in the mist, and pulled into the lot. Instead of parking by the office he went to a spot near the main entrance to the nave. He unlocked the high relief carved double doors. The giant domed space was gloomy, with only the palest of glows, like the phosphorescence of insects, from the immense ring of stained glass overhead, and he went to the robing room and turned on the single bank of lights that played on the altar screen. Returning slowly to the nave, he lowered himself to his knees before the immense maplewood cross suspended from its carved wooden screen. He didn't even need to look at it to know every meander and whorl of the faint honey grain, and the small nick where a chain had slipped and crushed the edge as workmen lifted the two-ton cross into place.

My God, have I failed You in some way? he prayed. Have I been too proud? Have I relied too much on Channing Pelt? I know when I took over Olive Grove from my brother, I promised You that I would build something greater than even my father had built, and it would grow in proportion to whatever You needed from my ministry offered up to you. Now I seek only to serve You, even if what You demand is my own humiliation before the world. If You need me to burn this sanctuary to the ground, You have only to give me a sign.

A seemingly bottomless wellspring of distress and dejection rising from within surprised even him.

I know the Devil is here, nearby, watching me and gloating at every mistake I've made. I know I can't begin to understand how to defeat him without Your direct help.

His mind kept returning to Channing Pelt and his unruffled revelations about the local power grab aimed at undercutting *their* campaign. On the surface the man had shown annoyance; after all, he had taken responsibility for much of the advance work. Yet Kohlmeyer had sensed something else, something perverse, something his colleague might not even have been admitting to himself. It was a kind of satisfaction, a mischief, that, after all, their holiest efforts had been outmaneuvered by men who were hip-deep, original-sin-deep, in the world of accommodation and civic compromise.

If the truth be told, Dennis Kohlmeyer knew quite well that Channing Pelt had always secretly enjoyed manipulating the pastor himself: outflanking him, or maneuvering him into a reluctant agreement, or simply nudging him along a course that Pelt had already laid out.

Am I on my own now? Kohlmeyer's heart cried out to the Lord. Must I do this utterly alone?

He knew there would be no melodramatic voice issuing from the great cross, not even a whisper within his own heart. God did not work that way. But he needed a sign and a direct order. And he knew how he had found such direction in the past. He stood up and climbed the twenty steps to the high lectern above the congregation where he sometimes offered the more dramatic Sunday sermons and where the big King James Bible of his father rested.

Now God's will would make itself known. Praying, he opened himself to the Holy Spirit and then lay his hands on the large volume, calmly accepting of what he would find himself led to.

3 For strangers are risen up against me, and oppressors seek after my soul: they have not set God before them. Selah.

4 Behold, God is mine helper: the Lord is with them that uphold my soul.

5 He shall reward evil unto mine enemies: cut them off in Thy truth.

So. The call to battle was sounded.

—-—

Teelee clutched a sleepy Catalin to her chest as she rested her forehead against the cool glass that separated her from the Kern Medical Center's trauma ICU where Jenny Ezkiaga lay behind glass in something like a wizard's workshop of tubes and wires running in all directions and a bandaging that almost obscured her face. It was hard to tell whether the tubes were pumping life in or out. Tears ran down Teelee's cheeks.

*She has a fighting chance.* A very dark East Indian doctor had been the one to tell her this. *It was a really bad accident, you should know that. The vehicle was so crushed it took almost an hour to cut her out.*

Why should she know that? Teelee understood intimately how badly Jenny drove, and she didn't want any vivid pictures of powerful mechanical saws and big pliers. She didn't want to envision the accident at all, not where it had taken place nor what it was that Jenny had hit. She just required them to go do their healing work at double time and accomplish one of the miracles of medicine that had become so commonplace. They needed to pay total attention to this one priceless being who was so very important that she absolutely had to remain on earth.

An older nurse came into the ICU and touched Teelee lightly in passing, just a hand on her arm, but it brought on a fresh bout of uncontrolled sobbing, which Catalin naturally joined in. The other nurse came out when she heard.

"I'm so sorry, miss. I think you and your little girl will be better off in the trauma waiting room. Come with me."

It wasn't far, and she followed, trying hard to be good. Maybe that was the deal, maybe God would help if she were very good.

A narrow room with blue plastic chairs and tray tables. Scattered magazines and a few broken plastic toys. A TV was playing an annoying game show but no one else was in the room and the nurse reached up on tiptoe to switch it off. "There's coffee there and bottled water. Please help yourself. I'll get a blanket for the little girl if she wants to lie down. What's her name?"

"Catalin," Teelee said.

"What a lovely name. We'll do everything we possibly can for your friend. You have my word."

Teelee couldn't trust her own voice any more. She could only sigh heavily.

As the nurse was going out, a man in a suit stopped her and they spoke softly. Then the nurse nodded in the direction of Teelee.

The man carried a rolled-up supermarket bag that might have contained nothing more than a box of breakfast cereal.

"Miss Green?" he asked.

She looked at him, her eyes unfocused.

"Does Miss Ezkiaga have a law partner?"

She shook her head.

"A paralegal or a secretary?"

She wondered if Sonny counted. "There's an investigator who works for her. His office is in the same building."

"Will you be leaving here soon?"

"I want to be near Jenny."

"They may not let you. Hospitals are drowning in rules these days."

"They'll have to drag me out."

"Your little girl may need some real rest," he replied. "You, too."

Was he friend or foe? Teelee couldn't tell.

"Anyway, somebody in the ER almost turned these over to the

police." He shook his head. "Miss Ezkiaga wouldn't let go of them as she was pulled out of the wreck. Since they've been issued *against* the police and the sheriff and the D.A. and just about every city and county official hereabouts, I thought they'd better not get handed over to the cops."

He winked at her, and she didn't know what that meant. At least he was bringing something to her that must have meant a lot to Jenny—maybe almost cost her life. She fought back a fresh bout of tears.

"Please give these to her investigator when you can." He watched her carefully as she took the bag from him.

She peered inside to see a clutch of legal papers encased in blue binders. Jenny'd gone north in a hurry, and she'd said it was to make sure she could get all the people out of detention, the ones the police had locked away. Now here was the purpose of her journey, rescued as she had been.

"If you'd prefer me to do something else with them, I'll try to find someone else."

"*No.*" Now that she had something of Jenny's, something that mattered, Teelee clung fiercely to the bag. He'd confused her at first, but he was irrelevant now. This was hers to take care of, just like Catalin.

"I'm all right now," Teelee said purposefully. "Thank you."

— —

## Artifact: 1939

I ain't gonna pick your 80-cent cotton
Ain't gonna starve myself that way

Gonna hold out for a dollar and a quarter

Till they take us back again.

> —Sung by Woody Guthrie in the union hall in Arvin, during
> a Communist-led Okie fieldworker strike, 1939[9]

— —

"When I stayed here, the night guy came on a lot later than this, but we can check," Jack Liffey said. "He had a name tag that said SLICK, can you imagine? Impossible to forget. He was way too young for 'Nam, but maybe the army still uses the damn expression. What's the name we're looking for?"

"Roy Sparks," Gloria said.

"Slick Sparks doesn't work for me," Sonny put in. "Dog just don't hunt."

"'Slick' was never something you were proud of," Jack Liffey said. "It was like Dipshit or Candy Ass."

"In my time, it was also what you called a dustoff, a chopper," Sonny said.

"Gentlemen," Gloria said. "All those ready to get out of the vehicle and go to the motel, signify by dropping the topic of Vietnam."

"Affirmative," Sonny said.

The motel was down off the bluff on old 99 and the fog was still largely overhead here, hovering about fifty feet up like an inverted gray sea that was churning slowly and could drop to engulf them at any moment. The light was eerie, starting to fade in the dusk and much more horizontal than light should ever be. There were no hookers of whatever sexual preference out patrolling business 99, and no road traffic at all.

"Let me go in," Jack Liffey said. "I've seen him."

"I'll be right behind," Gloria said. "Sonny, you go in back again in case he bolts."

A feeling of crystalline lucidity seemed to take over Jack Liffey, almost like a good mood. Everything was under control, and they would soon get Maeve back—he knew it. Somewhere, in some rational world, he felt himself sitting in a wood-paneled room explaining to a godlike presence why he felt so suddenly confident. It was almost like a drug. "Thanks, Glor," he said softly, as Sonny hurried away.

"For what?"

"For uprooting yourself and coming up here when I said I needed you. You got on top of things right away. I really needed that, and I love you for it."

"Are you okay, Jack?" Her brows furrowed.

"I think so," he said. "This is one strange town."

He touched her gently on the arm and they walked toward the motel office.

I knew decency would triumph, he heard in his head as he went in the door. And then his attention was focused entirely on Slick, kicked back and reading a superhero comic book with bottle-thick round horn-rims. It was him all right. Maybe twenty-five and hollow-cheeked in a way only old men with missing dentures were supposed to be. He suggested someone who lived high up in some West Virginia holler, near the coal mines, with lots of dogs under the porch. His eyes found Jack Liffey through the Coke-bottle bottoms but didn't seem to register any recognition at all.

"Can I help you?"

Jack Liffey looked back and saw Gloria just entering the door.

She just gets stronger and smarter, he thought. It was awesome, and he really liked having her as backup.

"I work for L.A. Gear," Jack Liffey said. "You know, the big sports shoe people."

"I guess." He was dubious. Jack Liffey decided there was something unwholesome about the man, the fastidious way he pressed a Post-it on the very panel he'd been reading and then closed the comic and set it down with an odd ironing-out gesture.

"We're traveling through the Valley picking subjects for a long-term advertising project on our best shoes. We're prepared to offer you a ten-year supply of any of our 'Luscious Gibbs' line and five thousand dollars just for helping us. You know who he was?"

"Huh-uh."

Thank god, Jack Liffey thought. He didn't have a clue himself. "It doesn't matter. Mr. Gibbs is probably the best-scoring basketball forward in history. He'll be visiting you himself with the TV people to follow up and maybe use you for the commercials."

That got his attention, and the young man sat forward. "TV?"

"If you look good on camera, there would be a considerable amount of money in it, and best of all you'd get to pretend to beat Gibbs in a one-on-one game. You know, you're wearing those hot In the Paint models and he's not, so you've got the advantage." Jack Liffey paused in his riff. "Got any idea how big this is, Slick?"

The man sat up and blinked nearsightedly. "I don't see so good without my specs."

"Doesn't matter a bit. We got our special effects guys. You'll look like a winner, trust me." At this point Jack Liffey glanced at Gloria. She stood there deadpan, letting him play out his hand. "My assistant, Miss Ramirez, will take notes."

He knew she always had a little spiral-bound notepad on her, and she didn't even glare at him for the "assistant" before bringing it out.

"Your full name is?" she said.

"Roy Elroy Gervaise Sparks."

He was dying to ask about the nickname but knew there was no percentage in it. Sparks offered his address and even his social security number. The expression "quiet desperation" was beginning to come into focus for Jack Liffey.

"Mr. Sparks, have you ever worn L.A. Gear products? It could help us clinch the deal and be worth even more money."

"I think so," he said. "Are those shoes you're talking about the ones with the metal holes and the silver rib-things like fins?"

"That's it."

"Why, I got a pair back at home."

"That's just perfect, my friend. Now we just need to get a photo of you in the shoes. It would clinch the deal, I'm sure. Once our people see it."

The man was getting excited now. "I close up here at eight and go home for an hour to eat. Could you take it then?"

"Perfect. Miss Ramirez here will get her camera, and we'll see you at eight, movie star."

A cuckoo clock went nuts all of a sudden, its avatar sounding six o'clock.

"What hours do you normally work, Mr. Sparks?"

"I do four to midnight when Vinh is off, like tonight, but mostly I do midnight to the morning. I'm night man. It's a double shift tonight. Is that a problem?"

"Not at all. Do you have any children?"

Something dark flitted past his eyes. "Huh-uh, no, sir. Do I need to for this?"

"I was just asking to be polite, Mr. Sparks. No problem at all."

Jack Liffey took the moist nervous hand before leaving, but Gloria didn't.

——

"Gibbs is a point guard," Gloria told him outside, with the fog hovering.

Jack Liffey laughed. "What the hell do I know about it? I could tell Slick had the IQ of a half can of cat food."

"It's nice to know he has the shoes, but here's something even better."

She held up a Hires Grape Drink can by the bottom. He hadn't even noticed she'd swiped it. "His DNA. I imagine the lab here is useless. I'll get it to L.A. Where I know they've still got the DNA from the baby's hand. We prove he's the father, then the tennis shoe really means something."

"Okay, you're a cop and I'm not, Sergeant Ramirez," Jack Liffey said. "Good catch. Let's not forget to pick up Sonny. He's still cooling his heels out back."

"I'll go to L.A. to take care of the can, but you two need to find Maeve," she said.

——

Jack Liffey insisted on checking Maeve's car immediately, before heading back to Sonny's. It was only a half mile away.

The car was right where they'd last seen it, but the Bakersfield cops were on top of things in one particular, despite the fog. A big sheet of sticky orange paper had been slapped officially across the doorhandle, keyhole, and the gap between door and side panel. DO NOT BREAK SEAL. REPORTED STOLEN.

Jack Liffey was impressed. But then, efficiency didn't necessarily mean intelligence.

The fog was indecisive enough that a few birds were coming out to have a look around even though it was still the dead of night. A feisty sparrow landed on the Echo's side mirror, fluttering and fighting for footing and pecking away viciously at its twin inside the glass.

"Even the birds in this town can't get it together," Jack Liffey said.

"Let's go home," Sonny said. "I'm as limp as a last-dance fiddlestring."

Chapter Sixteen

# THE OLIVE GROVE OATH

P astor Dennis Kohlmeyer entertained a childish urge to
lock the outer doors of the church and turn on all the
lights inside. Long ago, he had made his mother snap on
the night-light every night before closing his bedroom door. He
wondered exactly how you *did* prepare to fight the Devil, for he
knew the fiend was coming, there was little question of that anymore, and he would come unexpectedly in unexpected forms.

The pastor would stand fast, no matter what.

"The wicked flee when no man pursueth."

He left the nave by the robing room and hesitated when he
saw his blue robe hanging there, a powerful comfort in its own

way, but costumes were nothing more than another kind of night-light. He knew Satan would not be deterred by them, nor by ceremonies of any kind, despite Channing Pelt's photocopied rites. He wondered if he had let himself be talked down the wrong path entirely.

Kohlmeyer had a feeling that this particular challenge called for confronting evil with unfussy and completely ingenuous faith, the great hammer of the Protestant tradition. He closed his eyes for a moment and spoke aloud: "For God so loved the world, that He gave His only begotten Son, that whosoever believeth in Him should not perish, but have everlasting life." He felt strong enough after that to continue, restored, along the back hallway. He had to go through the school on his way to the infirmary.

The girl was held fast to her bed by padded restraints. He'd had his doubts but now he was certain that the Devil resided in this girl or wanted this girl for something—though he no longer had any faith in the rituals Pelt had given him. Her keeper was now Mona Rabenhorst, who sat patiently on a folding chair. She was alone, and though she looked quite fierce in her simple smock and hair bun, he made a mental note to find another Lady-Witness to stay here with her. He must leave no one alone in the face of the Devil, never—it was only sense.

"Good evening, Mona."

"Pastor."

"Has she given you any trouble?"

"Off and on. Don't let her fool you. She's conscious now. She's playing possum, but the Devil can speak his wiles through her at any moment."

He stood over the bed. He couldn't help thinking with a pang of remorse that this child looked worn down. Yet, despite what they had put her through, as far as he could tell, they had gained not an inch on the demon inhabiting her. In fact, Kohlmeyer had begun to wonder if this one scrawny girl were, for some unknown reason, Evil's main target in the town.

He was about to repeat John 3:16 aloud, when her eyes snapped open, staring upward, not at him. The faded blue eyes gradually seemed to gather awareness and then they found him.

"The chief creep, himself."

"My name is Dennis Kohlmeyer. I was ordained at Grace Abiding Seminary, and by that simple fact I bear the power of Jesus within me to combat Evil in all its forms."

"Goody for you."

"God loves you, Sue Ellen. God wants you back from the precipice. I won't make a fuss now, but God wants you to put aside all things of the Devil and of the material world and know true peace."

"Sure thing, Den."

He looked in her face and, overtaken with dread, saw a smirk that suggested nothing less than the words "irretrievably lost to God."

"Will you think about God's grace, Sue Ellen?"

"I'll send you a postcard." She rolled her eyes.

He turned to Mona Rabenhorst sadly. "You need someone else here to watch with you," he said. "We all require support in times of godlessness."

"It's not a problem."

"I believe we're entering a time of tribulation. I don't want you here alone."

"Thank you, pastor. Mr. Pelt stopped by—I think he wants to see you."

"Yes, of course," he said. But it was almost as if he hadn't quite heard her. He hurried away toward his office, but slowed in the hall, pretending to study the list of events on the school's big calendar board. He was feeling light-headed and heavyhearted, ready and hesitant at the same time. He knew the time had come to put aside his own weaknesses and all those who encouraged weakness in others, including secular meddling.

Give me a good feeling, Jesus, he thought. That's all I ask. A sense that I'm on the right road.

When he stepped into his study, Channing was standing there, waiting for him.

Channing Pelt looked up from the fishbone management diagram he was working out on the whiteboard, a bit startled.

"What on earth is that scratching?" Kohlmeyer said.

"It's just rationality applied to problems, Denny—even religious problems."

"Lucifer has scores to settle," Kohlmeyer said gravely. "Since his defeat and ouster from heaven, as you know, Channing, he delights in confounding us, even though we were made in God's image."

"Of course." Pelt seemed wary.

The pastor walked distractedly behind his desk, but found he could not sit. "He knows he has limited time. All right. I think you rely too much on the material and the conventional world, but I didn't fully realize it until today. Our enemy is ingenious, deceptive and dangerous, and he uses rationalism and everything else that falls within his path. Science, biology, carbon dating, metallurgy, spreadsheets—even what some deem common sense."

"Where are you going with this, Dennis?"

"We've seen the unmistakable signs of a holy battle arriving. For some reason, the Devil has chosen Bakersfield for this rehearsal for the end times. Someone has to stand up and bar his path in the name of Jesus. I don't believe you've ever taken this peril seriously as what it is."

"I've been right at your side, Dennis."

"That is true. But I think you've been so close, I haven't been able to see you truly."

The tall man with the buzz-cut came close to the desk, put his hands on his hips. "Dennis, what are you trying to say?"

Kohlmeyer took a deep breath. "One must bend to God's will. I'd like you to clear your office and be out of the sanctuary in one hour. Leave an address. Your outstanding pay will be sent on."

"I don't believe this. You're Section 8. You're going to take a lot of good people off into looneyville." Pelt shook his head in disgust.

"I can only do what the Lord commands me to. He loves us all, and undoubtedly He has another plan for you. This battle-field can have only one general."

Kohlmeyer registered the dismay on his companion's face but realized instantly it was only another trick of his adversary.

"Oh, don't quote crap at me like you're some kind of Pee-Wee League Jesus. Listen, for all your constipated intellect, Dennis, I've always stuck with you. Always. Even when you had your little slip with Nellie Stonemason."

"Yes, you are with the Devil now," Kohlmeyer said calmly.

"If I was God," Channing Pelt replied, "I wouldn't have a church with the likes of you in it. I wouldn't have a world with you in it, you dumb hick. Let's see how you keep things running without me when all you've got is that dimwit piety."

The pastor closed his eyes and began to pray to himself. When he heard Pelt slam out of the study, he stopped and looked around the room. It revealed nothing except its usual furnishings, a little dusty. It hardly seemed a likely setting from which to launch such a battle as he knew he must.

First he carefully erased the offending fishbone diagram. Pelt should have trained as a Boy Scout counselor or a school therapist. Certainly nothing that called for taking a direct role in accomplishing Salvation's plan. The pastor fell slowly to his knees and again prayed, seeking guidance now that he was as good as alone against all the wiles of Satan.

— —

Bulldog had had a little trouble with the gear and wrestled with the tall wobbly lever, though the fog was lifting a little. They all sagged in relief when they finally got to the street that held his office and coasted up behind Maeve's dwarfed Echo. She noticed it had a big parking ticket.

"I got a ticket."

"Not exactly," Bulldog said. As he switched off the ignition, the air brake tanks gave a wheeze and slowly exhaled.

She climbed down and walked over to peer at the orange door seal that said DO NOT BREAK SEAL. REPORTED STOLEN. As a Denver Boot, the label was a real failure, Maeve thought. She could rip it in two in a second, but the idea still made her nervous—as lawbreaking always did.

"You're still working for me," Maeve reminded Bulldog. "We know Toxie wasn't in that warehouse with us. So where is she?"

"Hey, kid, don't be a ballbreaker. Give a guy a chance to crack a welcome-home Coors, and then maybe I'll call around to wake some sleeping dogs."

They trooped into his office and Tammy seemed to give up

what had seemed her plan to jump Bulldog's bones instantly. She went though the curtain to a mussed double bed and was snoring like a wasp inside of a minute.

Bulldog got his beer and was into it immediately. "You want one, kid?"

"It'd knock me flat," Maeve said.

"That's what they're for. What was that incarceration all about, do you know?"

"I think it's about crazy people worrying about the devil. I guess they've decided we've enlisted in his army."

"Hey, none of that was legal. I know. Plenty of heads are going to roll on this eventually."

"I don't care about eventually," Maeve said. "I'm worried about Toxie now."

"Sure, okay, I get it."

He rolled up his sleeves as he sat heavily at his desk, and she read with surprise a tattoo on his arm that said GOOD CONDUCT.

"Hey, my dad has one of those."

"What?"

"The good conduct thing. From Vietnam, isn't it?"

He glanced down as if he hadn't seen his arm in years. "Just the army. It was supposed to keep me out of trouble, but it never worked."

"I guess my dad had the same problem."

"I bet I'd like the guy." He finished off the beer. There was a signboard above the desk that she hadn't noticed last time. It had two removable, replaceable numbers and said 38 DAYS SINCE LAST BAILSKIP GOT PUNCHED OUT.

She couldn't quite take it seriously, but with Bulldog it was hard to tell.

"What if I find out she's being held in Guantánamo with a thousand marines guarding her?" he said. "You still going to go after her?"

"Try and stop me."

He played around with the phone and finally dialed. There was quite a wait. "F.A., this is Izzy."

Izzy! Maeve thought. Isaac? Israel? Utterly impossible.

"Yeah, sure. Don't complain to me. Be mortified on your own time. You still owe me one—a big fucking-ass one, too. What's up with the cops and the kids?" He tucked the phone under his giant shoulder and began scratching various itches as he listened.

"Of course I know about it. *Señor*, where do you think I've been for thirty-six hours? You know me, I'm an ordinary drinking man, and they stuck me in with the hippies. Someone's gonna pay, but right now I have a question for you." He described Toxie as best he could, gave her real name, and asked if someone he called The Wrangler could locate her. "*Claro que no, hombre*—I mean *now*. I woke you up. You can wake him up. I'm here meanwhile, pining for the fiords."

He listened and frowned, then hung up.

"Fiords?" Maeve said.

"It's Monty Python. We're huge fans."

She was surprised she hadn't recognized the reference. "So this fiord guy'll help us?"

"Yeah, but I'm afraid not tonight. He can do anything in this town he wants. But it doesn't please him to call The Wrangler until morning."

"Is your name really Izzy?"

He sighed again. "I'm Tony, like the sign says. Legally. For general consumption and all. However, if you promise not to spread it around, at my bar mitzvah I was Isaac Rosenberg. In this business it's much better that my clients imagine a different family tree." He shook his head. "I got a feeling you can keep your trap shut, and anyway, you won't be around here long. Don't leak it to Tammy, please. I figure she's about as discreet as Geraldo on meth."

"Are you ashamed of being Jewish?"

"I haven't been Jewish since I was sixteen, girl. Why should I drag that whole fucking tin can if I don't believe any of it? Don't tell me you're religious."

"No, but I don't reject my own people."

"Fuck you, kiddo. Clients don't get no insult rights. You get the divan out there. I ain't waking anybody else, but I'll get you some blankets."

—-—

"I wouldn't leave tonight," Sonny suggested. "The Grapevine's gonna be socked in."

"Gotta get this sample in," Gloria said. "Tomorrow morning's the walk-in day at the police lab. Only time you don't have to get in some three-month line to wait for your results."

"Okay. I can tell you're stubborn. So listen, when you see those warehouses right after all the gas stations on the valley floor, it's gonna start getting thick as ever was, whiteout thick, just like we seen or worse. Slow to about twenty when you can't see much ahead but don't ever stop. Crack your window and use your ears. Stay out of the truck lanes, and if you can find a German car with those blue xenon lights, get behind it. Let *them* run up somebody's ass."

"Thanks, Sonny."

Jack Liffey walked her outside. "I wish you were staying, Glor. You've been amazing. I'm beginning to think I need a different job."

"Why?"

"Watching a pro work. Makes me feel like amateur night."

"Jack, you've been finding missing kids and talking them home for ten years. I catch bad guys. I do that and you do what you do. You do it good. The basketball stuff was good. I wouldn't tell you that if I didn't mean it."

"I worry about the fog, too," he said. "Be careful, Glor. I can't take any more loss."

"Find Maeve. That's your big worry. I'll be back late tomorrow night, maybe sooner."

He kissed her hungrily and finally let her go.

Inside, Sonny handed him a mug of green tea, which he frowned into.

"I don't know, Sonny. Are you sure this isn't just rinse water?"

"She knows what she's doing, your Gloria. Got more crust than an armadillo. Let's worry about getting a night's sleep. That there's green tea and it'll help you sleep. It's pretty much all-purpose, healthwise, except it won't make your pecker stand up."

"That's okay. He's getting a rest tonight."

— —

## Artifacts: 1950s

*Nigger: Don't Let the Sun Set on You in This Town*
—Sign widely reported to be posted at entrances to Oildale and
Taft, 1950s.

*IRS stands for In Range Shooting*
                    —Sign reported on rural Kern roads, 1950s.[1]

——

Maeve woke early, just as a weak light began tarnishing the room. She threw off the bedclothes and got on her knees on the sofa to peer out the barred front window through the reversed decal SDNOB LIAB. The fog had withdrawn to a respectable height, basically only a low overcast now. But it was obviously so unpredictable that no one knew what it would do next. What weirdness of temperature and dewpoint and pressure controlled its rise and descent?

She was determined to get Bulldog on the job as soon as possible and find Toxie. A shiny black crow startled her, gliding low past the window, way too black against the gray morning. She realized she hadn't even reflected much upon her pregnancy for a couple of days now. The thought came like a rebuke, and before she could stop herself she sat hard on the sofa and found herself crying, emotions gone all haywire.

——

Teelee fussed with the straps and lifted the sleeping Catalin out of the car seat in the early morning, so much heavier when she was dead weight. She'd taken the chance that the fog would hold off up at flag level until she fulfilled her mission. She owed it to Jenny, and she'd risk more than that for her. With the little girl cantilevered against her hip, she picked up the writs she'd been given and walked toward the odd little lampoon of a southern mansion in Oildale where Sonny lived.

243

A voice came from somewhere above. "Who's that being nibby so early?"

She picked up the writs and backed down the steps to look upward past the verandah arch to where Sonny Theroux stood on a small round balcony in a voluminous purple-striped nightshirt.

"Hey, Sonny," she called softly. "I got some law papers here that can't hardly wait. Straight from Jenny."

"Well, I guess it's gone peep of day. I'll be right with you."

——

Pastor Kohlmeyer had got himself up early from a restless sleep, wrapped himself in his green cotton bathrobe and slipped off to his small home study. An idea had announced itself between fits of anxious dreams. The fight that he knew was coming was going to demand absolute loyalty from at least a small band of believers that he could rely upon. Pelt's massive and undisciplined Sword of God would not do. He had to gather from within the church a select few.

For an hour now he had been reading and copying over early Christian creeds—the Nicene and Augsburg and Leyden, the Heidelberg Confession, even the Oath of the California-Nevada Evangelical Renewal Fellowship. He had transcribed and winnowed and cut.

He sat back and stared at the yellow pad where he had written out the final draft. He had worked hard and he was pleased:

### The Olive Grove Oath
I have been born again by trust in Jesus Christ, Lord and Savior.

I believe the Bible is literally accurate in all it teaches and that Satan is a living entity waging war against people of true faith.

I pledge, with Jesus as my witness, to fight Satan with all my worldly and spiritual strength, even unto my death.

Chapter Seventeen

# THE WORST ARE FULL
# OF PASSIONATE INTENSITY

J ack Liffey drove his pickup, retrieved finally from the cops,
toward the little K Street ghetto of bail bondsmen, only to
experience his heart plummet a foot or two in his chest
when he saw that Maeve's Echo was gone, tofu power and all.
On some superstition he parked precisely where she had been,
just in front of a badly dented Mack truck cab from the 1940s
that definitely hadn't been there the day before. As he got out he
discovered hard evidence on the pavement that he hadn't hallu-
cinated the Echo. His foot nudged a shred of the big orange
sticky label that the cops had plastered over the door handle. She,
or someone, had ripped it off.

Two of the local bail bond agencies appeared to be open for business. Both of the occupants professed to have no knowledge of Maeve's car, other than having noticed it parked there the day before. The second one he talked to, a bored woman with a pencil stuck in a tight bun of hair, hooked her thumb across the street to another bail shop and said the guy lived in back so he shouldn't believe the CLOSED sign, just knock hard.

BULLDOG BAILBONDS was the big sign across the street. And this beside the door:

As seen on local TV
Smart Bail to Start
Children's Play Area
Habalamos Plain English
Youre family to Me
All Collateral Taken
25 hours/8 days

He rapped hard on the screen door and was startled when an identical rapping came back at him from somewhere within.

"Hold your horses."

"No hurry," Jack Liffey called out. He felt he didn't want to start out on the wrong foot here, so he sat down on the porch steps and looked upward to study the eerily motionless underside of the fogbank.

He felt a rumble in the porch step before he actually heard anything, and eventually a diesel engine came down the track at the end of the street attached to four others and towing an endless string of freight cars covered by metal mesh. Something moved within. Cattle. He could have identified the contents by the smell alone, wafting a hundred feet from the tracks like a mobile fertilizer factory.

"What's the secret word?" a man bellowed from the other side of the door.

Jack Liffey stood up and considered. Please? *Pretty please?* "Maeve Liffey!" he called through the door, which came open immediately.

"What about her?" The guy in front of him was large, very large, and every inch of his bare chest and arms was covered with colorful tattoos. He wore multicolored jogging pants, but for all that, his face seemed to possess a sort of kindly beatitude.

"She's my daughter, bless her and all who assist her."

"Tam!" the fellow hollered. "It's the kid's dad!"

A woman soon hove into sight wrapping a man's robe around herself. She was in her late forties and only about half made up, badly needing either nothing at all or a whole lot more of whatever it was.

"Pleased to meet you." Jack Liffey couldn't read her expression but decided to believe she was, in fact, pleased to meet him.

"Do you know where Maeve is right now? Her car was out there yesterday."

"Come in, come in," Bulldog said. "The kid's fine. Do you want some coffee?"

"I wouldn't say no. Thank you. I need it and I couldn't find somewhere to stop on the way over here."

"From where?"

"I'm staying in Oildale with a friend."

"Ah," he said, as if that explained just about anything. "We've been taking care of Maeve. Or she's been taking care of us."

Jack Liffey laughed. "It often works both ways."

"We were held by the sheriff's people in a warehouse out east, with a lot of others, mostly kids. It was part of—I don't know what to call it—a kind of temporary insanity going on here. It happens in this place."

The man led him toward a kitchen nook and waved his hand toward an uncomfortable-looking built-in bench. "Sit. Java and toast's what we got."

"You sure Maeve's okay?"

"Snug as a bug in a rug." The man fussed with a suspicious-looking tin coffee pot.

"Where were you all being held, anyway? Sonny Theroux and I were hunting all over to find out."

His host's eyebrows went up. "Sonny's involved? That means Jenny Ezkiaga is, too. That's all good. And you can be proud, man. Your daughter actually busted us out of that warehouse, though they probably caught most of the others in the fog."

"Would you phone Sonny and tell him where they are?" Jack Liffey said. "Thanks to Jenny—who's had a pretty bad accident, by the way—he's got some habeas corpus writs to deliver. He can get most of the others out."

"That's too bad about Jenny—what happened?"

"I'll tell you all I know, which isn't much, but first I need to hear where Maeve's run off to. I hope it was straight home to L.A."

"No, not exactly," Bulldog said. All of a sudden, both men looked worried.

—-—

Two of Pastor Kohlmeyer's recruits stood in the church hallway. They looked uncertain. The taller one carried a cracked-open double-barrel shotgun over his arm, a valuable Merkel boxlock with hand-tooled silver all over it that had been his father's only legacy to him. The other man had a Smith & Wesson .38 revolver in a woven-leather holster on his hip like a Tijuana cop. They acted as if they were not quite sure they should be there.

"I can't see how a .38 is the best way for a Christian man to hold off Satan."

"I guess he can come at you in a lot of forms. Even a tough-skinned old demon'll get to thinking twice if he's got a butt full of double-ought buck."

The first speaker looked shocked. "Buckshot! What the heck did you buy that for, Tom? That'd tear a good-size duck down to confetti." He folded up the oath and handed it back.

The shorter man knocked softly because of the murmur they could hear within, then slowly opened the door of the pastor's office. He was on the phone.

"I'm not kidding you about the danger. This may be the beginning of a real fight, and Pelt has already betrayed us. I never really appreciated the secular poison he carried around in his head. The situation may become dire, and we can't count on any of the old plans."

The pastor listened a moment and then hung up softly with two hands. "Yes, Tom?"

"What should we be doing, pastor? There's a lot of grounds to guard around here and not so many of us."

"Until we get more men here, you and Al watch over the infirmary room at the school. I believe the Devil has clearly demonstrated he has a special interest in the young woman we've been trying to free from his influence. Her role in his schemes, however, is still uncertain."

"Yes, sir."

"When we have more men, we'll cover the perimeter. Don't underestimate Satan's wiles, Tom. Keep your eyes peeled. He's definitely coming our way, and he's prepared to confound our souls in ways we just can't anticipate."

"Yes, sir."

"It's all right, we have the power of Jesus with us."

The pastor could see the lingering questions in the men's eyes as they shut the office door. He still didn't, himself, have the answers to all the questions, but their duty was clear.

— —

### Artifact: 1950s

Steinbeck Cottage
Dusted Out by Cat

[exclusive to the *Gusher*]

As we announced in the spring issue of the *Glorious Clam & Gusher*, a deputed quorum of the ODCH convened at 121 Decatur Street on July 3 at 3 p.m. in order to affix a bronze plaque on the cottage once the home of Mr. John Steinbeck, the somewhat well-known author of several florid novels, a bona fide historical landmark of the Bakersfield area and favored drinking spot.

To the astonishment of all assembled, the deputation discovered that the cottage had been bulldozed to rubble the night before. The owner of the property, Mr. John Steep of Bakersfield,

when contacted by the Society, professed no knowledge whatso-
ever of the rude destiny that had befallen the derelict literary site.
In fact, he barely remembered that he even owned the semi-his-
toric domicile. Mr. Steep suggested that it may have been
destroyed by a disgruntled grower who had nursed a grudge
against the writer for many years. He went on to claim that Mr.
Steinbeck may even once have been a Democrat. We deny this
emphatically.

All assembled raised a toast to the much-maligned spirit of
Okiedom. As the intended brass marker no longer had anywhere to mark it was donated to the Beale Memorial Library in
downtown Bakersfield.

—Newsletter of the ad hoc Oildale Drinking,
Chowder and Historical Society[3]

— —

Maeve had heard Toxie talk about her stint of community
service inside the big flying saucer of God. For Maeve the whole
experience would have been worth no more than a shrug—it was
just a church, after all, one more extravagant waste of resources
in service of the age-old human longing to have a father figure
watching over you. She planned on doing the best she could with
the imperfect earthly father she already had, as long as she had
him. He'd acquitted himself pretty well recently.

It had taken her a long time to get to the church because she'd
chosen the wrong road leading west and found the suburbs
petering out into some winter crop that was still so young she
had no idea what it was. Miles and miles of frothy little leaves,
maybe carrots. When she'd seen what could only be I-5

approaching in the distance, like a conveyor belt of trucks, she'd known she had to turn back and maybe try Stockdale instead of Rosedale. Too many dales.

She waited along the side of the highway when she finally sighted the unmistakable church, watching what looked like a hive of activity within its grounds. An electronic message flashed over and over on its sign: SATAN, YOU'RE NOT WELCOME HERE! Clean-cut men with armbands and rifles were patrolling the parking lot, and the uphill entrance had been barricaded off with massive SUVs. She wondered if Satan was expected by road, and if so, what kind of car? Maybe a nice red Maserati, she thought, with that trident logo.

Making fun of these people was no help, though. Bulldog had finally made contact with the man he called The Wrangler that morning and found out that Toxie was being held here, a prisoner whose rights were being stomped on, out of a particularly putrid piety. It was odd how she could muster a kind of sympathy and even relish for just about any outlandish congregation of believers in the world—Jains, Zoroastrians, Dervishes—but couldn't do the same closer to home. Boring old Christians—though they didn't look so boring at the moment, strutting around with guns.

The pacing whitebread warriors she saw filled her heart with gloom, they seemed so zombified. She noticed that traffic had utterly disappeared on the highway in front of the church and wondered why. Starting her car again, she drove on to park in a deserted minimall just across the strangely empty road.

If I have any use in this world, she thought, it's to help friends in trouble. She wondered if this was just patterning her behavior on her father's. He'd probably identify his mission, if he'd use that word, as helping the weak, or the powerless, or maybe vulnerable children. But the ideas were akin. Your purpose in life couldn't be just having fun for a while and then getting mounds of dirt heaped over you.

She found a vantage spot in a breezeway between shops and watched the men patrolling the rim of the raised parking lot across the highway. One guy sat on the roof of a big-wheel truck, scanning everything around him with binoculars. Upon spotting the sentinel, she withdrew into the narrow space.

Luckily, she thought, whatever they were preparing for—vampire devil squadrons or whatever—nothing was really going to attack, so nobody was going to get hurt. And eventually everybody would drag their tails home to lock away their guns again and sulk. Unless of course the fog came down again, and they were all spooked into blind gunfire against unseen enemies. Anything that made a sound in the fog would probably get shot about a thousand times, like one of those crude Mexican drug-runner movies she'd watched on cable when she was practicing her Spanish. They always ended with a barrage of ugly insults and then some insane gunfight. She'd never really found a use for: *Si me picas, te quebras los dientes con mis huesos viejos!* If you screw with me, my old bones will break your teeth! But it was comforting to keep it in her repertoire.

She reminded herself that an infant had actually been killed in this town and, at least by widespread rumor, a number of animals had been ritually killed and mutilated. They were loony but you couldn't say their mobilization was based on nothing at all.

Her immediate problem was to convince the patrols that she wasn't Satan's handmaid when they noticed her walking slowly into their defensive perimeter. It was probably not a good idea to make a straightforward run for the church, nor try any hasty movements at all. She emerged from her cover and didn't even bother looking both ways on the quiet highway. She crossed quite deliberately with both hands open at her sides.

A whistle went off above. Some of the rifles swiveled around until they were almost pointing at her. As she reached the steep driveway up to the parking lot, a man came down the incline toward her.

"Hold it there, girlie!" He was holding a lever rifle, and luckily he kept it somewhat off target. It looked like the rusting Red Ryder BB gun from her dad's childhood that he'd never been able to part with and had kept hidden out in the garage.

"Who are you?" he said.

"My name is Maeve Liffey and I'm a friend of . . . Sue Ellen Crumm. I know she's in there and I need to see her."

"You can just turn right around and skedaddle, young'n. We're protecting this property, under strictest orders."

Maeve watched him for a moment. "I'm over two months' pregnant. You can shoot me and my baby right here, or you can call somebody who can make the decision to let me come in to see my friend. Otherwise I'm going to walk right past you." She could hear the edgy petulance in her voice, though she'd been trying hard for something a bit more grown-up.

"Wait there. I mean it."

He backed two-thirds of the way up the drive, keeping his eyes on her. He pulled out a cell and called someone.

How unreasonable, how feminine, it had been, she thought, to smack him like that with her pregnancy, but it seemed to have worked. Anyway, she didn't think there was any rational way to deal with idiots who strutted around toting guns.

As she watched the man whisper into his phone, she thought of an expression she'd read recently that had impressed her: The density of things becomes unknowable. That was just how she felt now—she faced an incomprehensibly opaque way of life that had petrified out here in the hinterland over generations.

She decided that the next time one of these men spoke to her she would act more demure, the way she imagined the teens of this church would behave. Hey, with recourse to movies of the week, she could probably come up with a passable prim Mid-American lass.

"Carlos!" a man's voice yelled. It came from somewhere out of sight. "Your guys are wanted out back. Someone's been sneaking up in that empty field."

This summons didn't seem to affect the man she could see. He clicked off his phone and came down the slope toward her.

"Girl."

"Yes, sir."

He stopped at a respectful distance, maybe worried she might be fixing to hit him with a lightning bolt. "What's your friend Sue Ellen's godless nickname?"

"Toxie," she said without hesitation, then wondered if she should have. Would a nice Christian girl have known that?

"Okay, you can come up. The pastor wants to speak to you. You walk ahead of me and, remember, keep your distance and no funny stuff."

She went up the drive, well wide of where he stood. The shallow climb winded her more than she expected—another side effect of the pregnancy. On top, the fog was lower, uncanny, almost touchable, obscuring the big church's roof.

Halfway to the building, the man asked, "Can you shift your shape?"

He wasn't calling for jokes about silicone implants, that was for sure.

"No, sir," she said. "I'm just me. Not anything evil."

"That's for the pastor to decide. Keep on walking. Go for that glass door."

She was a bit frightened by the aggression that filled the air. There were dozens of purposeful men walking here and there with shotguns and rifles, and wearing pistols on their belts. One man, who looked like a sorrowful banker, was distributing arm-bands made of cut-up white sheet, and other men were tying them on their left arms. A new group came out through the glass door with their rifles and fanned out in pairs toward the rim of the parking lot.

Her guard let her inside. "Stay in front of me. No acting up."

"Are you taking me to the pastor?"

"You're about to meet your betters, that's all you need to know."

She remembered a folk tale she'd read once of a mouse so frightened that it had run to the cat for compassion. Was that what she was doing? In fact, she couldn't really imagine these absurd people harming her. Her sense of optimism rose irrationally, as it often did—as if her dad would always be nearby to protect her.

"I will oppose Satan with all my worldly and spiritual strength!" Voices echoed this simple pledge as they passed her. Only a few looked at her curiously. They seemed rapt, or else confused. Neither attitude inspired any confidence. What kept the whole three-ring circus from being entirely comical was all the guns.

Now a younger man, buck-toothed and utterly earnest,

appeared and took over as her escort. She said nothing as he conducted her down a short hallway and then around a corner. He opened an office door only a few inches.

"I have been born again," he called into the opening.

A soft baritone came back from within. "By trust in Jesus Christ, Lord and Savior. Enter."

The door swung open, and she half expected to see the jaws of a giant cat opening to swallow her.

"Come inside. Let me get a good look at you. You say you are a friend of Sue Ellen Crumm."

"She likes the name Toxie Shock better."

"Come all the way in."

She realized that she was finally frightened, despite herself, and she tried to keep her knees from trembling.

A calm-looking man sat behind the desk watching her. He had wavy gray hair raked back from his forehead. Could it really be held like that by hairspray? He smiled without warmth. Be demure, she told herself.

"What's your name?"

"Maeve Liffey, sir."

"I recognize that as Celtic." He pronounced it with a soft C like the basketball team, not the ethnicity. He probably didn't know. "Are you a Roman, Maeve?"

She'd never heard anyone call it that. Though one girl she knew jokingly called the folks at her own church mackerel snappers. "No, sir."

"Well, then. Have you accepted Jesus Christ as your personal savior?" He leaned forward a little as if to watch for hidden signs in her demeanor or her reply.

"No, sir, I haven't." She wanted to keep him mollified but

would not lie. And even if she had fibbed, he probably had a bunch of trick questions to trip her up.

"How can you have moral behavior in your life without consulting Jesus and relying on Salvation's plan?"

He hadn't even said, Please, sit down. This was just too much. "You mean I won't know it's wrong to kill and steal and lie if I don't ask Jesus? I think wrong is wrong. And even Jesus can't change that."

He shut his eyes tightly, as if in pain. "Why are you here?"

"I came to see my friend and help her. That's all."

"Maeve Liffey, you yourself may be unaware that you're an emissary from the Devil. Have you considered that? Satan seems to have fastened fiercely upon your friend. She's resisted every effort to drive out the Devil and win her back to Jesus."

"I thought this was all about a dead baby. You know perfectly well she had nothing to do with that. She's just a rebellious girl who dresses Goth. I know dozens of 'em in L.A. I can bring her mother here to take her home, and you'll be rid of her. Then you can fight the real enemy, whoever that is."

"It's far past that, I'm afraid. This church is under siege now by the forces of darkness."

He's gone bonkers, she thought. It took real self-control for her not to say anything rude. She tried to cling to a love for all things human and to see some way to like this man and maybe find a way to touch him where he might be moved.

He picked up his phone and pressed a button on it. He was summoning someone who'd probably be bringing a straitjacket, she thought.

"You look for proofs, don't you, young lady?"

"What do you mean?" She heard, with chagrin, the suspicion in her own voice.

"It's not a trick question. But looking for proofs is an impertinence. God is beyond your chain of rationality, Maeve. It's faith that shines forth. A pitched battle for the soul of mankind is coming right here, perhaps a small one, only a forerunner, but we know we will win."

"Why would such a momentous battle happen in Bakersfield?" she asked.

"Because when new diseases of the spirit develop, we often seem to get them first here. Beyond that I can't say. Even asking may be an impertinence."

The door opened behind Maeve.

"Pastor?" The newcomer was a woman in a uniform.

"This girl is dangerous to us. Please take her and hold her . . . in the pantry at the far side of the church from the other one. Two of you watch her at all times, and beware of tricks. The Devil's handmaids must not be allowed to get together and multiply their powers."

As if, Maeve thought—if we were really devils—we couldn't communicate secretly as much as we wanted. And crush you jerks in an instant. But logic was not much good here.

"'The best lack all conviction, while the worst are full of passionate intensity,'" Maeve said, quoting Yeats at him.

The pastor was unperturbed.

No, I don't think I could find a bigger bunch of assholes anywhere, she thought grimly.

Chapter Eighteen

# A DRACULA MOVIE WITH NO DUBBING

G loria had pulled off Highway 99 and was driving
back into Bakersfield along an oblique boulevard,
though what had started out rural was now clearly
the industrial zone south of the city, car wrecking yards and pipe
fitters and a big reclamation company that seemed to sell only
used garage doors. Her eye caught on a little stucco box called
Lupe's Comida just off the road, and she pulled off beside two
much-dented American beaters on the dirt. It was midafternoon,
not mealtime for anyone, but they had a Tecate sign in the high
window and it beckoned to some recess in her psyche, being the
kind of place she liked but tended to avoid when she was with
Jack. She wasn't sure why, though his Spanish was terrible.

She locked up carefully, protecting the precious folder of DNA evidence under the seat. Inside there was a serving counter and a scattering of tables and chairs. At one table two grizzled men were sharing beers and what looked like bowls of *menudo*.

"*¿Qué transas aquí?*" she called at the empty counter.

A young girl who should have been in school appeared in a dirty apron. "*Sí, señora.*"

"Are you serving food or just the *menudo*?" she asked in Spanish. "*Toda.*"

Over her head was an extensive short order menu.

"Does your *machaca* have a lot of green pepper in it?"

"I think so. I can reheat it."

It was Gloria's favorite, but she realized it'd probably have been sitting in a big stewpot since breakfast, and nothing about it would be fresh, especially the egg. She had such a yen for it, though, she was tempted to follow the girl back and have a peek and a sniff. She settled for a beer, which she was directed to fetch herself from the big horizontal wet Fanta cooler along the wall.

"*Caballeros,*" she addressed the men after opening her beer. She asked if they would object terribly if she had the bad manners to sit down with them and trouble them with a few questions. Their behavior said, very subtly, that her request was extraordinary, like a chair suddenly deciding to talk to them, but, incapable of being impolite, they gestured to her to sit, and one actually reached to pull out the chair.

They were field hands for some giant agribusiness corporation, owned they thought, ultimately, by Exxon, and they were celebrating a few slack days between the planting of winter onion sets and the beginning of the thinning and tending. They lived in the exurb called Weedpatch just a few miles away. She told them she was an investigator and got right to the point, asking about the noisy protests going on in the Anglo part of what they called Bako.

*Señora*, they said, everyone with the least sense did their very best to stay away from these mysterious and most dangerous outbursts of the *gabachos*. And just last Sunday their priest had made a special warning. Who could say what was in the *norteamericano* mind, but this outburst had all the possibility of turning into another of the Valley's famous nighttime persecutions of *la raza*, with columns of trucks containing white *maleantes* driving through the Mexican areas honking and beating people up and shooting into homes. They had not had one of these in a very long time, but they were not forgotten. The oldest *gente* remembered the last one and told the younger *gente*.

What about *el diablo*? she asked. Why so much talk about him?

They both crossed themselves quickly. It was being said the devil had slaughtered a poor little *bebé* and was seducing white children into becoming *jipis*. One of the men shrugged and observed that the Anglo children were always loud and ill-behaved anyway, so why was this supposed to be any different? What was making the police and the *alcalde* so upset now was just a mystery. It wasn't like back home where you always knew what was going on and who *El Hombre Grande* was and who had to be paid off and how to keep the peace.

For a moment Gloria watched these two decent peasant farmers, born far away in some village in Sonora or Sinaloa, and she realized that for them America was, basically, an ongoing Dracula movie, in a foreign language with no dubbing, and without even the familiar cues that let you predict who might be bitten next.

She asked if they had seen any signs of the Devil themselves, maybe a mutilated animal, but they hadn't.

She thanked them and left them a five to drink on.

As she got into her car, she sat a moment, unexpectedly stricken by cultural displacement. She was Paiute, despite having grown up in their world and knowing it intimately. She wasn't sure what she'd been seeking, talking to them, but it had something to do with making a stab at standing a bit apart and gaining a new perspective on the mania being whipped up here. She was surprised to realize that she badly wanted, maybe even needed, Jack.

—–

Bulldog, Tammy, and Jack Liffey sat across the seat of the super-tall big-tire Ford that Bulldog drove angrily west across town toward the Olive Grove church.

"I'm sorry, man, *really*. Maybe I'm stupid, but it's hard to see the danger in sending her to a church."

"I suppose these folks are sincere about what they believe," Jack Liffey said, trying his damnedest, but not for an instant trusting his own sincerity.

They passed a shopping center that appeared to be closed, and he wondered if it was a holiday.

"A German philosopher once called Christianity a religion of slaves," Jack Liffey offered. Nietsche. "He was a pretty harsh judge. But it's amazing how reading the Bible selectively . . . . well, a lot of these people seem to think it's a religion of the masters."

"I don't know about that stuff," Bulldog said. "But we'll get your daughter. I promise you."

Jack Liffey appreciated that. He could use a bit of reassurance. This town made him feel like he'd fallen through the crust of his accustomed reality into something other. It only looked normal

on the surface here—the minimalls and suburbs and supermar-
kets. Then suddenly there'd be a book burning, a preposterously
literalist billboard about Noah's Ark, or a triumphalist march to
demand that the city outlaw childhood—all of it obstinately
mean-spirited and repellent. Once you'd broken through the
crust, you could see scorpions crawling everywhere. Hell, maybe
even devils, he thought.

—‑

### Artifacts: 1975

One seriously wounded
During melee on street

A 22-year-old Taft student remains in serious condition today
after being shot Sunday evening in a bizarre street fracas that
spawned even stranger events.

Authorities at Bakersfield's Kern Medical Center this morning
said Doug Henry, 22, was in serious but stable condition following
emergency surgery to repair a wound in his lower neck area.

Henry was wounded in a melee shortly after 6 p.m. in the
500 block of Seventh Street. Officers said the disturbance
involved three black men who had been recruited to play football at Taft Community College and a large group of whites. The
shooting triggered an ugly scene a short time later at the college
residence halls and prompted police to escort all of the college's
black students out of town for fear they would be harmed. . . .

—Daily Midway *Driller*, Taft, May 27, 1975

TC Officials express

Concern over incident

Officials at Taft College were shaken by the Sunday shooting episode that prompted all 13 of the school's black students to leave town fearing for their safety.

Taft police officers escorted all of the blacks to Bakersfield where they notified their parents that they had left school and did not intend to return. . . .

—Daily Midway *Driller*, Taft, May 27, 1975

— —

Maeve allowed herself to be incarcerated without protest in a roomy pantry that contained wooden shelves full of blister packs of tiny dispenser tubes of condiments and spices, plus vast numbers of paper plates, plastic glasses, and Styrofoam cups. Church supper central. She sat on a flimsy aluminum cot, lower and cheaper than the last one she'd slept on in the warehouse. A pair of tense biddies sat on folding chairs by the door, watching her with almost flattering suspicion. The two women held magazines but mostly glowered over them at Maeve, like lions who were being kept from the Christians. Or was it the other way around?

"My name's Maeve Liffey."

"I'm Myrtle Fine," the older woman said, polite by habit.

"Hush, Myrt."

"I'm in the twelfth grade at Redondo High in L.A. I'm applying to eight colleges. And I'm pregnant."

"The Devil's work," the younger woman said.

"A bad mistake," Maeve countered. "I admit it. What would you do about it?" She knew they'd never ignore that question.

"I'd go have the baby at a private hospital, if your family can afford it, and give the innocent one to a good Christian family," said the one who wasn't Myrtle.

It was a stock answer. They didn't really act as if she had asked them a genuine question at all, but it had been. One way of getting herself back around to the big subject.

"And you?" she asked Myrtle Fine.

"Where's the father?"

Maeve thought of telling her the father was a Latino gang-banger almost ten years older than herself who, in a vulnerable period of her life, had blasted her off her feet into abject sexual servitude with his testosterone-steeped charisma. How could she ever tell anyone but her father that—and even then the tale had had to be subtly reprocessed. Oh, girl, how did you ever let yourself get so carried away?

Now it all seemed like a strange dream she'd had. That time in her life had almost no reality to her. Except the bulge that she imagined already showing in her abdomen. "The baby's father is not in the picture," Maeve said simply.

"I'd keep it myself and raise it and love it," Myrtle Fine said, quite sincerely, as if she had lost an only child herself long ago.

"Myrt!"

"I *would*. A baby is precious beyond thought, beyond anything on earth."

"What if you'd been raped?" Maeve said. It was probably the only way she could get these woman to appreciate the degree of estrangement she felt these days from Beto.

"It wasn't the baby's fault," Myrtle Fine said. There didn't seem to be any ambiguities in her world.

"We don't know the facts," the other woman insisted.

"I know what this girl is telling me," Myrtle Fine argued. "Can't you hear her yearning to do the right thing? You are, aren't you, dear?"

"Sure," Maeve said. "But it's not always easy to know what's right—or know anything for certain." There was a sweetness deep within the whole gruesome experience of her domination and submission to Beto that she still couldn't understand, but she wasn't ready to lose it by rejecting it out of hand. She had certainly let herself go crazy over him. She wondered if it was ever possible to grasp the full nature of an experience as powerful as that. Maybe it didn't even have a full nature you could know, and the best you could do was grab a useful corner of it all.

She remembered her dad telling her to value the age she was now because it would never come again. He said it wasn't the age itself she'd eventually be aching for but a kind of not-yet-knowing, an innocence of how things turned out. Of course, she understood her father'd been talking about his own life at that point, thinking of a time when everywhere ahead he'd seen only open roads.

She noticed that both of her guards had their hair cut short, a woman-signal that usually meant good-bye to a lot. A kind of settling in to no further possibilities.

"It's not so difficult to know what's right," the one who wasn't Myrtle said sternly. "Killing a baby is wrong."

"The choices you pose are too easy," Maeve said. "It's wrong to kill, sure. It's wrong to steal a car. What about a soldier who defies an order to torture somebody? What about a starving family that steals a little milk for a baby?"

The questions shocked both women silent.

"Every time you set things up so they're easy for *you* to choose, I have a feeling you're creating a problem for somebody else."

"We do what God says is moral," Myrtle pointed out.

"Put him on the phone. I'd like to see what he says. And why aren't you selling your possessions and giving the money to the poor? Didn't Jesus say to do that?"

They both looked stricken.

"She really has been sent by the Devil," the other one said with sad calm. "Don't listen anymore."

But Myrtle was still on the case. "Look into your heart, dear. If you kill an innocent soul inside you, you'll be cutting a wound into your whole life that will never go away. Please consider your own soul."

What Maeve was actually considering was all the lonely dread and, paradoxically, the affection that she'd experienced with Beto—could she allow that to turn out to be meaningless? She had to find something worthwhile hidden in all the horseshit. She believed in that deeply. Salvage something real, even if the hurt never truly healed.

"I have to use the bathroom," she said.

—–—

"Jack took off like a scalded mule when he found out where his daughter'd gone," Sonny said. "He was just now on somebody's cell in somebody's car. I think I know the guy—he's a bail agent the size of a house with more tattoos than the Peruvian navy. But a good guy."

"We'll let Jack rescue Maeve. It's what he does best. Is this damn fog going to come down again?"

Sonny leaned forward in her car to peer upward. She hadn't given him time to think about much at his house. Once back from L.A., she'd just ordered him into her car and took off. "It's coming," he said.

"So, by nightfall," Gloria said tightly, "we'll all be lost in the damn pea soup again."

"That's the nut, lovely woman."

She glared at him. He looked unrepentant for flirting. "Let's get our business done. I'm going to make a citizen's arrest and you're going to witness it. Maybe if we deliver the killer to your local cops with a red bow around his neck, they'll simmer down and stop the Devil hunt."

"You got the DNA on him?"

She frowned. "Well . . . silly me. You need the mother's, too, for total. Then all the lines match up with the infant's and nothing's left over. Just having the dad's—what I've got is a very strong probability. But Roy and Rhea Jane don't know that."

"You're going to lie to the suspects." He grinned.

"Believe it or not, I have that intent."

They approached the Chester bridge and headed down toward the court of pygmy cabins where the couple they were after lived.

Luckily the belligerent tortoise was nowhere in evidence in the court. Gloria knocked at the door and they waited for a moment as somebody within went on watching *Wheel of Fortune*.

"Pat, I'll take an M." The moronic music tootled away, and Gloria rapped harder. The TV finally muted.

Gloria flashed her badge briefly when the door opened an inch. "Open up *now*," she said.

"I thought y'all worked for L.A. Gear." The Appalachian twang was Roy Slick Sparks, sounding uncertain.

"You thought wrong, dipshit. Don't even think of locking the door on us. We'll knock it off its hinges."

The chain pulled free and she barged in like half a dozen angry cops. "Sit down and shut up. *You*, turn the TV off. Eyes on me. Stay like that. Listen up." She recited the routine Miranda statement that just about everybody knew from TV cop shows.

Sonny watched the wife, a young stringy woman who seemed to have a bit more intelligence in her eyes than Slick, but her hair, her skin, and her clothing were uniformly bleached out, and she looked like the genetic end product of a millennium of overwork and exhaustion.

The young man wore round thick steel glasses and his cheeks were unnaturally collapsed, suggesting he'd lost his teeth in some locale where dentistry was an unknown science. These two were refugees from his homeland, very loosely defined. How did we ever allow this to happen? Sonny wondered.

"There's no point denying it," Gloria said. "We know you had a child and we know it's dead. It's all in the DNA evidence. Did you give birth right here?"

They just sat there, stunned by something too swift and too powerful to assimilate quickly. There were things embodied here—attitudes, fears, ways of being—that Sonny himself only understood as an anthropological tourist, though he told himself he was broad minded.

"What was the baby's name?" Gloria demanded. "I promise you, lying now will make everything worse. Just tell me the name of your little girl. I know you chose a name."

"Cloris Dana," the young woman said, her eyes cast down.

"Hush up, Rhea Jane. You know it were the Devil at work hereby."

"And whose brilliant idea was throwing in the Devil business?" Gloria said. "Yours, wasn't it?" She was addressing him now. "If you want to do this the hard way, we can separate the two of you, and I'll question your wife alone. You know how long she's going to hold out by herself."

"So I don't get to be in no basketball TV?" the young man said resentfully.

"No, but I'd say you've got a fine future in local TV news. Look at me when I talk to you. Both of you. Was it crib death? Or did you get angry at the baby's squalling one night and shake the poor thing to death?"

Sonny was impressed by Gloria's skills at intimidation, and he was curious all of a sudden how Jack made out when they disagreed about things. Her ferocity was something to behold, and it cooled his idle fantasy of picking her up on the rebound from Jack one day soon. Uh-huh, right after I get me a steel jock.

Without warning, the wife suddenly burst into hot, horrible tears, and the young man owned up to holding his hand over the baby's mouth to stop a colicky wailing, something that'd worked fine many times before. He hadn't meant to hurt her, but then he'd panicked because he knew what the police were like, and they were sure to blame poor hillbillies for murdering the baby even if it was a total accident or even a part of God's own plan. Poor hill folk always got the shit-sticky end of whatever was going down.

"All this innocence is very touching and all," Gloria said. "But you chopped off your own baby's hand and threw it into a truck. I predict people are going to start losing sympathy for you when they hear about that."

"I *told* you," the bereaved mother whimpered.

"Hey." He dealt her a little rap-and-twist blow like an elementary school noogie.

"Oww, Roy!"

"Do that again and I'll handcuff you to the toilet, Slick," Gloria said. "Just tell me why you chose that particular truck for your midnight deposit."

He sighed. "It weren't locked up, and the guy wasn't from around here, just some stuffed shirt from L.A."

Gloria turned to Sonny. "Go in the back and find the silver L.A. Gears. You'll know them."

"Under the bed," Rhea Jane said spitefully.

The young man eyed her with a scowl so extreme it looked like it would split his face open, but he made no further move to hit his wife as Sonny got up. It was great news, as far as Sonny was concerned. It ought to take the air right out of the Devil hysteria in town. Bless Jack's woman, titanium balls and all. She was the best.

——

Maeve checked the windows in the bathroom, but they were up far too high and the glass was wired. She locked herself into a stall and went ahead and plotted while she peed. If she was going to rescue Toxie, she had to escape her captors and then find the girl on the far side of the circular building, as the pastor had let on.

She wondered what the mention of a younger woman's gynecological needs would do to the old women. She'd soon find out.

"I'm bleeding," she called. "I need some Tampax. Would one of you get me some?"

She heard them conferring in urgent whispers, with the harsher one mentioning the pregnancy and saying it must be a

Devil's trick. But in the end, she went for some "sanitary tissues" and Maeve was left with Myrtle Fine. Maeve wondered if she was strong enough to simply overpower her. They'd taken her purse so she had no recourse to anything like the little tube of pepper spray her dad had bought her. She felt the pockets of her blouse and all she found was a dime. Franklin Roosevelt. One thin dime. And then she remembered reading that the dime was the one American coin thin and strong enough to be used as a screw-driver.

She looked carefully at the hinges and latch on the stall and quickly discovered something. By removing a single big screw, it looked like the inner handle of the spring-loaded latch would fall right off. Maeve grinned to herself. It was just too delicious an idea to pass up.

"Young woman, are you in any pain?" Myrtle Fine asked loudly.

"Some. It's just spotting, I'm sure."

"Be sure to let us know if it gets any worse. We don't want you in any trouble—being in the family way and all."

*There* was an expression that Maeve had never heard spoken aloud. Bun in the oven, she thought. In a delicate condition. "I'm sure I'll be fine, ma'am." She tried hard to sound like someone being brave as she leaned forward and fitted the dime into the screw. She tried both hands and squashed up all her face muscles with the effort, but the screw wouldn't budge. There was only one option now.

She edged slowly off the toilet, held the dime in place with the tips of her fingers and closed her teeth on it. By wrenching her neck around and enduring the stab of pain in her jaws, she broke the screw's grip and it started to unwind. Slowly she twisted the screw out. It was very long. As it got wobbly loose, she cupped a hand under the latch and both the screw and the little T-handle fell into her palm. Perfect. To work the latch from inside now you would need an ice pick or something similar to poke into the screw hole.

Maeve sat back and sighed. She knew she might have only a few more moments before the harder one came back. Very soon. She'd never really had trouble motivating herself, but now she sensed a holding pattern. She wondered if she'd become a hesitant person now that she was pregnant. Was everything in her life going to be about the damn fetus?

"Mrs. Fine!" She tried to put a bit of pain in her voice.

"Yes, dear."

"I can't stand up and I really feel sick." She pried the latch open with the screw and held it. "It's not locked. Would you help me up."

"Wait until Mrs. Minty comes back. We'll help you together."

"Please. I'm getting cramps."

"Are you having a discharge?"

The old woman pulled the door open and Maeve quickly pocketed the hardware and held out her arms for a boost, her head limp and nodding forward. The woman wasn't really very strong or weighty, and once Maeve grasped her arms, it was easy to yank her inside, swapping positions in a rapid twirl. Maeve tore her hands away and slammed the stall door on the woman. There was a gap of maybe eight inches beneath the door but she didn't think Myrtle Fine was going to be limbo-ing under it.

"Sorry, ma'am, but I've got to go now."

"Young lady! You'll regret this!"

But Maeve was already on her way out the bathroom door. No

one was in sight, and she took off along a dim curving hallway, leaving a shriek of complaint behind her.

— —

The bottom of the driveway was blocked by yellow sawhorses that said POLITE NOTICE, but once Bulldog stopped the truck, they could see a much more substantial blockade of hulking SUVs at the top. A man with a white armband sauntered down the slope and brought a lever-action rifle around toward them. With the windows rolled down, they could hear the chugging of engines, maybe generators.

"What's your business here?" Fingers of fog wisped down behind him from the solid bank just above his head.

Jack Liffey stepped out quickly. He'd been too long crossing town, worrying and fretting about Maeve the whole way. "You've got my daughter in there. I want her out now. And don't point that rifle at me, you putz."

Two more armbanded men appeared above, one with an over-and-under shotgun and another with an extremely intimidating assault rifle. The latter frowned and manipulated some control on his toy so all at once a red line zinged out through the mist. He swung it around to leave a bright dot bobbing on Jack Liffey's chest.

"Get that laser shit off me!" Jack Liffey yelled.

A big hand closed over Jack Liffey's shoulder from behind him. "I require you alive, my friend," Bulldog said earnestly. "Stay here."

Bulldog pressed down hard as if planting Jack Liffey's feet into the asphalt. Then he walked up to the sawhorse. "Gentlemen, my friend's daughter's name is Maeve. The mother is an L.A. cop. Unless you want hell to pay, I suggest you produce his girl."

"We answer to a higher authority. And this ain't godless Los Angeles, neither." But he punched a number into his cellphone. "Wait there."

"I was a Navy SEAL," Bulldog called. "You don't want me crawling around up there in the fog with a K-bar knife. You really don't."

"Were you really a SEAL?" Jack Liffey whispered.

"Fuck that shit," Bulldog said.

When the man finally got off his phone and came down the slope aways, he didn't look at Jack Liffey at all and kept his rifle skyward, the laser sight turned off. He spoke exclusively to Bulldog for some reason. "The girl is safe, you have my word. Nobody goes in or out tonight, sorry—but nobody. We have word the Devil is coming or he's sending somebody, who knows what form. The pastor has seen all the signs. Each of us has taken a solemn oath to defend our church tonight and that's what we got to do. The fog is coming soon and we're going to pull back now, just to the perimeter of the structure itself. If we are approached, we *will* shoot to kill."

"If I *were* the Devil," Jack Liffey said, "do you really think a rifle'd stop me?"

The man turned his head and met Jack Liffey's eyes for a long time, a variety of thoughts obviously passing though his mind. "We wouldn't know till we tested it, would we, sport?"

"Come on, Jack," Bulldog said. "Not here, not now."

Chapter Nineteen

# THE MAN WITH NO FAITH

The cops had not been amused, to say the least, not even Saldivar, the one detective she judged both competent and marginally open to reason. But they did take Slick Sparks and Rhea Jane Sparks into custody because they had no choice, took possession of the big plastic bag with the strange tennis shoes and noted the location of the footprint she reported, took the partial DNA report from LAPD's Scientific Investigation Division, and then they questioned Gloria and Sonny relentlessly while showing almost no interest in talking to the alleged killer and his weepy accomplice. To be fair, Gloria knew most L.A. cops would have reacted exactly the same way had their turf been poached.

"We could do you for obstructing a police investigation," Etcheverry grumbled.

"No you couldn't," Gloria said. "You could thank us for doing the obvious legwork nobody was doing. While you were busy harassing a bunch of kids with bad attitudes."

"L.A. is lucky it has so many crackerjack cops that it can spare a few to stick their long noses in other cities," Saldivar said.

"We live right, I guess. Honest to god, lieutenant, I'd prefer to do this without any disrespect." She stopped right there, before sarcasm crept in, whether intended or not. "We all drift off on the wrong tangent once in a while. I know first-rate detectives in L.A. who knocked themselves out on the McMartin thing and they're pretty sheepish about it these days."

"How about you, tough guy?" Etcheverry was addressing Sonny now. "You're going to be hanging around here long after your girlfriend flits back to *El Lay*."

"Yes, sir, I live in Oildale."

"You serve writs, I hear."

"Yes, sir, today I served habeas corpus writs on the police chief, the D.A., the sheriff, the jailer, and the head of the cult committee. I have some more if you feel left out."

"You show me just a hint of that paper, and I'll shove it so far up your ass it'll turn your eyeballs blue." Etcheverry glared at him.

Saldivar clucked in mock sympathy. "Don't tempt him, Theroux. We want to keep you happy. We insist on it."

Sonny hoped Gloria didn't vex them any further, and she didn't look like she meant to. He had to admit that he was powerfully attracted to the woman's swagger and strength.

"So where's you're pal, the other *pee eye*?" Etcheverry asked.

"He's out in the fog looking for his daughter. Jack's a good guy, lieutenant, really. His daughter's one of the kids they picked up, and she's pregnant so he's got a right to be a little worked up."

"Well, okay for that. We hope he finds her."

At the mention of Maeve, Sonny could see Gloria stir a little. "You know, lieutenant, the girl you're talking about is my step-daughter. I'd be obliged for any assistance. In all fraternal sincerity, cop to cop. From my heart, gentlemen." She poked herself in the chest with all her fingers, as if they needed the descriptive help. "Professional courtesy, I'm requesting it. In the end, I give you the full collar on the Sparks couple. It's all yours, not a word from me."

Saldivar watched her impassively for a while, then came to a decision. "Etch, you know where that other girl was sent, don't you? The one with the peculiar nickname."

"You really want me to do this thing?"

"Yeah, I do."

Etcheverry shrugged and picked up a phone and punched in a number.

To Sonny it seemed the cops were all moving with a dreamy indolence, even Gloria. He didn't really trust the two detectives, not in the end, because he'd been on the inside and he knew the power the position carried. He'd always had a recurring nightmare of dying at the hands of authority in some extravagantly undeserved way. Who ever promised you a just death, Sonny?

If it be now, he thought, 'tis not to come; if it be not to come, it will be now; if it be not now, yet it will come: the readiness is all. He would give up a lot for this couple he'd just met and the daughter that he hadn't met. They were remarkable people, so fiercely committed to one another across all the obvious rifts. For whatever reasons, he thought sadly, he had ended up with so very little for himself, in a town distant and alien from everything that had once mattered to him. Sometimes, Sonny Theroux thought, life just didn't pan out.

Without even looking out a window, he knew the tule fog was already descending to absolute whiteout, and tonight it would hold everybody's worst fears.

—–

They were doing their best to set up on the edge of the parking lot near the church signboard, but the fog was not cooperating. When Jack Liffey got close, he could see that the woman held a microphone with a badge that said KGET 17 plus the peacock logo that meant an NBC affiliate. The camera was only a few feet away from her and a young guy with long hair held a Sun Gun over his head pointed at the reporter's upper body.

"Might as well be in the driveway back at KG," the cameraman bellyached. "Sorry, Ellie, the whole world is scrim. I can't even see the sign. Maybe if you got right back into the planter."

The woman in her stylish Burberry trench coat high stepped delicately through crunching geraniums right up to the Olive Grove signboard, which had been turned off for some reason. The beam of the Sun-Gun defocused for the widest exposure.

"This is Ella . . . one, one-two . . . Ella Ella . . . Ella Keys, K-G-E-T 17. Lost in the fucking fog in West Bako."

"That's good. I had speed."

"Don't you dare!"

Bulldog's huge form plodded into the light all at once, blacking them out. "What the hell are you doing here?" he demanded of the reporter.

She made a respectable effort not to seem intimidated by a mountain-sized apparition appearing out of the fog. "Just doing our job. Got a problem?"

"There's crazy men with guns right over there ready to shoot anything that moves," Jack Liffey put in from behind Bulldog. "What've you been told about what's going on?"

The reporter hadn't noticed him. Now she was trying to size him up before speaking.

"Honey," Bulldog said, "tell him what you know or you can eat the microphone."

She batted her eyebrows once. "Somebody called the station a half hour ago to say a hundred armed men were out here defending some girl against an all-out assault by the forces of Satan. Do you know what any of that means? We went up to the church, but they wouldn't let us in and wouldn't talk to us, so we're about to do a stand-up right here and say what I just told you, then split. Give us the word if you think we should hang out a bit more, to see if a bunch of goat-foot guys carrying pitchforks show up, but basically I want to go home and have a drink with my boyfriend." She seemed to be mustering her courage. "Who are you?"

"I'm afraid we're the guys with the pitchforks," Jack Liffey said.

Abruptly the light went out, and, their eyes still dazzled, the world went out with it. "Gotta save battery," the lightman called. "Say the word, El, and I'll give you low power again for setup."

"It's okay, Julian," the cameraman said. "This is a crappy shot anyway."

"Who was it said he had a pitchfork?" the woman asked into the dark.

"I did."

"And who the hell are you?"

"I'm nobody." Jack Liffey was tired but he was determined. "My daughter is trapped in there with these pinheads and I need to get her out. Can you help me?" He worked at sounding like the kind of team player that he wasn't.

"How am I supposed to do that?"

"I don't know. Are you in touch with the police? Are they coming?"

"I doubt it. This is a lousy town to get your name listed in church bulletins as an enemy of Jesus. Who are you, anyway? I already asked."

"I'm tempted to say one of those enemies." His eyes were adjusting in the whiteout, and he could just make out nearby shapes. The woman was right where she had been, and she had her hands on her hips. "My job is finding missing children who're in danger, and now that means my own daughter. Well, not missing exactly. In there. You sure you can't help me? Take me inside as crew."

"They already refused us."

"I'll be your producer and talk us in. I'm damn good at that. Come on, what have you got to lose? How many Emmys have you got?"

"Leave the big guy behind, then. What's your name?"

"Jackie!" He'd been just about to tell her, but a familiar voice cut him off from somewhere out in the fog. He vaguely remembered hearing the chug of a vehicle coming up the incline in the wrong gear. "Are you here, Jack?"

"Over by the sign," Jack Liffey called. "Is that Sonny?"

"And me!" That was definitely Gloria.

— —

Maeve had undone the restraints she'd found binding Toxie limb-by-limb to the sides of a hospital bed in a narrow room that must have been the infirmary of a religious school attached to the church. But no amount of shaking had any effect on her friend. Toxie was obviously heavily sedated. Her skin was over-warm to the touch, a little clammy.

Maeve took the girl's limp hand and held it tight. We'll get through this together. She almost said it aloud. Maybe she *had* said it aloud. Sometimes, when you were alone and running on nerve, it was hard to tell what was real. She squeezed Toxie's hand with both of her own, and the sense of sisterhood she had gave her renewed purpose and strength. Listen, women, men's faces are grim and murderous while ours are loving. We do not give up, we do not break. She smiled. In the end, famously, we weave their shrouds.

Hormones, she thought. Wow! What a rush she was having! She recalled the face of the poor pastor who'd ordered Myrtle and company to take her away and hold her. He'd tried to seem firm and decisive but had looked wounded and lost. A man who was unloved, a boy who'd once hurt a sibling, thrown tantrums, demanded his way. Grow up, she thought. Then, fat chance.

"You've got me to reckon with, fella," she exulted. She glanced down. Toxie was unmoving, her breathing barely visible.

––

### Artifacts: 1980s

Local authorities came to believe they had discovered eight large child-molestation rings, each part of an interlocking underground of abuse, child pornography . . . More than seventy people were arrested. Hundreds more were implicated. Dozens of children were taken from their parents. . . . Allegations of murder, Satanism, cannibalism and ritual human sacrifice . . . During initial interviews virtually every child denied anything had happened. . . . Backyards all over Kern County were dug up by sheriff's deputies hunting for the tiny bones of sacrificed babies. Lifelong friends stopped talking to one another. . . . Naysayers faced the distinct possibility of being accused themselves.

—Edward Humes, *Mean Justice*, Simon & Schuster, 1999

Molestation inquiry tactics questioned

Brian Kniffen was just 6, a frightened and confused little boy, abruptly seized from his parents by deputies and wondering whom to trust.

"I miss my mommy!" he cried in a pitiful little voice captured on tape by the deputy district attorney and sheriff's sergeant interviewing him five days after he was taken into county custody.

It was April 13, 1982. Brian didn't know it, but he was becoming a key witness in one of Kern County's biggest criminal cases ever, the Kniffen-McCuan child-molestation case.

It was a huge case. It was the great-grandaddy of them all, the molestation-ring investigation the Sheriff's department and the district attorney's office cut their teeth on.

It is the foundation on which all other big Kern County group molestation prosecutions—mostly successful—have been built.

But events of the past four years have shown that foundation to be crumbling.

—Michael Trihey, Bakersfield *Californian*, April 13, 1986

"I concluded that, yes, the children had been grossly led in their interrogation. In fact, I would even go so far as to say they were badgered by their interrogators. . . ."

"They would take one juvenile, interrogate, badger them to the point of the juvenile saying, 'I don't recall.' The child would then be told, 'But your brother or sister tells us this. Isn't it true?'"

"It was just a situation of getting a child to, however slight, to say 'yes' or get them to shake their head or say 'uh-huh. . . .' And the next thing we know we have people being arrested from their homes.

—Denver Dunn, private investigator hired to look into "recovered memory" molestation cases in Bakersfield. Sidebar interview, Bakersfield *Californian*, April 15, 1986

— —

"The officers in charge decided any show of force would be a provocation right now," Gloria said. "Especially in this fog where people tend to run into each other a bit suddenly. Lieutenant Saldivar called over here and tried to tell them the police had the perps who killed the baby, but the pastor's not taking calls."

A small crowd had gathered at the church's sign now, lit to a diffuse glow by the headlights of several vehicles. The TV crew seemed to be waiting on the word of their leader, the woman in the Burberry who was sneaking nips from a number of little airline booze bottles from her pockets and getting slightly lit.

THE MAN WITH NO FAITH

Bulldog and Tammy had their arms around one another and whispered together. Gloria and Sonny were talking to Jack Liffey.

The reporter announced from the flower bed, "There's some kind of loyalty oath they keep repeating back and forth."

"You gotta have a mission statement these days," Sonny said. "Otherwise, you're just not happening."

"Jack, you got that up-to-something look," Gloria observed.

"I'm trying to talk our friend here with the mike into letting me play TV producer," Jack Liffey said. "Maeve's car is across the road. I'm sure she's in there. Anyway, they admitted it." He eyed the leather shoulder bag Gloria held against her side. "What can you give me?"

"Not my pistol. That's department policy. But here." She took out a little black leather pouch that contained a canister looking like an oversized Chapstick.

"Mace?" he said.

"Pepper spray. It's a lot stronger than Mace and quicker. Aim for the eyes. This one is set to stream rather than cone out. It won't blow back on you, and you can hit several people by waving it around. Don't worry, the effect is immediate. Anybody you hit in the face is blind and on his knees for thirty minutes. At your mercy."

"I'm surprised you never used it on me," Jack Liffey said as he pocketed the canister.

"I thought of it." She wasn't smiling so he gave up that line of joking. No point in going off message. Right now he'd do anything not to rile her. She'd come riding in like his own Joan of Bakersfield.

"Take care, please, Jack. I know you're going to go in there. Where Maeve's involved, nothing could stop you."

"Channel Seventeen," Jack Liffey called, turning to the TV crew. "If you want a story, I said I'll talk you in. Time to rock and roll."

"Hold on, Jack," the announcer said. She stepped delicately out of the flower bed. "They turned us back once and they've seen you. There's a lot of nervous guys out there with guns, and I've got a boyfriend at home I want to see again."

If you act with enough determination, he thought, armies will follow you. "Piece of cake. They're too distracted to remember me. This will go national. You'll see. Armed fundamentalists barricade church against assault of devils. Ella Keyes reporting from Bakersfield. Film at eleven. Next stop, major TV market."

She took a last nip and chuckled. "Intrepid reporter shot down in Jumping Jesus ambush. Unidentified body of man nearby."

"If it goes south, journalists everywhere will visit your grave," he said. "Stay close now. Come on, camera. And lights—what's your name, son?"

"Julian Walpow," the young man said.

"Stick with me, Jules. I'm charmed tonight. Let's have low-power ahead of us." Jack Liffey patted the lump of the pepper spray in his pocket for luck.

"You got it."

Julian wasn't able to light up much, but the faint wash on the asphalt showed parking lines that kept Jack Liffey oriented, and he led them toward where he remembered seeing the pastor's office . . . how long ago? Only a week?

"Let's not startle anybody," Jack Liffey said. "Who can sing? And, please, something pious. Know any hymns, Julian?"

"Do you count 'Smells Like Teen Spirit?'"

"What the hell is that?"

"Kurt Cobain."

"No, I don't."

Then the man with the camera started to sing in a pure and eerie countertenor.

> A mighty fortress is our God, a trusty shield and weh-
> eh-eh-pon; He helps us free from every need that hath
> us not overtaken.

The sound of that falsetto skirling out into the fog was so otherworldly and spine-chilling that he wondered if somebody might not squeeze off a few rounds just on general principles. But he didn't have the heart to stop him. They came to the last herringbone of parking spaces, with only a curb beyond.

> The old evil foe now means deadly woe; deep guile
> and great might are his dread arms in fight; on Earth
> is not his equal.

"*Halt!*" A hoarse bellow came from maybe fifty feet away.

Jack Liffey put his hand on the cameraman's tense shoulder until he stopped singing. A fog hush enclosed them.

"No *thing* passes here tonight!" This was decidedly not a countertenor.

"We're a television crew from KGET Seventeen, and we mean you no harm."

"Step away from here—now!"

"Listen to me," Jack Liffey called out. "We've come to offer you a platform so you can explain to the world what you're doing. That's important."

"We're locked down for the night! I couldn't change the orders if I wanted to. Maybe you can talk to Pastor Kohlmeyer in the morning. But you can't come in here now."

"I have my orders, too. We're approaching very slowly to talk. Don't do anything sudden, and we won't. I'll shine a light on me so you've got me in your sights. We need to get your story out there."

Jack Liffey had Julian go forward a few paces and shine the Sun Gun back on him and the ground at his feet. "Give me full power for a few minutes."

"I've got thirty-five on bright. Probably twenty-five now. And I'm wearing a second bat-belt."

"Good for you. Keep the light on me."

Jack Liffey walked very slowly forward with his open palms showing until the shape of a man emerged from the fog, looking like a young clean-cut banker, slumming in a red-checked lumberjack coat and cradling an expensive scoped deer rifle that was utterly useless in the fog. Beside him a much older man in a puffy ski parka sat on a folding chair with a big .45 pistol in his hand resting on his lap.

"Stop right there!" the lumberjack ordered. "I will do everything within my power to oppose Satan with all my worldly and spiritual strength."

"Amen," the older man said.

Jack Liffey opened and lifted his jacket, turning slowly to show them that he was unarmed, unwired, unanything'd. "This is all unnecessary now. The police have caught the killers of the infant girl. It was her own father. Shaken-baby syndrome—it happens all the time, but he panicked. He admitted writing the Devil note to try to divert suspicion."

"Why should we believe you? The Devil will be testing us with just such tales."

"If I'm a devil, why don't I just wave my hand and turn you two into flaming napalm? For heaven's sake, man. Use your head."

"We're sanctified and protected by our oath." It was the older man, his eyes going fierce and assured in an otherwise impassive face. It was easy to see where the real authority here lay. "Tonight we cannot be touched, no matter the wiles you employ. We have our instructions, and nothing you say can change them."

Jack Liffey took a pace forward and crouched slightly to touch the man's knee just in front of where he was resting the .45. "But I *can* touch you, you see."

"You cannot touch our immortal souls."

The lumberjack now brought the rifle to bear on Jack Liffey.

"I'll say it again: We're a television crew from right here in town, and I'm giving you your last chance to let the world know about the brave stand you're making here tonight. Our viewers want to hear it firsthand, right from you."

"We're not going to tell you a thing except to leave. Pronto."

There was no sound at all in the fog except the beat of his own blood in his ears. It was time, he thought.

"Okay," Jack Liffey said. "The magic word tonight is evolution." They were standing so near one another that he was able to spray both their faces with one short sweep of the little hissing canister.

Their screams were shocking in the soporific fog. Jack Liffey grabbed the barrel of the rifle with his free hand and shoved it skyward but there was no shot. Both men hurled themselves to the ground as if diving into a pool that would quench the fire in their eyes. He saw that they could barely get a breath, gasping as they pawed at their faces. He collected both of the weapons and hurled them far away into the fog. He had no intention of going in shooting.

The glass door was deadbolted, and he glanced back and saw a silver-beaded chain around the lumberjack's neck, the kind high school girls had once worn to hold the boyfriend's ring. The chain rippled and whipped as the man's neck snapped back and forth in his agony. Jack Liffey finally broke it and grasped the single silver key that came away with it.

The older man got to his knees and begged for help while the other went on shrieking and scraping his cheeks against the damp concrete.

Jack Liffey unlocked the door and swung it open. "You'll be fine in half an hour, gentlemen. It's just capsicum, the essence of chili pepper. Best not to rub it. Come on, my friends, we're going in. You can save the light now."

—-—

Pastor Kohlmeyer heard a commotion in the hallway and momentarily stopped praying at the small altar he'd put together in his office—really no more than an old tea chest with a tablecloth over it and a simple silver cross on top.

"I have been born again by trusting in Jesus Christ as Lord and Savior, and I believe that I am saved by the grace of God."

A voice through the door interrupted his prayer. This time there were clearly people coming his way along the hall. People—or something else, of course . . . . He had left instructions to leave him alone to pray. So, whatever it was in the corridor, it had to be evil. He'd always known that the devil had been waiting for him, just out of sight most of his life, lurking in the shadows—the shadows of his father's naïveté or his brother's resentments—waiting for an opportunity to ambush him with his own weaknesses.

He heard the peremptory knock, and before standing up asked quickly for strength and resolve. He regretted that he did not feel especially close to God this evening, nor especially strong, and he hoped that his entreaty would be granted. As he came to his feet, the door opened and a bright light flared into the dim room.

"I have been born again—" Then he recognized the man standing there. He'd been in the car with the bad-mannered Jennifer Ezkiaga a week earlier, and he'd stated flatly that he had not been saved.

"You can call a truce, pastor," the intruder said. "The police have caught the young couple who killed their baby. It was no more than a clumsy attempt to stop the baby's squalling. It happens. The father admitted that the note about the Devil was just window dressing, a diversion."

"I must do everything within my power to oppose Satan with all my worldly and spiritual strength. Take your lies and go from me."

"Why don't you telephone the police station. Ask for Lieutenant Saldivar."

That the police would be part of this attack on him as well! No, it didn't surprise him.

"Come no closer. Do you realize that you are doing the Devil's bidding?" There was something about the unbeliever's face that disturbed Kohlmeyer, the skin too pasty, his clothing too rumpled. He had the look of a sinner who had never even fought against temptation.

"Roll tape. Ellie, you're on."

"I do not give permission for this."

"Speed," the man with the camera said softly. A reporter the pastor recognized from local TV was holding out a microphone.

The unsaved man was holding something, too—a legal paper in a blue cover. "Sir, I am serving you with a writ of habeas corpus. If you are acting as an officer of the court of Kern County in the name of the anticult committees and holding any children in this building, the Superior Court of the State of California, County of Sacramento, Department Two, requires that you release them to me now."

"You know the Devil wants those innocent girls for his purposes. *You* want them, and you shall *not* have them." The pastor took the writ and hurled it into a corner.

"Then let's call in the police. Go ahead."

The police had always been such intriguers, Kohlmeyer thought. The council members. The mayor. You could never really trust anyone in civil authority. The mayor had turned on him already. His two loyal councilmen had backed away from coming tonight. His own assistant pastor. It showed the deep-reaching powers of the devil. Such betrayals were rarely so direct and straightforward, but tonight they were a big clinking bag of thirty pieces of silver.

"No police tonight. If you don't go away, I'll summon my armed support. You are of the Devil's party, whether you know it or not." There was nothing in the pastor's mind now but the fact that the man without faith had become the Devil's accomplice, bent on balking him and the whole crusade. He had to resist anything offered, no matter how seemingly ordinary or reasonable, no matter how lawful.

"Enough of your crap!" the Devil's man said. "My daughter is named Maeve Liffey. She's almost eighteen, has brown hair and freckles. She's in here and I require you to take me to her now."

"The Devil has targeted her as well as the other one—as you well know," the pastor said. "I mean to cleanse their souls."

—-—

He wasn't sure why he did it. He'd grown weary and then angry, and he was tired of trying to hold things together by his fingertips, and somehow the frustrations of all that annoying fog outside played a part in it, too. Jack Liffey snatched the pepper spray out of his pocket and blasted it directly into the pastor's face. The man screamed and clawed at his eyes as he crumpled into a heap on the floor. But Jack Liffey went on spraying for another ten full seconds against the man's hands and into his hair and clothing.

It was then that he heard the first gunshot outside the church, followed by others.

Chapter Twenty

# EVIL SPIRITS

T he echoes of the gunshots outside died away and everything stayed quiet for maybe half a minute. Then, as if reinforcements had just galloped up, a ragged fusillade began hammering away at the night. There was no way of knowing whether it was incoming or outgoing. Or just upgoing. Jack Liffey wondered what on earth anybody had to aim at in that fog, and why. He didn't know if it was just a panic firefight, with the defenders spooking, or if somebody were actually assaulting the church, and if so, who? He knew Gloria was smart enough to stay under some kind of cover out there, and the chances of getting hit from afar in a tule fog were just about zero. Still, he worried.

He had locked the deadbolt, coming in. He had no idea how many men outside had other keys, but probably not many, and he was just as happy if every last one of them was locked out in that rainstorm of lead.

First things first. He had left the pastor shrieking on his knees, involuntarily rubbing the capsicum extract deeper into his eyes. And he'd told the TV crew they were on their own now, he was looking for his daughter. Nonetheless, on the off chance of blundering into a real story, they were tagging along behind him. They'd probably got enough footage of the poor wailing pastor, anyway. In the dimness, Jack Liffey followed the curving hallway that apparently girdled the entire structure, checking any doors he could force open.

"If you see switches, turn them on," Jack Liffey called. "We're not paying the light bills."

"That spray is terrible stuff," the reporter said.

"I really don't give a damn," Jack Liffey said. "That man can go fuck himself."

There was another lull in the sporadic gunfire, like an offered truce, before the hammering took up again at a deliberate pace, as if potshotting visible targets now. At least one person out there had an automatic weapon he could hear rattle away now and again, and some of the gunshots seemed much farther away than others. Once in a while there was the very clear *thut* of a round impacting the outer wall of the building, sounding a bit like a cough, and now and then a sharper tinkle, almost a pretty sound, as small panes from the ring of stained glass overhead shattered. That pretty much made it obvious that the church was taking incoming. Perhaps the Devil had indeed called up his National Guard. Red goat-legged figures with Sam Browne belts and assault rifles. That would really be something to see.

More rounds struck nearby—*thut-thut-thut*—and then one punched startlingly right on through the outer wall to wallop an inner wall, too, and leave a small ragged hole.

"Gollywilkins," the reporter said, blinking bravely.

"Try the women's room there," Jack Liffey said.

He checked two utterly empty schoolrooms, and when the reporter reemerged into the hallway, she had an older woman in tow. "I found her locked in a stall. Ask her about the girls."

"Maeve Liffey," Jack Liffey demanded. "And another one that you might be calling Sue Ellen Crumm. About eighteen."

The woman seemed chagrined and was clutching the sides of her skirt with her hands. "Yes, they were in my care, but I failed," she admitted.

"Good woman, I am the civil authority here now." Jack Liffey thrust one of the folded up legal writs at her. "Defy this habeas corpus and go directly to jail. Produce the girls."

She gave in and led them through a maze of inner corridors to a wide green door that said INFIRMARY, but when she opened the door, she gasped. "I swear there was a bed right here with the Crumm girl in it. She was sleeping. Right there. See the shoe. That was hers."

A black hi-top tennis shoe lay on the floor.

"The bed had wheels?"

"It was a hospital bed. The other girl was way around in the pantry, but she escaped from us."

Maeve wouldn't go back there if she'd escaped. "Okay, folks—let's find a big bed and two girls in this place. It's not rocket science."

He motioned everyone to be quiet for a moment. They heard only the occasional bursts of gunfire from outside and a soft air rush from a heater vent. "Maeve!" he shouted at the top of his voice, and her name echoed off along the hallway. "This is your dad! It's okay to come out!"

—–

Two of the sacred guardians had made it back inside to find the pastor moaning on the floor of his study. One was a sheriff's deputy who'd served two tours with the National Guard in Iraq and knew about pepper spray. In training, his whole unit had been run far too slowly through a test chamber with both CS gas and pepper spray. He knew there was no neutralizer, but the best routine was still simple: a dish detergent to wash it off the skin and vigorous blinking to encourage tears to flush the eyes.

"Come on, sir, blink, blink. I know it hurts. You've got to do it as much as you can."

His partner for the evening, wearing a fancy Stetson and an old sheepskin jacket, stood in front of the small altar with his eyes closed, repeating his oath, as if confused by everything. "I believe the Bible is literally accurate in all it teaches—"

The pastor's moans mounted over the prayer. "Aghhh!" The indignity of it all didn't help him a bit.

Returning from the janitor's closet, the deputy used an old bandana to flush detergent solution from a plastic bucket over the pastor's face. "Who did this to you?"

"It was . . . that unbeliever. From Los Angeles. Something about one of the girls. Who is shooting at us out there?"

"The Devil has mobilized his legions, as you warned us. We can't see them, but they're everywhere. Morgan's in charge and we're mostly holding fire in the fog. Plumb crazy to shoot when you can't see."

All at once a few bars of the *Magnificent Seven* theme erupted in the room, startling them all. The man in the Stetson stopped repeating the oath and pulled a cell phone out of his sheepskin jacket.

"Stony." He listened. "Okay. Have you seen anything yet?" He said, "Okay," and "Yup," and then slapped the cell phone shut.

"Morgan called the police again," he explained. "Told them we were taking heavy fire. They could hear it, for pete's sake, right on the line. They promised to send help."

"Go stop the arm of Satan *inside*," the pastor forced out between involuntary gasps. "He's after those girls. The infirmary. I tell you, the Devil desires them and will stop at nothing."

The deputy guided the pastor's hand to the plastic bucket. "Keep swabbing your face, sir. And blink away. I'll take care of this. Watch over Pastor Kohlmeyer, Stony."

"It's a privilege."

"My sentiments, too." He gave an ugly laugh and headed out to do battle.

— —

### Artifact: 1989

"We wanted to ask James W. Boswell why taxpayers should subsidize his company's water bill, especially to grow more cotton than we need. But Boswell, who lives several hundred miles away in a plush Los Angeles neighborhood, declined to be interviewed."

—Ed Bradley, *60 Minutes*, CBS, November 1989. Boswell is the
largest grower in Kern County, in fact in the United States. You
can drive for half a day and never leave his land. Massive
corporate growers like him have taken billions of dollars out of
California's central valley and left little but impoverished
farmworkers behind.[9]

――

At first Gloria and Sonny had nestled low in the flower bed
with their backs to the Olive Grove sign, but as the gunfire built
up, most of it definitely incoming, they crawled around to the
backside of the sign. Bulldog and Tammy had been last seen scur-
rying down the driveway to the cars. There were still a number of
headlights setting the fog aglow all around them, which was
unfortunate. There seemed no gunfire in their immediate
vicinity, though, but gunshots were going off unexpectedly
around the compass. Like kernels in a pan of popcorn.

"We been scrooched up here a quarter of an hour," Sonny said.
"Maybe it's time to make a move."

"Christ, this town is an exhibit," Gloria exclaimed. "Does this
shit happen every fog?"

"Maybe Friday midnights outside Trout's over in Oildale
there'll be a good ol' boy or two shooting at the moon. Nothing
like this."

"Well, who the hell's out there? We can guess who's playing
defense, but who's shooting? I've counted twenty guns, at least."

"Beats me," Sonny admitted. "I think we can rule out the
Catholics, tired of being insulted as idol worshippers?"

There was a short burst of automatic fire somewhere east of

the big building. The church was no more than a looming presence in the fog, its mass felt in some strange tactile way rather than seen.

"Every religion busts your balls," Gloria said. "Even Jack's agnosticism."

He chuckled softly. "Now you're sounding like him. That's too philosophical for me."

"I reckon when I finally kick off," Gloria said sourly, "if I've got the time to realize I'm really on the way to checking out, there'll be nothing but a glorious feeling of what good luck. The damn thing's over at last."

He laughed softly again, brushing maybe accidentally against her shoulder. "Funny, I was just thinking how little luck I've had in life. Never found me a first-rate woman like you to care for. I know I need something out of this world that I'm just not getting."

Gloria leaned close to him, and he saw something he couldn't quite understand in her big brown eyes. "For God's sake, kiss me, man," she ordered.

He twisted around on the ground and in the secure damp shroud of the fog, they embraced. They pressed their lips together urgently, like teenagers, tentatively then wildly, using their tongues until they could barely breathe. She pulled back and averted her eyes but kept his hand tight in hers. "You're a good guy, Sonny, but I gotta tell you I'm too fucked up to take a chance on."

"We need one night together," he said. "Just to know."

"I don't think so. This is just the craziness of tonight. I've got my thing with Jack."

"That's something else. It doesn't interfere."

"It does for me."

They kissed again, long and hard, and his hand rested for a moment on her breast, softly circled the nipple, which was engorged and on fire.

"Don't say a word . . . don't say stop," he murmured to her.

They began to hear sirens in the distance, and she pulled a few inches away from him, gasping, and held both his hands to keep them off her heaving breast. "I thought the police here had all died." They were both panting so hard they could barely breathe.

—‒

They'd pretty much exhausted the schoolrooms along the interior corridor and everything else on the south side of the church, but Jack Liffey had no intention of heading back to the office area. Now and then there was still a *thwok* of an incoming round in the outer walls.

"There's still the nave," the reporter said.

"Strange place to hide, but let's look."

There didn't seem to be any way in from where they were. The oval inner wall of the encircling corridor was an unbroken surface marred by a long kitschy mural of a procession of life-size ordinary American types, heading off counterclockwise as if lined up for a blockbuster movie, though a lot of them carried Bibles or fish or other food. On their way to the feast, he thought, but bringing their own food along, just in case.

"They seem to know the way," Jack Liffey said, patting one of the earnest pilgrims on the wall.

"Slouching toward Bethlehem," the reporter suggested, which

took her up several notches in his estimation. Though she might have come to it from Didion rather than Yeats, the source.

"No rude beasts, please," Jack Liffey said.

She smirked conspiratorially.

Jack Liffey saw a quadruple set of doors ahead. They had small rectangular windows set into them like an operating theater. Just as they reached the doors, the mural did, too, and in the lead was a blonde Jesus in long white robes and sandals who was looking back over his shoulder and pointing ahead. A signpost beside Jesus pointed LIFE one way and DEATH the other. The mind boggles at the literalism, Jack Liffey thought.

The reporter yanked open the door to a dark echoey space, with the faintest hint of colored light filtering in from another ring of high stained glass. It felt immense, larger than any theater he had ever seen.

"Maeve, are you in here?" he bellowed.

"Oh, Daddy! I'm so *happy*! Over here! We're both okay!"

His heart leapt. It had been far too long since he'd heard her voice, and she'd said the magic word—*okay*. Though "over here" was wondrously optimistic in that vast black impenetrable space. *I am where I am*, the cry said. *I am at the center of being.* All his heart went out to that guilelessness. She was so very *there* in her innocence, feeling it, meaning it. Once again he wondered how this remarkable brightness had come from him.

"I'll be right there, hon. Can you see any landmarks?"

"I'm by a giant cross."

Well, what else? he thought. Then the Sun Gun came on behind him and its powerful beam swept over the acres of empty pews and bleacher seats, the glow finally settling on her, deep within the bowl. On Maeve. Without a doubt. She shone, leaning over a bed with hospital rails that took up most of an aisle almost beneath a gigantic hanging wooden cross. He sidestepped along a pew as fast as he could toward a descending aisle, clumsy in his haste, snagging and scattering embroidered cushions behind him.

"I see you, hon!"

"I've got Toxie here! They've done something to her! She's unconscious. We've got to get her help!"

"We will. I promise. Help is coming!"

Then he felt a carpet underfoot and someone found a switch that turned on a scattering of weak recessed lights in the ceiling far above.

Maeve fell into his arms and held him hard. "Oh, Daddy. They had us locked up in a horrid *warehouse*."

"I know about it."

The powerful light still played on them, and he could hear the murmur of the reporter talking far away in the nave, and he realized she'd begun taping, but it made no difference whether the world knew or not. Maeve was safe.

He disentangled himself from her spider-monkey grasp and felt the throat of the blue-haired girl in the bed. Here was the famous Toxie at last. Her pulse was strong and steady, and he used the moment to study her features, so many piercings, the spiky hair. Definitely a stormy soul.

From down in the nave, he could just barely hear some of the gunfire outside, seemingly very far away now. And then several faint police sirens arriving and cutting off.

"I think she'll be okay," he said. "I'm glad you escaped the warehouse. I'm not surprised you did."

"I cut away some insulation on the wall and then a man named Bulldog got us out by kicking his way through the metal."

"I've met him."

"You have?" She seemed astounded.

"That's where you parked, remember, and where your car was marked for impound."

"You mean that big orange sticker? I just tore it off."

He almost laughed at the charming obliviousness of her innocence. You run up against a police warning of a possible felony that's utterly irrelevant to your immediate needs: you simply tear it off.

A door at the far side of the nave slapped open hard, and the beam of the Sun Gun swung around to pick out two men coming in, shielding their eyes from the glare. They carried rifles and one of them looked utterly perfect for the role, with a sheepskin jacket and a Stetson.

Then the TV light became irrelevant as the main overheads came on. A corner of his mind realized that the ring of stained glass above them would look a huge hovering UFO to those outside in the fog, and he wondered if the clerestory window would now be a target. In the moment that he watched the windows nothing broke, and he heard no gunshots. The two riflemen who'd entered were coming his way cautiously, making their paths along two aisles in order to flank him in case he and Maeve decided to make a run for it.

"Hold on! *Stony!*" a distant baritone called, and Jack Liffey noticed that the pastor he'd pepper-sprayed had entered the nave from yet another doorway. The man carried an old double-barreled side-by-side shotgun, cracked open across his forearm, just the way you were supposed to carry it when you climbed stiles over country fences.

The pastor's whole face was red as a beet and his eyes were

slitted. He brushed his face now and again with the sleeve of his free arm. Jack Liffey was amazed that the man could see at all. He must have had tremendous force of will to ignore the pain.

The other two gunmen looked back toward their leader, then waited in deference. He walked past one of them, flicking his shotgun up so the barrels locked into place. "I'll deal with this."

Slowly and relentlessly, he started intoning, "I have been born again by trusting in Jesus Christ as Lord and Savior, and I believe that I am saved by the grace of God." There was more, but Jack Liffey tuned out, eyeing the shotgun.

Kohlmeyer's sights had gradually come around toward him. Discreetly he moved directly in front of Maeve to shield her from any sudden blast.

All of a sudden, the pastor flinched and ducked a little as if dodging the swoop of a giant bird, but the apparent vision or hallucination seemed to depart his consciousness without further incident. He finally came to a halt about ten paces away from Jack Liffey. He still wiped at his face with the back of one hand from time to time. Each touch wiped away tears that were streaming down his cheeks. His gray hair, once slicked back as if by a rake, was now wet and awry. The dark hollows of the double-barrel were aimed casually somewhere south of Jack Liffey's chest.

"Unbeliever," the man crooned at him. "Serpent. Conduit of Evil. Doomed Prince of the Earth."

"Sorry about the pepper spray. Really."

"Anti-Christ." He sobbed once. "You have so much on your side in this world, and I have only the power of my faith."

"Actually, that scattergun does pretty well in a pinch," Jack Liffey said. "Who are all these guys on my team?"

"NASA," the pastor said very slowly. "Hollywood. The Bakersfield Board of Education. The Kern County library system. Microsoft. All of secular humanism. Every password to success in the material world. The power of the Devil is everywhere. You reveal yourself to me—the same way I know a skunk is under the house."

Jack Liffey hoped he didn't actually smell. It was hard to keep up with all this. Out of the corner of his eye, he saw that the TV crew had crept closer to record this absurd confrontation. Great, he thought. He represented everything that this pinhead hated, and his martyrdom by gunfire would be recorded for the whole country to view, over and over. "I don't grudge you your worldview, sir," Jack Liffey said. "But be Christian, please. Jesus stood for love, did he not? Can't you allow me my own worldview?"

"Not if you're going to corrupt the souls of these innocent girls."

"My soul is my own to worry about," Maeve blurted out with indignation, stepping out from behind him, and he wanted to bang on her head, hush her, yell at her to run away. But he didn't dare disturb the universe in any way with this fanatic facing him.

"Young lady, how many times has your father spoken to you about coming to Jesus?"

"Once would be too many, but my father is the most moral person I know!"

"Focus on *me!*" Jack Liffey shouted. "Me!"

The pastor seemed not to hear either of them. The voices he was hearing were in his own head.

"Listen to me," Kohlmeyer insisted, a frightening listlessness creeping into his voice. "All signs suggest that the Devil has chosen that very girl in particular, Sue Ellen Crumm, the one who is sleeping. She must be very important to him in some way, for he has defied all the efforts we've made to force him to leave her body."

"Do you hear voices that tell you this?"

"The whole of Kern County is full of signs. But you know it already. *She* was full of signs herself when we examined her. *She* has the demon drawn on her body."

"A joke of a tattoo," Jack Liffey said. "Come on, man. What else have you got?"

"Proof? To an unbeliever?"

"I like proof."

"I suppose you'd force Jesus to let you thrust your hand into the wound."

"Like Thomas? It'd help. So would striking me dead right now for blasphemy."

There was a collective gasp from a number of people as Jack Liffey set his arms on his hips. "Why don't you ask Him to do that—before you try shooting me, that is." He didn't like the expressions flitting across Kohlmeyer's face, but he was going for broke.

"God never responds to taunts. Or demands."

"That's convenient. He never seems to respond to much of anything, does He? I imagine the folks at Auschwitz prayed damn hard for help. This ruckus of yours is over, pastor. We heard the cops arrive. Put the gun down before one of us gets hurt. We can sit down tomorrow and talk peaceably, if you want. I give you my solemn word."

"*Pathetic*. You believe I have any interest in the word of a toad out of the mouth of Satan?"

"I think you know how to use that thing in your hands

because I've seen the way you carry it. But I'll bet you've never shot a man." Jack Liffey took one long breath and began to move slowly sideways, to get himself as far away from Maeve and Toxie as he could. The pastor was smiling a little through the pain of his burning face, as if confident of the outcome of his titanic battle.

"But then, you're not a man," the pastor said. "Anyone can shoot a rattlesnake. A serpent. Even a toad."

Jack Liffey wasn't sure how to talk a man down from something this intoxicating, but he'd had a lot of practice with other men who were disturbed and unhappy. And he had a good memory for odd snatches of scripture.

"'There before me was a pale horse!'" Jack Liffey said. To keep the man talking as he moved away from Maeve. "'Its rider was named Death.' Do you really believe we're acting that all out now?"

"Of course not. Don't be ridiculous. There'll be many small battles before the Final Battle."

Jack Liffey kept sidestepping along the aisle until he was well clear of the girls. The shotgun had stayed on him. "I'm glad you don't think we're part of some Middle Eastern fever dream, man, but what happened to trusting in the Lord? Why do you need a weapon to feel in control in your own house? Why don't you put it down, and we can discuss this, one to one."

Kohlmeyer's half smile came back. "Oh, Devil. I can quote better than you. 'Our struggle is not against flesh and blood, but against the rulers, against the authorities, against the powers of this dark world and against the spiritual forces of evil in the heavenly realms.' Ephesians 6. I realize you're probably somewhere else, Satan, safe and far away, and only speaking to me through this poor man's body. Yet we know that it's sometimes necessary to strike against the unseen through the seen. We need only remember that Jesus, through his death on the cross, has defeated you already. One use of this crude earthly weapon may just be a tiny recapitulation of Jesus' victory against you."

"I'm just a man, Pastor Kohlmeyer. Blood and tissue." Jack Liffey opened his arms. "I try to do my best. You can sprinkle holy words on me all night, you can try to drive out the evil spirits—but you have no right to harm this body."

"No, *Dad!*" It was Maeve's wail. Fiercely he tried to will her to stay silent and still.

Kohlmeyer's eyes had gone to Maeve for a moment, and Jack Liffey used that moment to step closer to the shotgun.

"Stay there, Maeve," he commanded. "Kohlmeyer, look at me! *Look. At. Me.* What you're doing is wrong, even if you mean right. Even if you're certain that God is guiding you and sending you signs—you're reading those signs wrong. Look in your heart where your humanity lives. For God's sake—for real. We're both men."

The pastor was staring at him now, and Jack Liffey openly took another step closer. The twin gun barrel rose a little, aimed directly at his heart.

"Is it a delusion or has this all happened again and again in our lifetime?" Jack Liffey said. "Do we have to repeat the murder of the innocent ad nauseam?"

"I don't know what you're talking about, devil," the pastor said softly.

"Okay, let's try this. You can slaughter me and everyone living in your head will praise you. But you'll only become another news photo in that endless gallery of American killer freaks."

"Daddy, *no!*"

"We don't see this the same way," Kohlmeyer allowed.

In that instant, it seemed all the doors slammed open and big black insects with dome heads and bug eyes swarmed into the nave.

"You with the shotgun, drop your weapon! *Now!*"

The pastor half turned, and Jack Liffey knew enough to raise his hands and show that they were empty. Never argue with a SWAT team that was riding hard on adrenaline and testosterone.

Two red dots began to dance and weave on the pastor's wet robe. Concentrating, Jack Liffey thought he could see the laser beams themselves sparkling on the dust in the air.

"Please stay calm, sir," Jack Liffey said softly. "Please. Those are laser sights on your chest. Don't make any sudden movements and we'll both be just fine. We can talk tomorrow. Who knows, maybe you'll turn out to be right about things."

"The Devil speaks so fine . . ."

"You have a count of three to drop your weapon!"

Kohlmeyer never got his count because he started to swivel the shotgun back toward Jack Liffey, and in that moment both the dots blossomed into splashes of red across his chest, and his eyes came wide open in surprise. The double crack of two closely spaced shots came an instant later. The pastor's shotgun clattered onto a bit of wooden floor in front of the altar, and Jack Liffey took one slow step and kicked the firearm farther away, as the pastor sank to his knees with a sob.

Jack Liffey stayed frozen until the newcomers had swarmed over them both.

## Chapter Twenty-one

# DECISION

Perhaps it had been a miracle of God, Jack Liffey thought, although not very seriously. He was unaccustomed to considering the arrival of a SWAT team, or anything else really, as having much to do with divine providence. The cop who was probably one of the shooters looked chagrined now, his plexiglass eyeshield thrown up as he dangled his shortie Heckler & Koch MP-5 assault rifle with the ungainly laser sight down at his thigh. He was arguing with Lt. Saldivar, who seemed upset about the body that now lay on an ambulance gurney covered with a Mylar space blanket.

Maeve clasped Jack Liffey hard around his chest and talked a mile a minute, telling him about her plans to help Toxie finish high school and something else about helping Toxie's mother learn to read, but his head was too busy swimming with events and he barely heard her. In fact, the event that had most significantly caught his eye had occurred just a moment before. It had been a single glance of longing and sexual regret that had passed between Gloria and Sonny Theroux at the door of the nave. It had been hard to mistake and harder still to get his mind around. And there'd been the suggestion, somehow, that they'd been holding hands until just moments before they entered and had let their hands part in guilt. Amazing how little the mind needed to process an observation, he thought. Or was he just projecting his fears of losing her?

Jack Liffey reached out suddenly to grab Saldivar's arm. "Lieutenant, who the hell was shooting at the church?"

Saldivar's eyes came around like a searing blast of rage. Jack Liffey supposed it was because, in Saldivar's mind, he had been the cause, or perhaps just a witness, to the entire police debacle.

Mainly Jack Liffey just wanted to go home and return everything in his life to the way it had been before.

Saldivar sighed. "We think a couple of local gangs had a longstanding bone to pick with this church. They used the fog and the damn devil campaign as cover."

"I tried to talk him down," Jack Liffey offered. In the corner of his eye he saw Gloria approaching, just ahead of Sonny. His great friend, new friend. He wished he'd never stopped in Bakersfield, never.

The policeman turned away and Gloria kissed Jack Liffey on the cheek. "Good to see you're okay, Jack. I love you."

"Dad!" Maeve blurted out. "I think I've made a really big decision. I'm going to keep the baby. I have to, no matter what."

Chapter Twenty-two

# CHOICE

Perhaps it had been a miracle of God, Jack Liffey thought, although not very seriously. He was unaccustomed to considering the arrival of a SWAT team, or anything else really, as having much to do with divine providence. The cop who was probably one of the shooters looked chagrined now, his plexiglass eyeshield thrown up as he dangled his shortie Heckler & Koch MP-5 assault rifle with the ungainly laser sight down at his thigh. He was arguing with Lt. Saldivar, who seemed upset about the body that now lay on an ambulance gurney covered with a Mylar space blanket.

Maeve clasped Jack Liffey hard around his chest and talked a mile a minute, telling him about her plans to help Toxie finish high school and something else about helping Toxie's mother learn to read, but his head was too busy swimming with events and he barely heard her. In fact, the event that had most significantly caught his eye had occurred just a moment before. It had been a single glance of longing and sexual regret that had passed between Gloria and Sonny Theroux at the door of the nave. It had been hard to mistake and harder still to get his mind around. And there'd been the suggestion, somehow, that they'd been holding hands until just moments before they entered and had let their hands part in guilt. Amazing how little the mind needed to process an observation, he thought. Or was he just projecting his fears of losing her?

Jack Liffey reached out suddenly to grab Saldivar's arm. "Lieutenant, who the hell was shooting at the church?"

Saldivar's eyes came around like a searing blast of rage. Jack Liffey supposed it was because, in Saldivar's mind, he had been the cause, or perhaps just a witness, to the entire police debacle.

Mainly Jack Liffey just wanted to go home and return everything in his life to the way it had been before.

Saldivar sighed. "We think a couple of local gangs had a long-standing bone to pick with this church. They used the fog and the damn devil campaign as cover."

"I tried to talk him down," Jack Liffey offered. In the corner of his eye he saw Gloria approaching, just ahead of Sonny. His great friend, new friend. He wished he'd never stopped in Bakersfield, never.

The policeman turned away and Gloria kissed Jack Liffey on the cheek. "Good to see you're okay, Jack. I love you."

"Dad," Maeve blurted out. "I think I've made a really big decision. I'm going to have the abortion. I have to, no matter what."

# ENDNOTES

If you wish to vote on Maeve's momentous decision in the last two chapters, please go to www.jackliffey.com.

*The Devils of Bakersfield* is a work of fiction. However, the artifacts presented within the work constitute a reasonably fair portrait of a peculiar geographical area of California that has displayed repeated waves of oppression and intolerance against outsiders and minorities. Not all the artifacts included are up to the highest standards of historical scholarship. In order not to muddy the well of history, the notes below clarify where some were obtained, or condensed, or even reimagined from suggestions in

the historical record. I only "reimagined" where there was virtually no chance today of obtaining an accurate exemplar of any
original, at least for an amateur historian like me.

1  Quoted in Edward Humes, *Mean Justice*, Simon &
   Schuster, 1999. A stunning work of reportage.
2  Slightly adapted and condensed from several
   sources.
3  Reimagined from a variety of oral and secondary
   sources. [The second of these, the report from the
   chowder society, is based upon a genuine, and gen-
   uinely strange, California drinking and historical
   society that is over a hundred and fifty years old
   and does indeed mark historical sites with plaques.
   It goes by the dog-Latin name of *E clampus vitus*.]
4  Adapted from secondary sources.
5  Adapted from *L.A. Times*, July 23, 1922.
6  In Devra Weber, *Dark Sweat, White Gold: California
   Farm Workers, Cotton and the New Deal*, University
   of California Press, 1999.
7  Condensed somewhat from source noted.
8  Gerald Haslam, *The Other California: The Great
   Central Valley in Life and Letters*, University of
   Nevada Press, 1994.
9  Quoted in Mark Arax and Rick Wartzman, *The King
   of California: J. G. Boswell and the Making of a Secret
   American Empire*, Public Affairs, New York, 2003.